A TALE (

Robin Kingsley

Robin

MINERVA PRESS
WASHINGTON LONDON MONTREUX

A TALE OF WHALES

Copyright © Robin Kingsley 1994

ISBN 1 85863 126 2

First Published 1994 by
MINERVA PRESS
1, Cromwell Place
London SW7 2JE

2nd Impression 1995

Printed in Great Britain by
Ipswich Book Company, Ipswich, Suffolk

A Tale of Whales

AUTHOR'S NOTE

I wish to acknowledge a group of faithful friends who have read rough drafts and manuscripts of my writing, given valuable criticism and encouragement: Barbara Eso, Valerie Clark, Knud and Bente Nielsen, Anne McLean, my wife Corisande, my sisters June Simington and Anne Armitstead and my brother-in-law Peter Armitstead. My special thanks to Knud Nielsen for giving me the opportunity to discuss many aspects of writing over our regular meetings for elevenses and for his assistance with proof reading.

I also wish to give thanks to other special friends. To Doctor Jerald Bain, an eminent Endocrinologist, who has allowed me to use his first name in the story knowing that it will identify him. To Bob Melville, for many years the owner of Otter Bay Marina, for agreeing to let me use his name and one of his 'overheard' comments. To Lionel and Diane Field for letting me use the name of their boat, Heron. Last but not least, I owe a debt of gratitude to all the young men and women who have told me their stories during thirty years of medical practice.

ABOUT THE AUTHOR

Robin Percival Smith was educated in England and was posted to Vancouver after joining the Royal Canadian Air Force in 1958. He practised Family Medicine in Richmond for ten years before taking up an appointment at the Student Health Service of the University of British Columbia in 1971. He retired from practice in 1989 to pursue a life long passion for cruising his sloop Tremethick II on the west coast of Canada. He has chosen to write under the name Robin Kingsley, his given names, in fond memory of his father who was named for the author Charles Kingsley.

For

Corisande, Anthony, Keith and Christopher

CONTENTS

Page

PROLOGUE

Never Satisfied II log for
Monday July 8th 1984

Dead calm in the Central Johnstone Strait on the west coast of Canada; that's a rare event! As I passed the channel to Port Neville a pod of killer whales were heading north. A small whale left the pod and swam towards the boat. About three hundred feet from the boat it jumped clean out of the water showing off its juvenile white belly, a spectacle it repeated several times. I felt that there was some recognition between this superb young animal and the boat. Then all was quiet and I saw his fin heading back to join the pod.

The water looked like a sheet of ice and the sun behind my back was warm. I rigged a rope to the wheel for self steering and put my feet up on the seat. The gentle rocking motion, the warm sun and the position contributed to my sloth. I awoke suddenly and terror stricken at the approach of Stimpson Reef beacon dead ahead, but even before I could take evasive action the boat lurched to port to miss the reef, which slipped by to starboard. I looked down over the starboard side and saw a dark shape in the water and a fin which disappeared under the boat. A minute or so later a small whale jumped clear of the surface of the sea in jubilation.

September 1970

A hot Indian summer morning, the misty air still, the glistening dew on the grass, the scene surveyed from the patio as I sipped coffee from the steaming cup on the table beside me. On call for the clinic I was feeling trapped and wished I could be transported to the cockpit of my boat, Never Satisfied.

Andrew appeared at the window bringing milk and cereal to the table, tousled hair over a sleepy face,

"Never satisfied, Dad?" His voice trebled with conceited laughter at his own play on words.

"What's on for you?"

"The usual."

He liked to play baseball in the field behind the house with his two friends Brian and David.

"Who's the new boy?"

"That's Alex."

I had noticed this fourth player a day or two after Labour Day pitching to them and they were having difficulty hitting him. Notable because of his long red hair straggling down to his shoulders under his baseball cap, a carotene face on strong shoulders and a surprisingly tall skinny body, taller than the other three.

"First week at school go well?"

"Yep."

"Who's your new teacher?"

"Mr Dixon."

"What's he like?"

"Okay."

During the weeks I had noticed Alex leave when I arrived home. I thought it coincided with his time for supper until I arrived home early one afternoon. As I entered the house from the carport I heard the front door close. Then I noticed that on weekends he never came into the house.

"Why does Alex always leave when I arrive home?" I asked Andrew at lunch time.

"Don't know," he said in that unforthcoming way that children seem to go through life.

"And he never comes into the house with the other boys."

"I guess she's afraid of you, Dad."

"Why would she be afraid of me," I said at first not noticing the change in gender. "Did you say she?"

"Yes."

"A bit young for a girl-friend aren't you?"

"Alex is not my girl-friend," he growled, "she's one of the boys."

CHAPTER 1

Alexandra's story

Mr and Mrs Arthur Jones, with their daughter Alexandra, moved to the suburb of Vancouver south of the river on the flat delta lands of Richmond in late summer. She was a solitary girl and missed the boys that her father encouraged her to play with in Vancouver. He did not want a daughter and had brought Alex up to be a boy and did not hide it from her.

She was standing in the dormer window of her attic room, with its plain white-painted walls, cotton patternless drapes and dark wood trim, made more austere by the plain desk and two wood chairs, one at the desk and the other at the foot of her bed. The polished hardwood floors were carpetless and the simple pinewood bedstead had no box spring; instead there were plank boards on which a thin palette mattress was covered by a fawn comforter. Her thin cotton pyjamas were neatly folded on the single pillow. Even the built-in wall cupboard was kept with ordered neatness, with her clean simple clothes folded and lined up.

She saw three boys playing baseball in the field at the back of her house. She took her glove from the cupboard, put on her cap at a jaunty angle and went into the field. Standing in the outfield she waited, the girl servant, to be useful saving them from having to stop and recover the ball. They took a break, starting in the direction of the smallest boy's house and Alex started to walk home.

"Hey, you!" The small boy shouted to her. "Don't you want a drink?"

She walked towards them and followed them into a back yard where Andrew waited for her.

"I'm Andrew," he said looking up at her, "this is Brian and David."

They made shy glances in her direction as Andrew looked her in the eyes waiting for her to speak.

"Alex," she said; her untidy hair made her appear boyish, "we've just moved into the old farmhouse."

She was surprised by the ease with which he invited them all into his house and the way he offered them all a drink, just going to the refrigerator and helping himself and handing round the cookie jar. This was not even a mealtime! She was not allowed between-meal treats and was never given pop.

They took their drinks into the garden.

"Do you want a go at bat?" Andrew asked her.

"That's okay," she replied rejecting the offer, "but I'll pitch for you."

"We should let her," Brian said, smiling at David and Andrew, "then we can hit easy."

When her father discovered that she could throw and catch a ball like a boy he encouraged her, and when she made the baseball team as a pitcher he was inordinately proud and attended all the games. He set up the back yard so that she could practise and he pressured her to hone her skills.

There was no way that Brian could be prepared for his ordeal. As her tall thin body wound up to pitch, her shoulder muscles rippled as she let her fast ball go.

"I like to watch the first ball!" he said to Andrew, who was not fooled since Brian's bat had not even moved.

Brian swung and missed the next pitch. The third ball seemed faster than ever but his pride was partly restored by fouling it back and he was confident he would do justice to the next. Alex pitched him a well-concealed change-up which he missed by a mile and Andrew fumbled it into his glove.

David took the bat and did not fare any better. Andrew at the plate had the advantage of experiencing the speed of her pitching and with a bit of luck managed a line drive past her on the first pitch. So began the challenge to hit Alex, the occasional cause for hands held high in celebration, and they adopted her as 'one of the boys'.

It was Andrew who insisted on including Alex in everything he did with Brian and David; and Andrew who walked with her to school each morning.

"Alex," Andrew said, "would you come sailing with us this weekend?"

"I don't think so."

"Why not?"

"My father would probably say no."

"I'll come home with you and ask him."

"No," she said sharply.

She had only once taken a friend back to her own house and they were playing in the front room when her father came home. That night at supper her father had said to her, 'When I come into this house your friends must leave'.

"No, but I will ask my mother to ask him if I might miss church just this once."

"Church!"

A morning ritual had developed by tacit agreement, always parting company before reaching their classroom. They would have no contact during their school day, Andrew staying with his friends, while she kept to herself.

"See you after school?" he said and she raised her hand in affirmation.

She entered the school alone and went to her locker to put her lunch away.

"Good morning, Sir," she said politely to Mr Dixon as she passed him at his desk.

"Good morning, Alexandra," he replied, wondering why she always used this formal address each day.

There was a strange aura about Alexandra which he could not put his finger on. She was always polite, well-behaved and gave him near perfect work. 'Almost too disciplined and serious', he thought. She would answer his questions but never asked any of him. She would sit still and quiet, rarely smiling, a face without readable emotion, two blue eyes set in the pallor of her freckled face; only the eyes reflected pleasure at his praise.

He had met her father once and asked him if Alexandra was a happy child, observing him wince.

"Alex is a happy boyo," he said in his sing-song Welsh voice. On the rare occasions he had to speak to her sharply, her blank face would turn on him. In trying to draw her out he teased her once.

"I'll have to speak to your father, Alexandra," he said, but seeing the transitory terror in her eyes felt disturbed.

She stood apart from the other girls, having no special friend amongst them. He had been surprised to see her walking home with three boys in his class. He followed them and watched them play in the field at the back of their houses. She seemed more at home in male company, although in his classroom he had not seen them together.

When they got back to Andrew's house from school they stayed in the field behind his back yard. She was pitching to David with her back to Andrew's house and he hit her high over her head. Turning around she was astonished to see Andrew's father within a few feet of her. He was not much taller than her, his dark brown hair receding made his head appear larger above his long narrow face and aquiline nose. He was looking at her and seemed about to rebuke her. Assuming he was annoyed at her for playing with the boys she tossed the ball to Andrew, gathered up her belongings and went from the field into her own yard. She was afraid of all fathers and had never spoken to Andrew's. She would like to go sailing with them to be with Andrew; a friendship unlike any experienced before.

She went into her house by the back door to find her mother finishing the preparation of supper.

"Can I help you?" she said, already knowing the answer. Her father did not want his son helping with woman's work.

"No, Alex, you go to your room and start your homework."

"Mother, I have been asked to spend the weekend with Doctor Barlow and his son. Do you think Father would let me?".

"We'll ask at supper, now go along."

In her attic room she put her glove and cap in her cupboard on their hooks, set her books down in the centre of her desk and pulled up the hard chair. Even now she had started to question the differences between Andrew's home life and her own.

She had once asked her father if she might have a mirror in the room but he had refused, saying that vanity was a sin. When her mother had tried to dress her in a more feminine way he had become angry and insisted that jeans were entirely adequate. Once her mother had washed and dried her hair, then brushed it out and gathered it in a ponytail. When he saw this feminine apparition he went into a rage and told her mother that he would have none of this false vanity in his house. She had thought this odd because her mother always dressed in cotton frocks which made her look so young and fresh. At night her mother would put her hair in a ponytail and dress in one of her nighties, transforming herself into an eager teenager.

She heard her mother call for her to come down to supper. They stood at their places at the dining table. Alex and her father were similar in physical stature; he was over six feet with broad, strong shoulders and had played lock in the rugby scrum. He was a big man, but not fat. He gave the grace for their evening meal and they sat down.

"I hear that Doctor Barlow has invited you to go sailing with them this weekend?"

"Yes, Father."

She felt her pulse quicken, knowing and hearing his anticipated refusal.

"Well, I think that would be good for you."

She was speechless for a moment at the unexpected reply. She looked down at her plate knowing that her face could not hide her joy.

"I will learn the prayer and recite it to you when I return on Monday evening."

He nodded his approval and they ate supper in their customary silence.

Alex liked going to church in spite of her father's insistence on having to learn the 'Collect' for the week, which he made her recite to him after the Sunday morning service. She rarely made a mistake now because an error was good reason for disciplining her.

'Monday evening,' she thought to herself, 'three whole days'.

As Alex walked to school with Andrew next morning they were both jubilant with her news.

"You have just won me ten dollars."

"How come?"

"I bet Dad that you would say yes, and he thought that he was so sure to win."

"Why was your father so sure?"

"Because he said you were too shy to speak to him so you would never agree."

"What's your father like on the boat?"

"He's a demon when we're sailing!"

"Are you serious, Andrew?"

Andrew laughed at her and changed the subject.

"We'll sleep in the forward compartment so we can talk. Will you mind having the loo between us?"

"The what?"

"The loo, the toilet; it's called the head on a boat," Andrew said with a leer, "will you mind if I watch you?"

"Not if you let me watch you!" she said, punching his shoulder.

"I usually get up and pee over the side."

As they laughed together, Alex, still concerned with Andrew's father, could not be deflected from the subject.

"Will he mind my coming?"

"Who?"

"Your father."

"No, he'll love it!"

"Dad, I mean, John," Andrew said - his father liked to be introduced by his first name, "this is Alex."

"Hi, Doctor Barlow," she said taking his outstretched hand, "thank you for inviting me."

"It's a pleasure, let's get going, we don't want to be left behind like Douglas last year," John said, and turned to Alex, "sometimes on long weekends the ferry becomes so crowded some pedestrians have to be left behind."

The drive out to the ferry was a revelation. Andrew kept up a stream of criticism of his father's driving and she wondered what sort of reaction would come from her father if she behaved like that. But instead of getting mad Doctor Barlow just smiled or told him to shut up.

At the ferry terminal she lined up behind Doctor Barlow to pay for her ticket.

"I have already bought your ticket," he said to her. "Is that the only money you have?"

"Yes, but I was given it to pay for my fare, Doctor Barlow."

"You hang onto it; you'll need it in the store when you get to Otter Bay."

She looked at the five dollar bill in her hand and frowned. It was the first time she had unassigned money in her hands. She was never allowed money of her own. Any presents were put into her account at the bank and she never saw it again.

She sat in the Tsawwassen ferry terminal eating silently. Andrew and Doctor Barlow talked and laughed together about what to do and where to go on the weekend. It suddenly occurred to her that they were friends. She found herself relaxing with them but was unable to use his first name. She continued to call him Doctor Barlow and made sure only to speak to him after he had addressed her. 'Who knows when the next slap on the face will come,' she thought.

Never Satisfied was a 25 foot sloop with a V berth forward and the marine toilet between the two bunks. This was quite private when Andrew and John were on board alone. To John's surprise Andrew took the front starboard bunk and put Alex's gear forward on the port bunk.

"We can be forward together, eh Alex?" he said, looking at her nodding head.

"But Andrew, what happens when Alex wants to go to the head?" John said, pointing out the marine toilet between the bunks.

"She says I can watch her if she can watch me!" he said, smiling at him.

"Andrew, let me hear what Alex would like."

"All right by me."

"I'll just check out *Heron*," Andrew shouted as he dashed off.

John showed Alex how to operate the marine toilet, stressing the importance of leaving it on "dry bowl" otherwise it would overflow and sink the boat.

"Are you sure you wouldn't like the forward bunk to yourself?"

"No," she said, "I like Andrew's company, Doctor Barlow, and I'm not shy about bathrooms and things."

"Alexandra," he said pompously, "my name is John, please don't call me Doctor or I will think I'm still at work!"

"Please call me Alex," she mimicked his voice, "or they will think I'm a girl!"

John raised his hand swinging it as if to slap her face but stopped just short of her left cheek. Her head did not move, but a look of terror crossed her face as he smiled down at her. Andrew, seeing this as he returned to the boat, shouted at her.

"Alex, you idiot, you're supposed to duck. Just as well Dad practises karate."

Alex knew that if she had ducked when her father went to slap her face she would be severely disciplined. During the inspections of her room any failure to live up to his rigid standards had been punished with a slap across her face. If the sting made her cry he slapped the other cheek or if she ducked her head he would get angry and put her over his knee. He trained her to take her punishment like a man, without flinching or crying.

She felt she had been outrageously undisciplined with her cheeky remark and by her home standards would have been punished and deservedly for once. She debated whether God would find her unfit on the day of judgement because she had not been duly punished. Her father said it was God's will that he punished her and to ask forgiveness in her prayers. She was to realise later that something snapped inside her at that moment of no impact.

"Come on, Alex," she heard Andrew say through her thoughts, "meet Jim and Jessica on *Heron.*"

It seemed to Alex as she followed Andrew down the dock that he was charged with excited uncontrollable energy as he urged her to 'come on, Alex'. As they approached *Heron*, Andrew started to shout to Anne who was sitting in the cockpit smiling at them. She could not remember the conversation, only the atmosphere, an impressionist painting in the shadowy light of dusk. The obvious pleasure in Andrew's eyes that he was once again close to Anne, sitting beside her and introducing her. 'Does Anne mean a lot to Andrew?' she wondered. The feminine lovely Jessica from whom she had felt that tinge of antagonism. Big Douglas, frighteningly strong, and tall Jim arrived at the boat in their dinghy after setting the crab trap, whatever that was. Douglas was so huge and Jim a similar build; and yet an absence of fear.

"This is Jim, Jessica's twin," Anne said, introducing him. "He's the older!"

"Douglas, this is Alex," Andrew said.

"A girlfriend, Andrew!" he said. Alex found him scary as he continued. His gruff voice issued out of his bearded face. "Do you know how fickle this lad is, Alex?"

"Alex is one of the boys, Douglas," Andrew said emphatically.

Alex was surprised at the ease with which she was able to talk to Anne and use only first names. But then no one told her their last name and she thought of them as Douglas, Anne, Jim and Jessica *Heron*! She felt exhilarated as the four of them set off to the little store to buy treats for the weekend. When she got to the store, what confusion she had felt at the choice! She ended up buying the same things as Andrew, but keeping three dollars back because the novelty of having money in her own pocket exceeded the pleasure of the treats.

On Saturday morning she was up early. As she was dressing she smelt the fragrance of bacon for the first time. At home she would be sitting in front of a bowl of porridge, the breakfast that never varied. She went into the cabin to watch John laying the strips of bacon on paper towel.

"Good morning, Alexandra." He greeted her with a sly smile.

"Good morning, Doctor Barlow," she replied, and grinned back.

She watched him as he deftly broke two eggs into the pan, feeling unusually relaxed in his company. He wore an old bathrobe and slippers.

"How do you like your eggs, Alex?"

"Any way, thank you, John."

She did not know how to reply because she had only eaten a boiled egg previously. Andrew's sleepy head appeared from forward. "Blinded, Dad."

"As if I didn't know!" John mumbled.

He put her plate of eggs, bacon and toast in front of her.

"Eat whilst it's hot, Alex, and don't wait for us."

After breakfast she asked John to show her where they were going on the map.

"Chart," he corrected her and set it out on the table. "You look at that whilst I get dressed, Alex."

The gown slipped from his naked body and he dressed.

"I figured you were one of the boys, Alex."

"I am."

But the blush on her cheeks betrayed her.

They set off for the marine park at Portland Island after breakfast and while she had gone forward to watch Andrew attach the jib sail to the forestay she heard the motor start. She watched Andrew release the dock lines, pushing the boat away from the dock. Since she had never sailed before she didn't know what to do. She asked if she could help but they told her to sit still and watch.

"Andrew's going to raise the main sail," John said to her, "he's attaching the rope to the head of the sail and will pull it up; that rope's called a halyard. The sail on this boom," he said, slapping the boom above his head, "is the mainsail and these ropes attached to the boom are the main sheets which in turn are connected to the traveller."

John continued to describe each step that Andrew took so that the maze of ropes began to make sense to her.

John sat beside her to explain the principles of sailing and then Andrew handed her the tiller, both talking at her at the same time. After a while, she proclaimed that she was surprised how easy it was to sail the boat. She wanted to know if all sailboats moved as well as *Never Satisfied*. John and Andrew both laughed.

"You wait till we fly the spinnaker!" they said in unison.

They anchored with *Heron* in Royal Cove on the northwest side of Portland Island. Anne made them a pack lunch so that they could all go ashore to explore the island. As she looked back at the boats from *Heron's* dinghy she saw that *Heron* was much bigger with *Never Satisfied* a cygnet to a swan nestled alongside. She was restrained, not because she was anxious, but because there was so much new around her to take in, talking seemed unnecessary. Once on shore it seemed natural that Jim teamed up with Andrew and she found herself in company with Jessica. They followed the boys in silence listening to their patter and occasionally Andrew would turn back to explain something to her.

At first Jessica had been formal and stiff with her and she, who was not used to female company, had not made it any easier with her reticence. By the time they reached Kanaka light and were sitting on the rocky promontory eating their lunch the barriers were breaking down. Jim and Andrew were sitting on the top of the light eating their lunch.

"Are you Andrew's girlfriend?" Jessica asked.

"I don't think so," she said, confused by the question, the concept foreign to her, "Andrew always says I'm 'one of the boys'."

"Do you like him?" Jessica persisted.

Of course she liked Andrew but the way Jessica had said "like" had implied something else.

"Why do you ask?"

"Oh I don't know, Alex; as soon as he and Jim get together I feel cut out. I don't think Andrew even notices me."

They watched the boys finishing their drinks and Andrew start to climb down followed by Jim.

"What's Jim like?" Alex asked Jessica.

But before she could answer the boys were within earshot. Jim looked at Alex.

"Andrew says you like to play baseball, Alex?"

Jim took off with her leaving Andrew with Jessica. She found walking back with Jim less constraining than with Jessica. She enjoyed walking back with this strong boy; a novel experience to look up to him. She could chatter with boys about sports and as the discussion became argumentative she backed up her jibes with physical jabs. Formality turned to informality as the walk progressed and just before they got to the dinghy she almost managed to get him to fall in the water directing raucous laughter at him. Jim did not retaliate and she did not appreciate the reason for his gentleness towards her.

Back on the boats, John in the cockpit and Anne in the galley, were busy preparing the evening meal and Anne asked Alex for her help. It was a novelty to be given a knife and told to deal with the vegetables and salad. She was finding the camaraderie between them all a confusing experience.

Happy hour started at six o'clock.

"Get me a beer, Andrew," John asked, "Alex, what do you want?"

"Coke please."

"And a coke for Alex."

Andrew appeared from the cabin with two coke cans and a tankard of beer. He passed a coke to Alex, put his down and took a deep draught from the tankard before handing it to John.

"Just making sure it wasn't off," he said to John and grinned at Alex. He moved quickly to sit down, avoiding John's foot.

"What do you think of the new Quebec premier?" Douglas asked.

"Bourassa; smart, educated and a federalist. Should be all right," John replied.

"My teacher thinks they should separate," Jim said, looking at Andrew for his view.

Anne passed up the crisps and nuts to Alex and sat beside her.

"Robin Lee Graham got back home all right," Anne said to her, "the boy who left California five years ago in his small boat."

"Oh yes," Alex replied, remembering she had read about it, "the one in National Geographic. Would you let Jim do that?" They were interrupted by raucous laughter at one of Doug's jokes.

"Did you see the interview with the man with three buttocks!" Andrew asked Douglas.

"No, but I did enjoy Woody Allen on Ed Sullivan, paranoid from the talking elevator."

Alex listened to Jim, Andrew and Jessica vie with each other for the most outrageous story. 'I wonder when the axe will fall', she thought. No axe she noted; John and Douglas seemed to encourage them.

They ate supper squashed four a side along the table in *Heron's* cabin, Alex sitting next to Anne across from Douglas and Andrew.

"This is good," she told Anne, "what is it?"

"Goulash!"

"What's that?"

"Everything I could find I needed to finish up!"

"Never have her soup," Douglas told her, "I swear I saw her put cat food in one time."

His gruff voice made Alex take him seriously until she looked at Anne.

"Don't you criticise Anne, you're lucky to have such a good wife." Andrew stretched himself up trying to look as tall as Douglas.

"What did I tell you, Alex," Douglas said ignoring him, "fickle - all Anne has to do is feed him and you've lost him."

After supper they stayed at the table to play hearts. Alex seemed to own the Queen until Anne sitting next to her gave her some hints on tactics. Either the help or the luck of the cards changed her fortune although Douglas won and they all accused him of cheating. The kettle boiled, Anne made them hot chocolate and handed round the cookies.

"Time to turn in," Anne said to the twins, "then we can have our night cap in peace!"

Alex followed Andrew to their boat where they changed into night clothes. She stood in *Heron's* cockpit and watched him in the cabin go up to Douglas, shake hands, "good night, Douglas," he bent to kiss Anne, "good night, Anne," and hugged John, "good night, Dad."

"Good night, Alex," she heard in chorus from them as she turned to follow Andrew back to *Never Satisfied's* cabin where he turned and hugged her.

"Good night, Alex, sleep tight," he said and got into his bunk.

At home she would leave the kitchen table without a word and happily make her way to bed where she could express herself without reprisal. She heard John, Douglas and Anne arguing and laughing together, 'so much laughter', she thought as the gentle rocking of the boat sent her to sleep.

On Sunday, Andrew asked Alex if she would like to join Jessica and himself on shore, but she declined the offer, sensing Jessica's relief. Douglas had asked Jim to help him and anyway Alex wanted to fish with John. She rowed him to the rocky shore where he told her the cod lingered. After a while there was a screeching cry from the trees, the ungreased axle of a pram wheel, that took her attention.

"What's that, John?"

"An eagle," he said, "its cry betrays the size of its claws." He handed her the binoculars to watch the eagle sitting sedately on a bare branch with its white head and protruding yellow beak curved like a scimitar.

"He's big; what do they eat?"

"Children!" he said, teasing her.

He took one of the small rock cod and threw it into the sea. The eagle opened its wings, dipped down, banked and descended towards the water gliding fast and smooth across the surface. Suddenly its claws were down in the water bringing up the fish. It rose in the air, flew towards shore and stood on the rocks over its prey eating with greedy slashes into the meat. She thought of her father. The gulls, sensing a meal, stood off like sentries awaiting their chance. The crows, more aggressive, chattered and flew down in feigned attack on the eagle who opened its wings with a lazy flap warning of the danger of too much closeness. She was fascinated by this drama on shore; her frown turned to a tentative smile.

"I've never seen anything like that!"

"Nature can be very cruel," he commented and reeled another cod into the boat, bonking its head and removing the hook; her expression squeamish.

"The Indians," he said, "had a way of justifying their action by asking understanding of the fish. They believed that fish or animals gave themselves to the hunter. They accepted them with special prayers or speeches to the animals. They were careful to put the fish bones back into the water, believing they grew new flesh on the old bones."

"How do you know about Indians?"

"Stephanie grew up with them as a child and she was always comparing the two cultures."

"Who is Stephanie?"

"She was Andrew's mother, my wife."

Her expression changed, unable to deal with his momentary grief or perhaps just her child's uncertainty when faced with death.

"Did you notice the kingfisher over there in the tree?" he asked, pointing in its direction, "watch it dive and you will see a fish in its beak."

"It looks like a Haida Indian carving, Alex."

"What's a Haida Indian carving?"

"Has Andrew shown you the work by Bill Reid at home?"

"No."

"Ask him to show you next time you visit and you will see what I mean."

Back at the boat she waited for Andrew to return to ask whether there was a book about birds on the boat that she could borrow. She saw them get into the dinghy on shore and went to *Heron*'s stern to help handle the dinghy. As Alex took her hand to pull her up, Jessica squeezed it and whispered, "Thank you."

This weekend of her awakening passed too quickly and they were driving back to Richmond. Sitting in the back of the car alone as if in her own room, she brought the images of the weekend into her mind. Rowing out to fish, the eagle on its perch but not least sitting at the table, open chart in front of her secretly watching him slip off his robe and dressing as if she were not there. The embarrassment at being caught out! Her eyes crinkled watching the curls of dark hair over his collar, imagining his face, large forehead and brown eyes that sparkled with interest; she caught sight of them in the rear view mirror.

"What are you thinking, serious one?" John asked her.

"Nothing much," she replied, a blush on her face belying her fib.

Now back at Andrew's house, they, saying how much they had enjoyed her company and she, wishing she had the courage to show John some tactile affection, took her leave, saying thank you which she knew did not fully express her feelings.

As she walked through the field to her back yard and entered her house she felt the chill enclose around her. She briefly told her parents how much she had enjoyed herself. Her father insisted she write a note to Doctor Barlow. She went to her room, sat at her desk and did as he told her.

CHAPTER 2

John's Story

Alex left us and by the time we had eaten supper and prepared for the morning it was bedtime. Some evenings before sleep I discussed the events of the day with Stephanie even though she had died three years before. Some mornings she would visit my dream; a portent for a happy week ahead. I found myself talking to her again.

"I did not find Alex as competitive for Andrew's attention as the other boys," I said aloud, "she turned the tables on him, spending time asking me about sailing, navigation, weather and came fishing with me. She wanted to know about all those aspects of boating taken for granted but making comfort for the inexperienced. When we were fishing she asked me who you were."

Memory took me back to meeting Stephanie at the university.

We were so young and vibrant when we met; Stephanie from a small town on the coast of Vancouver Island, surrounded by a horde of twenty five thousand others and yet lost in the vast loneliness of the university. The first week attending the Anthropology course she was sitting waiting for the class to begin. I had to catch her attention, I knew I must get to talk to her, so I sat next to her and introduced myself. Images of her recurring hourly during the few days to the next class brought new meaning to 'the tickle of the rub of love'. The thought of her shy smile made my knees wobble like jelly and I longed for her to appear around the next corner. My own crude poem to her written from consciousness of an overwhelming desire to sit at her feet and stare. Carefully written and folded I took a place beside her, shyly passing the note to her, watching her read and frown.

When I took Stephanie home in the third week of university to meet my parents she had an ease with them that surprised me. None of the tentative shyness of our whirlwind courtship. I picked her up at her residence in the afternoon. Her shyness melted as we drove to the East side of Vancouver to our house on Windsor Road. She asked me about my parents and whether my sister Mary, who was her residence advisor, would be there. I had expected reserve with my parents and had practised my excuses for her. There was no need.

She went straight to the kitchen to help my mother, chatting with her as if they were old buddies.

"Do you have brothers or sisters?" my mother asked her.

"Four sisters and then a brother," she replied raising her eyebrows at my mother, "I was eight when he was born!"

"You live in Port Hardy?" Stephanie nodded. "Out of the way isn't it?"

"No, it seemed settled after living on our floating house which was towed from one logging camp to the next. That's where I met all my Indian friends."

"What's the origin of Kurri?" I asked her, it was her surname. "Finnish, from Sointula where my grandparents moved to join the communist colony early in this century."

All through dinner she kept us amused with excerpts from letters she received from her Indian friends of her youth. Her love for and interest in their culture were given with illustrations from their beliefs and traditions which she had gleaned as a child. My mother turned to me, eyes alight with humour.

"It's like having the best after dinner speaker in Vancouver! Are you in residence, Stephanie?"

"Yes."

"What's it like?"

"Awful food, hard squeaky bed," she retorted, "can't say I like it much." Her eyes twinkled at Mother, "except for my adviser."

"Are you allowed to stay out?" Mother asked looking at the clock.

"I think so, Mrs Barlow."

"Would you like to stay here the night?" Stephanie's expression requiring no response. "Let's phone Mary and let her know."

When I said goodnight to my father and kissed my mother, Stephanie bent to kiss my father's cheek and I was surprised to see my mother rise and embrace her as if she were an old friend.

I said good night to Stephanie at her door, lingering as long as possible.

"Would you like to come again next weekend?"

"H'm, every weekend," she replied putting her arms around me and hugging me, "I feel so comfortable with you all."

"Have you been to the Symphony on Sunday afternoons?"

"I've never been to a live concert, only heard some of the music on radio."

"Shall I get tickets for you for next Sunday?"

"I'd like that," she replied, putting her arms around my neck and pulling my face to hers, "good night."

I had enjoyed the school dances, tending my duck's tail carefully and admiring the result in the mirror. I was inconstant, no one girl, and I would follow all the girls with my eyes, a penchant for long fair hair, seeking the eyes that reflected a common will to fool around at the evening's end. This was different, the lust was there but I wanted more than self satisfaction. Even after that first stay overnight I knew she was my lifetime partner.

The whirlwind progress of our love made me expect that Stephanie was already experienced. Consummation, although tentative at first, was wanted by both of us and her shyness overcome by the time we went to the drug store together. As we left the store Stephanie gave a memorable performance of the pharmacist's smell-under-his-nose disdain when serving us. I think she would have repeated it for my mother if I had not forbidden it!

The second symphony concert of the season ended with a performance of Rachmaninov's Second Symphony. The performance had swept both of us up to a new plane of listening enjoyment and its romanticism was hard for new lovers to resist. Returning home, the mixed melodies working their spell, she followed me to my room, locked the door and started to remove my clothes. She would not release me from her arms certain of love's consequence and swept towards it by choice. I opened my eyes to see her bliss and felt the quiver of her body just before she fell into a deep sleep. Her breathing so regular and her expression so calm I knew that the miracle of conception had touched her.

After Thanksgiving I went to Port Hardy to meet her parents and her sisters. Her father towered above me, Stephanie's eyes gentle and kind looking at me from his face.

"I would like to marry Stephanie with your permission."

"She's only eighteen, John, and you not a year older." A Finnish lisp to his speech. "You've only known each other a few weeks."

"How long had you known Mrs Kurri?" I asked innocently.

"I can see the little vixen has been talking," his eyes sparkling, "I suppose she has already agreed?"

"We would like to marry at Christmas," I said boldly, "shall I get her so we can talk together?"

She entered the room and kissed him. "Thank you, Father."

"Why so soon, are you sure?"

"Absolutely," she said and then blushing with eyes down, "and almost certain you are a potential grandfather."

"Your mother's daughter!" taking her in his arms. "Are you wanting to marry because of the child?"

"No, because of the father!"

I had not expected to be married by Christmas, the father of a son before the start of second year university or feel the generosity of parents who took us into their home and insisted that we both continue with our studies. As Stephanie finished university a nurse, I entered medical school, and my mother continued to look after Andrew during the day even though we had moved to our own small rented house in Richmond. Stephanie tolerated my long hours of study, never dissatisfied and Andrew was growing ever more interesting. At last finished after five years, internship over and into practice in Richmond, we were able to plan for our future. Listening to her chide at the demanded patience of our self-made circumstance, our unity was cemented undiminished. Stephanie thankfully stopped nursing to look after Andrew, and as the practice expanded in this growing neighbourhood at last we were able to plan our future family.

Whether it was the eroticism of the movie or just the meshing of desires that night, there was an intensity of gratification for both of us.

"I haven't felt like this since Andrew was conceived," she said.

"Now I remember, the afternoon of the Rachmaninov concert," I replied.

"They used his music in the film tonight too," she joked. "When do I get a pregnancy test?"

"Why bother, we both know the result."

I took Stephanie to the hospital in early labour as soon as the membranes ruptured and brought my mother back to the house to care for Andrew. All excitement and happiness as I returned to the office to see patients during her long afternoon of labour. Then the phone call from Frank to say that the labour was obstructed, the baby in some distress and he suggested an immediate Caesarean section to which I agreed.

At the hospital, our baby daughter stillborn and Stephanie uncontrollably bleeding her life away, the world became blurred with outrage. She did not regain consciousness and there was no chance for Andrew and I to say good-bye to her. I was so emotionally unprepared that for days I was unable to contain myself or function in such a hostile world. Poor Andrew, how to explain to you, and yet in his innocence, he started the rehabilitation for his father by gently saying, "We have each other, Dad."

Time present.

After we had finished our meal on Monday evening Andrew remembered his claim.

"You owe me ten bucks, Dad."

"What do you mean?"

"You bet me ten bucks that Alex would not come on the boat if I asked her," he said triumphantly, "and you've lost."

"Really, I thought we were just joking."

"Where's my ten bucks?"

I felt a touch of annoyance, 'was it losing a bet with him?' I wondered, 'or the intrusion of a stranger in our relaxed companionship?' Certainly I had lost enough bets to Andrew and it had become my way of supplying him with pocket money. He had to be careful to win since he knew I would never forgive him a loss. When Brian or David had been on the boat I felt the competition for his attention; a competition that I never won leaving me mildly bitter at the end of the trip, with Alex it had been different. Andrew at twelve was small for his age, as yet beardless, his high pitched voice in conversation belied the maturity of its content. He read endlessly with concentration, retaining quotations and had an appreciation of its content that surprised me. On the boat we would read to one another in the evenings. He liked to play with words and would challenge me to give synonyms honing his punning wit. Recently he had started to play with word associations, rather than synonyms.

In public he would refer to me as Dad, but in private when we were discussing, I was berating or he was resisting I was always John. When I was angry with him in the sense of disciplining him he had an aggravating way of saying 'Dad' like a sergeant-major addressing 'Sir' to an Officer Cadet! I believed in correction by reason for children and became the butt of his mimicry; a device he used to turn my pique to humour. Early in our boating experience my insecurity made me Bligh-like in treating my crewman, blaming him for my own errors. He told me I was 'A demon captain' and I replied 'who else do I blame?' my own form of apology. Over the three years of experience it had become an easy bantering relationship with accusation and threats never to be taken at face value.

When I arrived home on the following Friday evening I found Alex sitting in the family room.

"Alexandra, what are you doing here?"

"Andrew asked me to supper, Doctor Barlow, " she replied, "and to stay overnight."

"Well that's nice, Alex."

"For me too, John."

As I got the spare room ready for her I wondered why Andrew chose to ask her. He had never asked other friends to stay, although Brian and David had both visited the boat with us. I could see no difference in the way Andrew treated her compared to them. When I went to check on Andrew before going to bed I found her asleep on the floor of his room with the pillow and comforter from the spare room bed. In the morning she was bright and cheerful, the complete contrast to Andrew.

"Did you sleep all right, Alex?"

"Fine thanks, John."

"Weren't you uncomfortable on the floor?"

"No, I've always slept on a hard bed, your bed is too soft and anyway I like his company."

As fall turned to winter she stayed over more frequently until it became a weekly routine. We would have Saturday morning breakfast together since Andrew was incommunicado for some time in the morning. I started to look forward to our Saturday morning discussions when she would ask about my growing up in Vancouver or my marriage to Stephanie.

"Was it difficult to manage after...?" Alex asked.

"Yes, particularly the first few weeks before Flora came to run the house for me. Have you talked to her often?"

"After school sometimes."

Mrs Flora McKenzie was the widow of a fisherman lost at sea some three years before. She was tall and stately with conservative reserve, a strong prudish strain and Scottish to the bone. She had consulted me one year after marriage because she had not conceived and I was about to refer her to a colleague for investigation of infertility, when she was widowed.

"She was a patient of mine. I like to think that I gave her some help while she was grieving Rod's death."

"She told us you helped."

"She returned the favour when Stephanie died. She cut her hand and after I sewed it up she talked to me and offered to keep house. She came the next evening to our house to meet Andrew and discuss terms; I didn't know what to offer, nor she what to ask!"

"Andrew likes her," she reassured me.

Flora gave him lunch, got the evening meal and instructed Andrew on how to get it ready when I got home. I would hear him imitate her Scottish accent.

"Get away with you, Andrew, with your teasing," Flora would say.

Rushing home one Friday evening Andrew greeted me.

"Dad, would you look at Alex's ear? She said it was bleeding and she can't hear that side."

I was in a hurry as I examined Alex's ear. Seeing that the drum was perforated, I discounted the red area in front of her ear, assuming she just had a cold.

"Have you had a cold, Alex?"

"A bit of one," she said after hesitating, her face expressionless.

"These will help," I told her, handing her a supply of antibiotics from my bag. "The ear drum will heal."

"But what's wrong?"

"You've perforated the ear drum. When it heals the hearing will come back. It won't take long."

That Friday evening the Women's National Volleyball Team was playing a match at the university gym and I had volunteered to be present in case a physician was needed. I rushed them through supper and took them both with me. I listened to them discussing 'this sissy game' as we drove out to the campus. As the teams were warming up and the women started to practise spiking and digging she was impressed.

"They hit the ball hard don't they?"

"You wait until the game starts, Alex, and watch how they block those spikes at the net or dig for the ball off the floor." I watched her face during some of the longer rallies and saw her interest become more and more intense as the final and deciding game came to its conclusion.

"A sissy game for Alexandra?" I inquired.

"Doctor Barlow, I've never seen it played like that. Do they play volleyball in junior high?"

"Yes, I think the program starts then; why?"

"I'm going to play volleyball next year," she said with a determined look on her face.

Now that spring had come Andrew and I spent most weekends on the boat, sometimes just relaxing or doing all the maintenance jobs getting ready for the summer. I still enjoyed time alone with Andrew and had asked him not to request company too often. Then I noticed that I was beginning to miss Alex's company, so when Andrew told me she was allowed to come on the long weekend in May I was unable to hide my pleasure.

She awoke early on Saturday morning at Otter Bay and was up before me. She had watched me light the stove before and putting the methyl hydrate in the burner, I saw her set it alight. I got up anxiously, trying to take over, but she held her ground at the stove, not allowing me to and determined to master it. With the kettle on she set the second burner going and put the bacon into the pan.

"I didn't ask you on the boat to be my maid," I said, displacing her from the stove, "I'll make you breakfast."

"Will you let me do it one morning by myself?"

"That's a deal," I told her.

We set off in late morning with a brisk southeast wind which died as we were half way across Swanson Channel on a port tack. We came about and were drifting with the tide when I warned her.

"Get ready, Alex, there's a strong southwester coming towards us."

"How do you know?"

"You can see it coming," I said, pointing to the ruffled water a hundred yards away, "we may need to drop the jib if it's as strong as I think."

As the wind caught the sails our speed increased. A strong gust hit the boat and made it heel suddenly, knocking her back against the winch and her left elbow caught the side of the cockpit. I saw her wince with the pain.

"Andrew, go forward to bring the jib in," I instructed, "Alex, let the jib sheet out."

She took a loop of rope around her left wrist.

"No, Alex!" I shouted at her, but it was too late, her wrist was already drawn towards the winch and locked in.

I watched the rope bite into her and crush her hand against the winch. A deep breath drew into her lungs ready for a scream at the pain but I quickly brought the boat up into the wind and the weight came off the rope releasing her wrist. She let her breath go silently.

"Control the jib," I shouted to Andrew as I loosened the halyard and turned to her, "are you all right, Alex?"

"Yes, John," she replied, "nothing broken."

I could tell she was lying and fighting the tears back into her eyes.

There was no time to console her as the wind continued to pick up and Andrew came back to take some of the mainsail in with the roller reefing. She got up to try and help.

"Stay where you are, Alex," I said sharply, "until I have a chance to look at your arm; lucky we're in protected waters and the sea's not a factor." Andrew nodded his agreement.

Andrew took the helm as the boat scudded along more comfortably under the reduced sail.

"Let's see your arm," I said, taking it gently, feeling for damage to the elbow and then looked at the rope burn on the wrist and hand. I examined each finger and then the hand and wrist, "I don't think it is fractured, Alex, but I bet it hurts. I'll put it in a sling until we can get the plaster out for a cast," I said to her, winking at Andrew, but she knew from Andrew's face that she was being teased.

She took her hand back and wrung it out to try and make the pain go, punching my shoulder with her right fist.

"No worse than a baseball hitting you."

"You must be Dsonqua's daughter."

"Why?" she asked, "and who is Dsonqua's daughter?"

"The forest giant who stole children."

"Another Indian story?"

"Yes, specifically Kwakiutl but the same type of myth occurs in various forms up and down the coast. The 'Sasquatch story' probably has the same origin."

"Tell me more about Dsonqua."

"Tonight around the fire if you remember to ask me."

When we were settled at anchor protected from the southwest wind and warmed by the sun I showed Alex why she must not wrap the rope round her wrist.

"If a gust of wind had hit us at the time your arm was locked in the force would have broken it," I said, feeling squeamish at the thought of it. "You were lucky!"

I had not expected so many boats in one bay or that one yacht club would raft ten boats together across the bay, talking to each other through loud hailers, disturbing our peace. I saw Andrew get the fog horn to blow it every time the loud hailer was used. Other boats joined in blowing their horns with humour but in protest until the loud hailers were turned off.

As we walked ashore the children, in a rush to see who could get to the horse barn first, had soon left Anne, Douglas and me behind.

"Would you consider bringing Alexandra with you this summer?" Anne asked.

"Why do you ask?" I replied.

"Well, Jessica sometimes feels left out when Jim and Andrew get thick as thieves."

"You know he always calls her Alex."

"Because she's one of the boys," Anne said, "but that will change soon, or haven't you noticed!"

"You know Anne, I have never seen Alex in the company of another girl except for Jessica on that weekend at Portland Island and this weekend. I don't think she has ever had a close girl friend."

"Has she become Andrew's girlfriend?"

"No, they are like brothers together and Alex is the more talented athlete; holds her own physically."

"What do you think of the idea?"

"Why don't you put the idea in Andrew's mind; you have a great influence with him," I said, "I certainly would be happy to have the extra crew."

'If it was Alex,' I thought to myself.

As evening came the tide rode up the beach, the fires were alight and the smell of hot-dogs pervaded the air. As darkness fell a huge moon rose, lighting the bay which was further illuminated by the lanterns on the boats. The kids had made fires on boards which they floated out into the bay only to bombard them with rocks to put them out. We sat on logs around the fire until late at night and I attacked Anne about her disciplining of children.

"All disciplining of children should be done with reasoning," I pontificated. "And it is fundamentally wrong to strike a child; not even your spur of the moment anger can justify it."

"I don't agree with that. The occasional spanking never did a loved child harm." Anne answered whilst Douglas remained strangely quiet.

"Is that what you do, Anne?"

"Not myself, that's Doug's responsibility and with his big hands they usually come back contrite," she said, smiling at Douglas.

The children sat listening, making faces at each other or whispering laughter back and forth behind their hands. Doug sat silent, his eyes looking at the twins as if to will them to be quiet. Alex's expression, formless with discomfort at the argument, suddenly brightened.

"Tell us about Dsonqua, John."

"Some say Dsonqua lived in the forest, others that she lived in the sea. Some say she was he, even though the pendulous breasts were a constant feature. All agree that she had sunken eyes and a round mouth with thick lips as if about to make the sound 'ooooh'. All agree that she was a giant, some say with a basket on her back into which she put the stolen children. These she took to her lair, ankle tied and hung upside down from the roof. The smoke from the fire wafting through their browned bodies preserved their meat for winter food.

"Some say she has a daughter named Lexa who had never been known to shed tears. Some say that the first hero to arrive who could make her cry would be rewarded by Dsonqua with great wealth and riches.

"Chief Fullmoon had fallen on bad times, the salmon had failed to come to his river and he had to trade away part of his copper to get food for his people. Several children had disappeared from the village and not returned so he knew that Dsonqua must have a cave nearby. He ordered one brave warrior to be selected to find her and make Lexa cry. Wander was the smallest and weakest of the braves but the most cunning. The other braves decided they could sacrifice Wander on this useless quest and sent him to the chief.

"Wander saw a trail of mussel shells leading to a cave and knew the children must have thrown them out as Dsonqua made her way along the trail in order to lead him to them. As he entered the cave he saw the children hanging by their ankles, the tears from their smoke filled eyes forming puddles beneath them.

"'I have come to make Lexa cry and take our children home.'

"'You will not succeed,' Dsonqua cackled, measuring in her mind the meat from his body.

Lexa sat by the fire on a smooth rock bench looking at Wander with an expressionless face. Wander sat beside her, she looked lonely and unloved as his eyes fixed onto hers. He did not know why, but from his heart he asked,

'Will you be my sister, Lexa?'

"He saw her eye glisten, a small tear collect on her lower lid, slip down her cheek and hiss as it hit the hearth."

The story finished, their absorbed faces alight from the flames of the dying beach fire.

"Is that the end of the story?" Jessica asked, puzzled by its inconclusion.

"Yes."

"But what happened?"

"That's for you to decide when you go to your bunk to settle for sleep."

On Sunday we all felt crowded in the bay. We decided to go further south to explore D'Arcy Island. The pilot book mentioned that it had been a leper colony until recently, the old wooden buildings still standing, no glass left in the windows and daylight visible through the roofves. Douglas warned the children to be careful of open wells hidden by the undergrowth, getting angry with Jim's overeager explorations and correcting him sharply several times. Alex was walking with Anne, her chatting eyes sparkling and face animated with their conversation. Jim came rushing past them.

38

"Jim," Anne said, halting him, "you'll feel your father's hand if you're not careful."

I saw all animation leave Alex's face as if a 'Noh' mask were placed in front of it. Her eyes betraying her fear for him, Jim looking at her as if to say 'it's not that bad'.

Back at the boats, nobody had been in need of rescue from the wells, a lazy atmosphere covered both cockpits.

"There they blow!"

Andrew quickened us into action with his mimicry of my reading of Captain Ahab. We stood to watch the pod of killer whales pass down Haro Straits, close to our shore, feeding as they went. Three tall fins of the adult males joined by the four smaller fins of the female and juvenile whales; the sighting always a treasured event of a weekend.

On Monday morning, the early sunrise flooding the cabin woke Alex. She came to the main cabin to light the kerosene stove sitting on me as I threatened to get up to do it for her. She put the kettle on and sat back on the foot of my bunk and hugged herself against the cold penetrating her T-shirt.

"Put on my dressing gown, Alex," I said, staying in my sleeping bag, remembering my promise to let her cook the breakfast.

The kettle boiled, she made coffee, handing me mine and taking hers to sit in the sun in the cockpit. I got out of my sleeping bag, dressed and joined her in the sun, my dark blue sweater absorbing its radiant warmth.

"Do you want it back?" Alex asked.

"No. I'm warm enough."

"The breeze not making you cold?"

"No, excited."

"Why?"

"Spinnaker day," I said, to find my own excitement reflected.

"First time for me."

All went well until we reached the entrance to Swanson Channel where the wind veered just as Alex at the helm was arguing with Andrew. She let go to attack him and allowed the spinnaker to wind itself around the forestay.

"Alex!" I shouted in anger, "attend to your job."

My irritation was accompanied by rumbled grumbles at her for her inattention as I unwound the sail from the stay. Once more the 'Noh' mask descended, short-lived this time, as Andrew put his face close to her ear and whispered,

"Demon."

Mouthing the word clearly for my benefit.

It didn't take long before Andrew started to pester me about Alex coming for the summer cruise, so I knew that Anne's seed had taken root. When I doubted that Alex would want to spend so long with us he assured me that I was wrong. After some discussion we decided that I should go to talk to her father about the trip.

"Dad, don't call her Alexandra for goodness' sake!" Andrew pleaded, "and stress that she is needed as a crewman, man!"

I had met Mr Jones briefly when attending school functions and I had not warmed to this large blustery man. His Welsh accent reminded me of one of those brutish second row forwards of my rugby days. Alex must have mentioned the intent of my visit.

"So, you are asking whether Alex can come boating with you for six weeks this summer?"

"Yes," I explained, "I have been able to take all six weeks of holiday from work so that I can make an extended cruise this summer and I really need an extra crewman."

I stressed the man and saw a hint of a smile on his face. "Ah yes, but why Alex?"

"She and Andrew, my son, have become good friends. Alex is as good and as strong a crew as any boy I have had on the boat." I noticed that he was now smiling broadly as I added, "and I don't expect her to just do galley work or cleaning. I need her for the sailing."

"What do you intend to pay her for all this work?"

I was taken by surprise, since thought of payment had not entered my calculations.

"How much would you expect me to pay her?"

"Fifteen dollars a week."

"How about ten dollars?"

"Agreed," he said, looking pleased with himself.

I was glad for Andrew that he would have the company of a friend, particularly for the second phase of our cruise to Queen Charlotte Straits. *Heron* would be returning after Desolation Sound.

Did I really need the extra crew? I could have handled the boat on my own. I was not certain of my feelings towards her. Was I looking for a substitute for the daughter I had lost when my wife died in childbirth? I was fond of her and enjoyed her company even though she was reserved with me. This puzzled me for she seemed comfortable calling me John and yet there was a stiffness to her if I tried to get closer. 'It must be her age', I thought; Bob at Otter Bay had teased her on the May weekend.

"You're starting to grow in all the right places I see, Alexandra!"

Andrew and his friends had a habit of using a tea towel, a wet one preferably, to inflict a whip-like sting on the unsuspecting, and Alex had become as expert as the others. On the Friday before we set off they were washing up after supper when Andrew caught her. She never complained but caught my eye with a grin just before she got her revenge.

I had been to the store to pick up three sets of longjohn thermal underwear, having heard how much colder it could be when we got to Queen Charlotte Straits. I laid them out and picking one up held it against Andrew to make sure that the size was adequate.

"You must be kidding if you think you can make us wear those," he said, contorting his face, "what do you think, Alex?"

"Ugh! They look horrible!"

I sent them off to put them in their tote bags.

That evening when they went off to get ready for bed, I heard shouts of derisive laughter then muffled inquiries. They both appeared modelling their underwear and making derogatory remarks about the flaps various! I noticed how tall Alex had grown and that the longjohns were a bit short for her.

CHAPTER 3

Andrew's Story

Andrew would feel her tummy trying to catch hold of a foot and Stephanie would educate him about the coming baby. Andrew would draw some of the Indian tales of human origins from her and she would tease him with legend.

"Where did I come from 'Injun' style, Mum?" he asked, unable to pronounce the word Indian.

"Indian, Andrew, not Injun," she corrected him, "Dad blew his nose into a mussel shell."

"Greenies!" As he said it he curled his upper lip in disgust; or was it disbelief.

"Then you just grew and grew and I had to find bigger and bigger shells."

"I thought I came from inside you."

"You did, when you got too big for the clam shell," she pointed to the geoduck shell on the mantle, "Dad put you inside me."

He could remember the morning when he saw her face contort at breakfast.

"I won't be home at lunch, Andrew," she said quietly, "the baby has started to come. I'll make sure John is here to keep you company."

"Okay, Mum."

"Andrew."

"Yes, Mum."

"Be sure to look after him," she said and added, "promise?"

The last time he had seen her and the promise he was keeping like a sacred trust.

When Alexandra came into his life in the field he had felt a kindred spirit with her. He made friends easily, enjoyed a crowd around him and yet treasured his solitude at home. His father was his best friend but there were secrets he kept from him like the promise to his mother. The trio friendship of the sailing weekends with Jessica and Jim had made him wish for a sister. There never seemed to be a time when he could talk to Alex alone, Brian and David were always there. The invitation to her to come sailing was made to have her to himself; his sister to tell, taunt, tease but mostly trust. The first weekend she stayed overnight lying on the floor of his room they talked and he told her of his promise to his mother.

"Do you miss her, Andrew?"

"Occasionally," he replied, "sometimes after school I still come into the house and start talking to her before I remember she's no longer here."

"What did she look like?"

"Often I can't remember," he said. She looked up at him, at the soft tears on his cheeks, "so I have to go to John's room to see the photograph."

Alex was disturbed by him. 'Boys and men don't let people see them cry', she thought.

"Until last weekend I didn't believe you really liked to go with John. I thought you had to go."

"Don't you like your mum and dad?"

She could not answer, the truth would be disloyal to her parents and she would not lie to him. He turned the lights off and she soon heard his regular breathing of sleep. The door opened, John came across the room, looked down at him, touched his head and left the room. She held her breath, terrified that he would be angry with her for not being in her room, his visit unexpected; nobody came to check her at night.

Andrew brought her home after school every day, even when the field was unfit to play baseball. Brian and David would join them in his room where they would sit on the foam cushions made by his mother instead of chairs and play cards or board games set out on the floor. Disputes were settled by wrestling and since he was the smallest he rarely won, even against Alex.

There were times when she would lie on the floor bringing the cushion under her chest. He noticed that she would not fight them at these times.

"Why do you lie on your stomach like that, Alex?"

"It's comfortable; I like it sometimes."

"And you don't fight me when you lie like that," he said, seeing her expression change, "and..."

Before he could continue she was on him, she was angry, pushed him on his back and sat on top of him.

"Yeah, is that so!"

Some Fridays John would not be home for supper and Flora would stay to eat with them. They got her to tell them about Scotland or her husband Rod or the trips when she had gone fishing with him.

As winter came the long nights were times for sailors' dreams and reminiscences. Once they told her about their first cruise.

"I can still see Robert Stoltz, the boat builder, standing on the dock waving 'good-bye' as we headed out of Steveston Harbour into the Fraser River," John said, opening the story. "The outgoing tide swept us along the river from one red buoy to the next; a brisk northwest wind in our face as we came down the river. We could see the lighthouse structure at the entrance to the Fraser River channel, the size of the waves increasing as the river water tumbled into the Gulf of Georgia. The fetch raised by the northwest wind against the tide made the waves grow until we could no longer see over them when in their trough."

Andrew took up the story.

"It was unbelievable, Alex, and scary when the waves started to break above you. It was like magic to find yourself above the breaking water as the boat was lifted up on the crest of the wave. Then the waves got shallower and the wind on our beam as we set our course to Porlier Pass and as the crests of the waves stopped breaking the quiet was eerie. We heard a blowing sound with spray shooting in the air. Suddenly, not 200 yards ahead, there was another spout of water, this time accompanied by a large black back and tall fin of a killer whale as it broached the surface of the sea."

"I remember Andrew asked why they were called killer whale after trying to reassure him that we were in no danger."

"Yeah, Dad, you didn't know it was because they killed other sea mammals. I found that out when I discovered that killer whales were really large porpoises, not whales."

Alex's eyes were focusing from one to the other as they told their tale. She wondered if embellishment over time and telling had deepened the troughs like a fisherman's story of the 'one that got away'. John took up the narration.

"The sail across the gulf to Porlier Pass in 12 to 15 knot winds on a reach was exhilarating. When we got to Porlier Pass we couldn't understand why we were at a standstill."

"You couldn't," Andrew corrected John, "you made the same mistake in the Power Squadron exam!"

"Quiet son," John told him in mock annoyance and turned to Alex, "we took the Power Squadron course together and I forgot to change Pacific Standard Time to allow for our summer time when reading the current tables. We had arrived at Porlier Pass one hour too soon! One hour later we started to creep forward. Once we were through the pass we went into Clam Bay to anchor."

"I left Dad on the boat and took the dinghy to explore the channel to Telegraph Harbour that runs between Kupfer and Thetis islands. We should go there again, Dad, it was neat. But the night that followed was awful."

"Why so?" she asked John.

"Just after we turned in, a wind started to blow from the south. The flapping sound of rope against the mast awoke me. I went up on deck, the stars had disappeared behind a band of cloud, the wind was starting to make the sea hit against the bow. As it strengthened the boat yawed from port to starboard, increasing the sound of waves against the hull. I went forward to let out more anchor rope, traced all the sources of noise where the ropes were hitting the mast and frapped them. I went back to my bunk but the wind increased; the whining in the rigging denied us sleep. The strong wind persisted and we both experienced a change in mood to anger induced by the relentless wind. I remember thinking 'so this is wind madness'."

"What a wretched night," Andrew said to Alex. "In the morning, do you remember, Dad, we looked out and saw a patch of still water in the southwest corner of the bay; if only we had anchored there!"

"We had so many lessons that holiday, didn't we, Andrew?"

"Yes, we never missed listening to the weather forecast at six each evening and recording it in the log after, that did we?"

When Andrew asked Alex to stay overnight she would approach her mother to intercede for her with her father. At first she sensed a reluctance from him but as successive Fridays rolled by there was a cheerful acceptance. She still looked boyish, clean but untidy and showed no sign of femininity. She could not tell Andrew about her father's disciplining of her, although she noticed the frequency of her punishments lessened through winter and spring and she was rigidly obedient.

By New Year her visits had become routine. Andrew would return to his house on Friday afternoon with Brian and David. He would watch for Alex coming across the field carrying her valise, his uncertainty relieved as soon as he sighted her. Brian and David would return to their homes about the time John arrived home and he would have her to himself. After supper they would talk together or Andrew would read to her, imitating the voices of the characters; ever the actor of his dreams.

Andrew's love of words, to play with their order often leading to a muffled clarity, landed him in trouble with Mr Dixon. He waited for John's return to unburden his troubles; an act that would remind John of Stephanie.

"Dad," he said one evening mid-week before John could get his coat off, "I've had a terrible day. Mr Dixon didn't like my story about Annette Bay. He said it was all mixed up, called it a mumbo-jumbo of words. I was so mad I told him what I thought. He sent me to the Principal."

"Just what did you say, Andrew?"

His coat off now, he stood in the sitting room.

"I told him," Andrew hesitated and continued quietly, "that he was an old goat!"

"What did the Principal say?"

"Not much," he replied glumly, "it hurt. I thought Mr Dixon partly to blame."

"Did you deserve it?"

Andrew did not answer, went up to John and hugged him for comfort, although he knew that John would never intervene unless he had been unfairly treated.

"Have you apologised to Mr Dixon, Andrew?" John asked him gently.

"Do I have to, Dad?"

Already knowing what John expected of him.

Andrew always felt better for his confessions to John; absolved by them. Next morning he apologised to Mr Dixon who took the story out of his desk.

"I've made some suggestions for you. I hope you will rewrite it, Andrew, so that you can read it to the class. I realise that I was partly to blame; I didn't understand how important it was to you."

Andrew would sleep in on Saturday mornings even though he knew that Alex was up early. He sensed that Alex enjoyed breakfast with John and would ask her what they discussed.

"John said you never see Jim and Jessica in Vancouver," she said, "only when you go to Otter Bay."

"What did John tell you about them?" Andrew said with a sleepy voice, looking at her sitting against the wall on one of his cushions.

"He told me that Douglas was a lawyer in Vancouver. He said he used to be a fisherman and went back to university when he was older."

"Did he tell you that Anne works near him at the university now?"

"He said she is a social worker who looks after kids who've been abused." She looked at Andrew, "you like her, don't you?"

"I like the others too." He felt around the bottom of the bed for his dressing gown. "Must pee, Alex!"

He gathered the gown around him and rushed out of his room. She sat back wondering and hoping they would ask her to the boat again. She had liked Jim and Jessica, was a little afraid of Douglas, not knowing that his gruff manner hid a soft centre and Anne, she had seemed pleasant.

Andrew would have liked her to stay Saturday nights as well.

"They will not often let me miss church."

"Do you have to go to church?"

"Don't you ever go?" she inquired. "Do you believe in God?"

"Someone out there," he said vaguely, waving his hands to the sky, "standing over us with angels and things."

"I talk to someone inside me," she answered, perplexed by his idea, "he tells me what to do; what's okay."

"I talk to myself when I'm really upset, like last week with Mr Dixon and then I tell John."

When Alex saw the altercation between them ending in Andrew leaving for the Principal's office, she felt her empty stomach sensation; the panic induced by her father.

"What did John say?"

If she told her father he would punish her again. She could hear him send her to her room and feel the waiting fear, humiliation and his sensed pleasure as he punished her.

Andrew told her about his talk with John and his apology next day.

"Don't you talk to your Dad?"

Alex would not answer him and he already knew it from the set of her face. This was not the first time he had come up against her stone wall.

"Don't you?" he repeated, knowing it would anger her.

Her eyes blazed at him as she fought him to the ground, sat on his chest and pinned his arms above his head holding him there until her anger dissipated.

Andrew had asked Alex twice to join them on the boat before her parents allowed her to go on the long week end in May. On D'Arcy Island he was walking with Anne talking about lepers when she changed the subject.

"Do you think John would ask Alex to come with you for the cruise this summer?" she asked, "so much better if there were four of you."

"I'll work on him," he promised her.

Lying on their bunks that night, Alex and Andrew snug in their sleeping bags against the chill of a May night, she noticed that he was unusually quiet. Andrew was considering the suggestion made by Anne. He did not realise that there was a conspiracy between Anne and John so he was tentative in his attitude towards inviting Alex in case John did not welcome the idea. Alex turned to look at his trance-like face staring at the cabin ceiling.

"Why so quiet tonight?"

"Just thinking; planning actually."

"Will you tell me?"

He turned on his side looking her in the eyes.

"If I work on John would you like to come on the cruise with us this summer?"

"I don't think my father would let me."

"Why, are you going somewhere else?"

"No, we never go anywhere."

"Would you want to come?"

"Of course."

"I'll work on Dad then," he said, then smiled at her, "I should warn you, Alex, that John is not the same benign skipper on a cruise."

"How do you mean?"

"He drives his crewmen during the long sails."

"I like sailing."

"The crew must obey or else."

He was teasing her now.

"Or else what?"

"The lash," he said, holding his face serious until he turned away from her.

CHAPTER 4

The Cruise

Alex did not know what had passed between John and her father when she got home after their meeting. Her father looked pleased.

"I'm only agreeing because Doctor Barlow said he needed a good crewman and that you were as good as any man," he said and looked proud of her, adding, "and I have negotiated a salary of $10.00 per week for your work on the boat so mind you make a good account of yourself, young man."

Alex was leaving the school on the last day, having said good-bye to Mr Dixon. She was pleased with her year and looking forward to junior high in the fall. The school was quiet, most of the students had returned home and as she went through the door out into the car park area, she saw David and Brian slipping round behind the gym. Curious, she followed, finding them with a can of red spray paint with which they marked the white outside wall with a garish good-bye. It was unfortunate that the principal should happen around the corner, catching them red handed. At the principal's office both Brian and David insisted that Alex had not been responsible and he reluctantly allowed her to leave, indicating that he was not certain that he believed them. A note from the principal was delivered to the house in the late afternoon.

Her father arrived late that evening when she was ready for bed. She watched him read the note, his head nodded and his eyes narrowed. A sneering smile across his face told her she would not be spared.

"I'm disappointed with you, Alex; I've a good mind to cancel your sailing trip."

"Please, father."

"You'll accept my punishment?"

Alex lowered her eyes in acceptance and went to her room to wait for him. The severity of his beating with the pain greater than the humiliation almost broke her will to remain silent; that determination not to show him that he could hurt her. As he left the room, sensing the pleasure he derived, she was touched by the irony of his pronouncement, "May God forgive you".

She saw David and Brian on Friday morning and asked what had happened to them. Their parents had been stern but they suspected they were hiding their amusement. They would have to paint the whole side of the school under the supervision of the janitor. They told their parents that Alex had not been responsible and insisted that she should not be included in the punishment. They had not asked what had happened to her and she did not tell them. She knew she would have to be careful on the boat if she were to hide her disgrace from Andrew and John. When she went home she found the letter on her father's desk in which the principal had exonerated her and she said out aloud, "May God forgive you, Father."

Once at Otter Bay John and Alex sorted the supplies and carted them to the boat in the wheelbarrow. Andrew, ever restless to get away to *Heron*, left them to entice Jim to go to the store for his candy and pop supplies.

"You can go with him, Alex."

"No, it's okay, anyway my father said I must earn my pay."

They worked systematically stowing the supplies of cans, dry goods, vegetables and packed the ice box as full as possible. John was just finishing stowing the last of the supplies when he heard her start the outboard motor. She checked the fuel tank which was full and got the hose to fill the water tank, sun showers and wash down the deck and cockpit.

"John, which jib do you want?"

"Let's wait until we see how much wind there is tomorrow."

"Do you want me to get the jib and spinnaker sheets rigged?"

"Thank you."

"I'll need help with the spinnaker sheets."

When they finished rigging the spinnaker sheets John saw Jessica approach the boat to speak to Alex.

"John, can I go to the store with Jessica?"

"Sure, but, Alex, ask Andrew to come and help me please."

"What do you need?" she asked eagerly.

"For you to ask Andrew to come!"

When he arrived a few minutes later, John asked him to help with preparation of the evening meal.

"Where's our crewman?" indicating that she should be helping.

"Alex is not our personal slave," he replied, a testiness to his voice.

"The work will be shared equally between us and she has been with me for the past three hours without a break."

After they had been to *Heron* for happy hour and returned to *Never Satisfied*, Andrew cooked dinner without complaint or mouthing of 'demon'.

Andrew went to bed early that evening. Douglas and Anne arrived for a night-cap and Alex was too excited to turn in. She sat quietly in the cockpit listening to them discuss routes for the next few days, deciding to make the long leg to Pirates Cove in the morning.

"What time shall we leave in the morning?" Anne asked.

"Up early and away at eight, I think," John replied, and so it was agreed.

"Time to turn in, Alex," John said to her.

After they left, John got ready for bed, checked the toilet, touched Andrew's sleeping head and looked down at Alexandra's smiling face which seemed to be asking 'did I do good?' and he thought 'real good'.

Waking to the sound of a fresh wind across Otter Bay from the southeast charged John's enthusiasm at the early hour of six, knowing that a spanking good sail is the ideal start to a holiday. The weather forecast confirmed that the winds would remain moderate to strong all day. Alex was already awake and hearing John she dressed and sat on Andrew to wake him.

"Alex, go away!"

He was irritated at her for waking him.

"Time to get up, I want you both to shower before breakfast," John said to them and Alex gave him a 'told you so' look. Andrew grumbled from his sleeping bag, reluctant to shed its warmth.

They were away a little ahead of *Heron* out of Otter Bay and had a fast reach across Swanson Channel with Alex taking the first turn at the helm. They were to take turns on watch, half hour for Alex and Andrew and one hour for John turn and turn about. John sat beside her making sure she would steer a course that would allow for the northward current in Swanson Channel and noticed her bruised wrists.

"Do you bruise easily, Alex?"

"Yes," she said, and to redirect his attention added, "Look, I think *Heron* is catching up on us."

The wind backed so that they were running up to Captain's Passage into Trincomali Channel where the wind lessened. *Heron* with its longer hull had caught up and was within hailing distance. As if by tacit agreement both boats started to get ready to hoist their spinnakers. Andrew rushed forward to attach the halyard to the head of the sail wanting to beat Jim to the punch whilst Alex was ready at the halyard.

"Ready!" Andrew yelled, looking pleased that he had got ahead of Jim on *Heron*. Alex hauled on the halyard and up went the spinnaker. They heard the gales of derisive laughter from *Heron* before they realised what had occurred. Andrew had mistakenly attached the halyard to the clew of the sail so that it was going up sideways and it looked comic.

"Let it down, Alex," John shouted testily, "Andrew, you'll need to repack it."

He was irritated by Andrew's mistake and grumping to himself all the time that Andrew took to repack the spinnaker. His mistake corrected, Andrew shouted.

"Ready, Alex!"

The sail filled, their speed picked up and calm returned to the cockpit. John looked at Andrew sternly.

"Twelve lashes for you tonight, Andrew."

"What did I tell you, Alex?" Andrew said to her, standing beside her at the tiller. "The captain's a demon!"

Alex was at the helm when they arrived at Pirates Cove. John stood beside her and suggested she go beyond the entrance so that she could see the chalk markers on the island, a guide to the narrow channel into the anchorage.

"When you leave the marker buoy to port make a 90 degree turn to port, Alex. I will go forward and guide you in."

"Couldn't I go forward and you take the helm?"

"Nope. Strictly turn and turn about, Alex."

She followed John's occasional signal and took *Never Satisfied* through the channel and brought her alongside *Heron*.

"What would you have done if I had steered her on to the rock?" she asked him when he returned from the bow.

"Same as Andrew!"

"John was really angry with Andrew about the spinnaker," Alex said to Jessica as they were on shore.

They reached the notice board near the dinghy dock and were reading about Brother XII who was head of the immoral religious sect on the island for six years from 1927 and told of the arrival of Madame Zee who carried a bull whip to maintain order. Jim watched her wince as she read and her face echoed her real concern for Andrew.

"So, Andrew, you were in trouble with John, we heard him tell you that you would have twelve lashes; is that true?"

Andrew smiled, but Jim had been watching Alex and had sensed that she had been taken in so he asked her seriously.

"Ever seen twelve lashes given, Alex?"

"You don't really mean it do you?" she said anxiously.

"Oh yes, after supper John will have Andrew stripped to the waist, tied to the rigging and then you'll see the cat out of the bag!"

Andrew turned away, unable to keep a straight face as Alex surveyed Jim's and Jessica's grim looks.

As Andrew rowed her back to the boat noticing her silence and worried expression he realised that she might have been taken in by Jim's teasing.

"Jim was having you on, Alex."

"About your punishment?"

"Yes, Dad would never hit me, let alone whip me. It was after reading one of Alexander Kent's books that we started to joke about lashes."

"Does he never punish you?"

"Yes, he grounds me occasionally when I really go too far, but mostly he reasons with me," he said, imitating his father's voice, "you watch, at some time tonight he will show me how to avoid the same mistake."

When they got back to the boat she was still upset and went forward to her bunk to think. She heard Andrew laughing. They were on the foredeck where John was showing him how to identify the head of the spinnaker.

"She thought you were going to give me twelve lashes. Jim really fooled her."

"She's right, I'm going to. You deserve it!"

"Ha ha, Dad!"

Alex felt intense relief as she heard them laugh about her and they reinforced her belief that she was treated at home quite differently to them. That night as she sat in the cockpit watching the clouds racing over the moon and feeling the warm wind on her body John sat quietly beside her.

"Alexandra, did you really think I could give Andrew twelve lashes with a whip?"

She would remember that he sounded terribly hurt. "Doctor Barlow, I didn't know what to think after what Jim had said," she replied, not able to face him.

"I have never struck Andrew. I suppose if I was angry enough with him I might, but never cold bloodedly. I do know that I could never strike a girl or woman, that would be inexcusable."

She had wanted to put her arms around him so that she could hide her face in his body and feel him hold her tight but her reserve would not allow it, and she turned her face away from him and sat quietly thinking, 'I'll get you, Jim.' Later when she said good night, she longed for that evening hug and approached him with that intent but could not, feeling frustrated as her face became expressionless.

Over the next few days every time she made a mistake she would hear a chorus from the twins and Andrew.

"Twelve lashes for Alex!".

'How could they understand the chill that goes down my spine every time they say it?' she thought angrily, 'how could they know that each time I momentarily relive the fear of waiting for the pain inflicted by my father.' At one point she felt driven to remove her jeans and moon them. As the days went by she began to accept it with the humour they intended and then of course they stopped.

The short trip to Silva Bay next day was marred by a change in weather and by evening the rain was torrential. By morning the air temperature had dropped even though the rain had stopped.

"You will need to put on your thermal underwear for crossing the straits."

"Do we have to, Dad? We'll be warm enough won't we, Alex?"

"Do as you're told," he ordered as Andrew mouthed 'demon' at Alex.

At Smuggler Cove, where they planned to stay two nights, she was joshing with Jim on shore when he called attention to her untidy appearance so she attacked him and wrestled with him. As she sat on top of him pinning his arms above his head, she was aware that this big strong boy had given way to her again and he was looking uncomfortably flustered, mistakenly thinking he was an easy mark. Later she saw him leaning over the side of the boat. 'Revenge!', she thought and had given him a well-judged push, laughing heartily at him as he swam back to the boat. But this was too much for gentle Jim who came after her, picked her up and she remembered flying through the air before hitting the water with a splash. When she got back to the boat, more dishevelled than usual and very cold, not even Anne was sympathetic.

"You deserved that, Alex!" she said, laughing down at her.

Anne called from *Heron* for her to come across. When she got there, Anne had a bowl of fresh warm water ready and told her to put her head down over the bowl and shampooed her hair.

"I've been waiting for this opportunity, Alex. Now I'm going to make you look spectacular."

Alex lay back with her hair spread out to dry in the watery sun. Anne brushed it for what seemed forever until it had a sheen to it. Then she gathered it in a hair slide and made her look in a mirror. She smiled into the mirror and looked at Anne then back at the mirror.

"Here," Anne said handing her a belt, "thread that in the top of your jeans."

She did as she was told and tightened the belt letting her T-shirt fall outside her jeans.

"Oh Alex, aren't you proud of your beautiful body?" Pulling Alex towards her, Anne put the shirt inside her jeans so that her slim waist accentuated her developing breasts and hips. "Now you look stunning," she whispered.

"Do I?" she answered, looking puzzled.

"Jim thinks so, or haven't you noticed?"

"Do you think it's true that John never spanks Andrew?" she asked Jessica as they walked on shore.

"Yes, don't you remember at Portland his arguing with mother? Are you spanked at home?"

"Rarely," she lied, "Doug spanks you though."

"Dad spank us!" she said with laughter, "Can you keep a secret, Alex?"

"Sure."

"I remember the first time; Jim and I were terrified. I remember quaking as I lay over those huge thighs and his telling me to cry out loudly. He never touched us! The cries were for impressing Mother and he told us to be suitably contrite when we went back downstairs to apologise for our wickedness; we became good actors."

The change in weather brought good wind to the coast making the sailing marvellous. She enjoyed her time at the helm but even more sitting on the forward cabin hatch just listening to the trickle sound of the water on the hull and the slip-slop noise made by the trailing dinghy. She was able to speculate about what a normal life should have been and resolved that there would be no further beating of her body at home. When in the evenings John would teach her about sailing, seamanship and navigation, treating her like a mate to make decisions and be assertive, her resolve became firmer.

When sitting at the bow she would fantasise how she would tell John or Andrew about her home but whenever she tried her mouth would dry-up, words would fail her.

They anchored at Laura Cove and put a stern line ashore on this hot sweaty afternoon, the only boat there.

"Time to swim, Alex," Andrew shouted to her.

She saw him with Jessica and Jim naked diving into the water. She had just recovered from her shock when she saw Anne standing ready to dive with Douglas, both naked.

'Wow!' she said to herself, looking at John's nude body facing her.

"I will put on my swim suit with you if it makes you more comfortable," he suggested to her.

'Oh no!' she thought, 'they might suspect.'

"It's okay."

She faced John, took off her clothes with no opportunity to make them tidy without revealing the cause of her discomfort, and jumped sideways into the water. She had never skinny-dipped before and the experience was lovely as the water cooled, soothed her and she felt free. As the others scrambled up onto the warm flat rocks they lay on their stomachs sunning their backs. She stayed in the water until they were all settled and then went onto the rocks below them, nearer the water and laid face up to the sun. She compared Andrew's hairless body to Jim's plethora of pubic hair and then her own small breasts and wispy hair to Jessica's full development, totally ignorant of its significance.

She heard John and Anne discussing the meal, sensing that it was time to return to the boat before unwelcome eyes could see her disgrace. By the time the others returned she was dried, dressed and had rinsed her hair in fresh water which she brushed with the hair brush that Anne had given her at Westview. She looked over to *Heron* and saw that Jim was busy brushing out Jessica's hair for her. She sat between Andrew's knees and handed him the brush. She caught Jessica's eye, knowing what she was thinking, and later they contrived a change of hairdressers.

They left Laura Cove reluctantly but John and Douglas felt that they should see as many anchorages as possible before they had to part company. At Walsh Cove, another of those hot still days, they had needed to swim on and off during the afternoon to keep cool. She enjoyed Jim's attentive company, talking to him, although she realised she did more listening than revealing and had sneaked her first tentative kiss.

They talked about his feeling for Jessica as he probed her for her feeling for Andrew of whom he was becoming a little jealous. As he talked about the frustration of his competition with Jessica who he could not but love she became aware of her similar sisterly feeling for Andrew.

Like Andrew, she had fallen under Anne's spell. She noticed how the ever open Andrew would like to sit close to her. She imparted skills that her own mother could not or would not do for her and all through their time together Anne kept exposing and then filling the ignorant gaps. Simple things like the washing of her hair, the polishing of her nails and above all the preparation of food, all denied her by her own mother. Her gangling body was assuming a new grace and her mind a new subtlety under Anne's tutelage.

That evening at Walsh Cove after they turned in, she lay sweating naked on her bunk listening to John, Douglas and Anne talking in the cockpit, the forward hatch wide open for the slightest wisp of wind. She could stand the heat no more. She went up on deck through the hatch, stood momentarily looking at the small islands of the cove illuminated by the moonlight, then dove into the water leaving behind her a mass of phosphorescent sparkle. As she stopped and turned to look back at the boats treading water the phosphorescence was all round her. She had acted like a catalyst as they all came tumbling into the water. They swam to the pool between the islands that shone like The Blue Grotto where the moonlight hit the blue milky water of Toba Inlet. The beauty of the island in the moonlight, the silhouette of their naked bodies and the echo of their voices would stay in her memory. When Jim lay beside her on the cool rocks and ran his hand lightly down her back she felt an electric shock; a horse's flank to a fly bite, her muscles twitched. His hand sprang back and she was more disturbed by it than his first tentative kiss. She closed her eyes, hoping they would leave her to sleep here for the night on this cool rock.

The last afternoon with *Heron* at Octopus Islands she would have liked to have gone fishing with John and Douglas but they did not ask her and she, ever reticent, was unable to impose herself. Instead she went ashore with Anne to walk in the forest and as they picked berries for supper Anne talked to her about the various berry bushes.

"Do you not get on with your mother?" Anne asked her.

"She does everything for me."

"What do you mean, Alex?"

"This is the first time I have helped to cook."

"Really!"

"I've peeled my first potato on this trip," she said and saw Anne's look of disbelief, "and put a cooking pan on a stove for the first time when I went with Andrew and John on the boat."

"What did you do with yourself?"

"I played baseball and did my homework," she replied, "my father always wanted a boy. He makes my mother treat me like a boy."

"Have you never had a girlfriend?"

"No, Andrew is the closest friend I've had, he is like a brother. He can certainly irritate me like Jim does Jessica."

As they were back at the beach and getting the boat launched she felt a despair when she could not say or show Anne the gratitude she felt nor was she able to tell her how much she would miss her the next day. As she tried she knew her face was blank again, revealing nothing.

They docked to get fuel and water at Blind Channel and bought some loaves of their famous bread but did not stay, preferring to go up to the Crawford anchorage at Greene Point for the first night alone. Alex and Andrew were missing Jim and Jessica, but more acutely if less obviously, Anne.

The influence of Anne on Alexandra over the past two weeks was not obvious to John at first glance since it had been so gradual. At Blind Bay he watched her walking across the grass; her hair bouncing, her tall and graceful body was beautiful. He shivered and asked himself, 'is there a waste of shame in my looking', wondering whether Andrew had noticed.

They anchored at the Crawford Anchorage in a tiny bay that hid them from the world. Before bed, John read to them the Kwakiutl legend of how the raven got its cry Gwa-Gwa-Gwa, which means don't-don't-don't. They wanted him to read some more but he insisted that they tell him a story. He told them that he expected them to tell him a new story every night if they wanted him to read to them.

They powered from Greene Point to Forward Harbour and up the dead calm Johnstone Straits, not knowing the luck of the weather. As they turned into Port Harvey they did not like the look of it and instead continued down Havannah Channel to the abandoned Indian village of Matilpi and anchored for the night, feeling the Kwakiutl story more acutely than before.

At first their stories were meagre and not too imaginative but as they journeyed northwest through ever more spectacular terrain, visiting Indian villages and taking in the atmosphere of the land, their imaginations began to flower. They took time together during the day to discuss their next story and no longer content to give a spontaneous account, they had started to write them in the note books purchased at Powell River; the ones they had meant to keep their own log of the cruise. The stories of thunderbird, Transformer, raven and mink encouraging them, although they chose to weave their stories around killer whale, heron and woodpecker. So the evening ritual of hot chocolate and stories continued to the end of the cruise.

She would never forget Matilpi, waking early in the morning with stomach cramps, wondering what was happening to her. She managed to stay quiet until sunrise and then feeling stickiness between her legs had to get up to the toilet. That was when she noticed the blood trickling down her inner thighs, feeling faint and fearing that she was dying.

The aspirin worked well, allowing her to sleep during the passage to Minstrel Island. John bought her some sanitary pads with a belt at the little store. She felt desperately embarrassed at having to ask John for help when she could not understand how the belt connected to the pad. She was sitting on her bunk bent down by the cabin ceiling and naked from the waist, the silly belt with its contraptions hanging down the side of her hips.

"John, I don't understand how this works!" she said to him from her bunk, hoping he would hear.

Trying to sort out how a sanitary belt works with the pad in the confined forepeak of a 25 foot boat from the instruction sheet that assumed 'what every woman knows' was similar to putting a Bren gun together blindfolded. As he tried to sort it out for Alex, the perplexed look on John's face started her infectious giggle, sending them both into uncontrollable crying laughter. Poor Andrew, it was some time before he could get any sense out of them.

John seemed nervous as he started to talk about female anatomy, drawing line pictures of the vagina and uterus and how they related to the bladder and bowel. He illustrated the ovaries where the eggs start their journey down the tubes into the uterus. He drew the scrotum, testicles and penis of the male showing them what would happen as they matured through puberty. He explained to them the changes in their bodies, where and why they were developing new hair. He told them about the differences in their hormones that were inducing the changes and why she had started to bleed that morning. He explained how the male passed his sperm into the female during sexual intercourse and how the fertilised ovum developed into a baby inside her uterus.

"You can ask as many questions as you like," John said, "sex is a private matter, your questions should be kept for when we are alone together. Now, Alex, we will have to put you in isolation for two weeks."

"What do you..." Startled by the suggestion, her humour returning as she appreciated the tease. "Why?"

"It is an old Kwakiutl custom for a girl at puberty to be isolated for two weeks bound with cedar bark cloth. During your isolation your prayers will set the course of your life."

"I'll get the dinghy ready, Dad, we can put her in there."

"Don't forget to make a cover so we can't see her," he said, but they were already finished with the game and were heading up the dock, chattering, pushing each other, the morning's fear and frustration healed with reason. Alex was walking like a bow-legged cowboy, unused to the inconvenience of padding.

Later during the day, Andrew, ever ready with tricky questions, asked for more details about sexual intercourse. "Can I practise with Alex, Dad?"

"I could not give you permission to do so. That would be for Alex to agree," John replied, not getting upset at Andrew's question. "Would you agree, Alex?"

"I won't let anyone do that to me," she said making a face. "It's... it's dirty."

"Oh yes you will, Alexandra! Eventually," he prophesied.

At happy hour Andrew started to ask more questions about changes at puberty. They had obviously been talking together and Alex was still intrigued about the Indian puberty ceremonies.

"Why?" she asked.

"A coming of age ceremony; also a time to educate girls about being women. You are quite different Alex; look at your hair, nails and the way you dress. You are now capable of having a baby and must attract a male. You are the giver of life; men can't do the same. Men can be born and they can die, but cannot give life."

"I don't want to attract!" she said emphatically.

"Not even Jim?" Andrew accused.

"Who brushed your hair for you, Alex?" John asked her. She blushed with embarrassment.

"Many tribal societies have elaborate ceremonies for young women at puberty usually with isolation, sometimes even degradation and suffering."

"What about boys?" Andrew asked, "do they get to be isolated?"

"The puberty rites for boys are usually worse. The elders take the boys out to the forest to initiate them into the rigours of hunting.

One of the old Chiefs of the Kwakiutl told of his initiation which started at the age of six. There were about ten boys taken out into the forest by their uncles. Their fathers were not allowed because the elders felt they would be too soft with them. They were given a short stick to be held in their mouth and instructed never to let it drop. They were driven naked into the cold river and felt the lashing from the spruce bow to make their backs bleed. Old urine was poured into the wounds making them burn with fire. Then they were pushed into the river to wash it off, the stick still held in their mouths so they could not cry out. Training that gave them the discipline to endure unexpected pain and accept it."

Her attention was deflected by the initiation rituals for boys that John was relating to Andrew. 'Was that what her father was doing for her; make her endure the unexpected,' she wondered. He certainly brought her up as a boy.

"In African tribes," John continued, "circumcision is practised as a ritual at puberty which must be born with silent bravery."

"What's circumcision?" Alex inquired.

"Removal of skin from the end of the penis."

"We'll do that for you tomorrow, Andrew," she said making a face at him.

"Or in women skin from around the clitoris," he said, leaving Andrew looking squeamish on both counts.

After getting ready for bed, sitting in the cabin drinking hot chocolate, John's laced with brandy, instead of reading a story he told them:

"The Nuu-chah-nulth chief planned the potlatch for his eldest daughter Axelnadar to take place during the winter ceremonials following her first menses. The planning for this most important potlatch had started at the birth of the child. He intended to invite all the tribes around him from as far away as canoes could bring the guests. He went out into the forest to fell a score of cedar for the beams of a new house. Those beams were ninety feet long because the house would have to be large enough to accommodate all the guests. He started to collect wealth; money to pay for pilot biscuits and sugar and four huge cauldrons to use to cook for the expected company; above all, blankets to distribute at the potlatch.

"Eventually he went to Victoria to purchase his potlatch gifts taking $2000 in gold. There were twenty bales of blankets, eighty boxes of pilot biscuits and ten barrels of sugar. He drove a hard bargain with the trader, loaded his supplies onto canoes and took them back to his village. Axelnadar was taken by her mother and other women of the tribe at first menses to an isolated cabin in the forest where she was stripped of her clothing. Her mother anointed her with oil and wrapped her in a Hudson's Bay blanket. They sat her on a sweet smelling bench of balsam wood and plucked the short hairs off her eyebrows. Her hair was ceremonially coifed by weaving tiny clumps of hair into many plaits; the ends fixed with white mountain goat hair. In the end there were ten rows on each side. They bound her middle in soft cedar bark cloth and she was forbidden to scratch herself with her finger nails even though she would feel something sticking to her. Around her neck they attached a bone comb to use on her scalp, thus avoiding a break in her ritual. Four days she sat on her bench neither eating or drinking, only allowed to dip a clam shell in water to moisten her lips. After the four days they took two of the plaits out, now allowing her to eat only hard foods like dried salmon. They told her that if she ate soft foods when her babies came they would die soon. Each day two more plaits were removed and she complied rigidly with her mother's instructions until at last all the plaits were removed. The cedar belt was taken from her waist where she found miniatures of bow and arrow, cabood, canoe, salmon spear and bailer which would ensure her the prestige of a first born son. Naked she took the forty stones from her mother which she dropped at intervals on the way to the river bank to wash which would give her a long life.

"As the potlatch approached, the beach of her village was so full of canoes of the guests that new arrivals would have to find space up the river. The speeches of welcome by the chief and replies by the visitors went on for many evenings until at last all had been welcomed. Then the dancing commenced ending in a great tribute from Wrablord, the young hunter son of the neighbouring chief. Axelnadar was drawn to him by the love bond spirit which she could not resist, not yet aware that she was already betrothed to him. The Great Chief distributed his gifts to all those guests and members of his tribe in honour of his daughter. This ceremonial potlatch would be remembered and spoken of for a hundred years."

They were silent. John began to think it was due to disinterest.

"What's betrothed?" Alex asked.

"Engaged to be married."

"Was Axelnadar me?" she asked with secret smile.

"What do you think?"

"Was I Wrablord, Dad?"

"No, Andrew," she turned on him. "Wrablord was a hunter, not a runt."

The story captivated Alex totally and instinctively she identified with Axelnadar. She had listened to sex and reproduction with objectivity and distaste; now she listened to this spiritual story appreciating the changes in her attitude and body that would allow her to grow a child inside her. Finding Axelnadar's sexual attraction, attributed to the love spirit echoed in herself during Wrablord's dance, disquieting; compelled her to make that unkind remark to Andrew.

Alex and Andrew fell in love with the Indian village of Mamalilaculla, which means "place of eating killer whale", the moment they set foot on shore. This village with its long white clam shell beach, the old long house remains, totem pole and sea wolf carvings at the chief's house, glowing hot in the sun, opened her imagination. The bees of the mint spread grass meadow with all the fruit trees gave a humming aura to the place. That night when the wind started to blow and she was unable to sleep, she lay awake allowing her stories to rove in her imagination made vivid by the atmosphere of the village. Next evening in the still water of their sheltered anchorage, the wind noise in the trees, her story had a spiritual quality.

"Big Figure lived deep in the forest behind the village. Nobody visited him because they were afraid of him stealing their children. He had married his wife Missfrog many years before and now she was no companion to him, just sitting in the stream behind their house croaking her hideous song all day.

"'It's time to capture our food for winter,' he said to Missfrog as he walked towards the village. As he got near the village Big Figure slid into the tall grass and slithered towards the chief's house where

Rea the chief's daughter was playing. He caught her and when she tried to cry he slapped her face and took her back to his lair where he tied her upside down by her ankles.

"As she hung upside down she felt her heart slowly migrate into her mouth and knew it would not be long before it fell onto the floor and she would die.

"'Big Figure,' she whimpered, 'I will make a bargain,' but he seemed to take no notice. 'If you let me down I promise I will never tell anyone or leave you.'

"Big Figure looked at her.

"'Can I hit you with my big stick when you deserve it?'

"She agreed so he smiled, cut the ankle ties and sat her on his knee. Rea was glad to be upright and kept her bargain for many years, but she grew sad because he would use his big stick for no good reason and she longed to return to the village.

"Alone one day she was sitting on a log with tears on her cheeks when an old Indian stopped beside her.

"'Why are you so sad?'

'I promised Big Figure never to leave him and I cannot break my promise.'

'I will help you,' he said, 'you must take Big Figure to the beach at the village tomorrow. On the beach there will be a killer whale. You will persuade him to eat some of the whale.' Rea looked down at her feet thinking and when she went to reply the old Indian had vanished. Next morning she asked Big Figure to take her to the beach and with much grumbling he agreed. When he saw the succulent whale on the beach she did not have to encourage him as he tucked into his favourite meat.

"After such a large dinner Big Figure became sleepy and the hot sun on the white beach made a perfect bed. As he slept she saw the old Indian gliding towards them. He nodded to her, signalling for her to remain quiet and then reached down to touch Big Figure's left ear. The old Indian vanished, Big Figure gave a huge sigh and was still. When she touched the giant he had turned to stone. She knew that the Transformer had visited and the villagers gathered round happy to see Rea's safe return and Big Figure no longer able to steal their children. That is how the village got its name; 'Place of eating Killer Whale.'"

As she finished she was pleased to see that her story had caught John's attention, even though at the time she had not realised that it was an allegory of her own life. Her purpose was to gain his attention because she wanted to learn to fish for a salmon. She knew that Andrew disliked that sort of activity and made her request sound like a reward for her story.

They trolled in the dinghy taking the oars turn and turn about, talking to the sea to give up a salmon. The excitement was in her eyes as she felt the strike and watched the black and silver fish jump some thirty feet behind the boat and once or twice more as she played it into the boat.

"Will you take it off the hook?" she asked.

"No, Alex, that's your fish."

The squeamish look on her face was replaced by determination as she took the fish bonker in her hand. When it stopped moving she pried the hook out of its mouth with pliers and sat back looking pleased.

"Can we fish for another?"

"Only if you're prepared to take out the hook when it's alive so you can put it back in the sea."

"Why?"

"You must only take what you can eat. Do you know how to clean the fish?"

"No, but I'll do it if you show me and we can ask the salmon's forgiveness."

"What do you mean?"

"There's a Kwakiutl prayer to the salmon in your book. Andrew was reading it to me the other day."

She convinced herself that the salmon had allowed itself to be caught, giving himself to her. Cleaning its bloody guts and taking the fillets from its flank had again made her feel unclean until that evening she asked John for the legends to read to them the prayer to her salmon, Swimmer.

'We have come to meet alive, Swimmer.
Do not feel wrong about what I
have done to you, friend Swimmer, for that is the reason why you
come that I may spear you, that I may eat you,
Supernatural one, you, Long-Life-Giver, you, Swimmer.

Now protect us that we may keep well,
that nothing may be difficult for us
that we wish to get from you Rich-Maker-Woman. Now
call after you your father and your mother and uncles and aunts
and elder brothers and sisters to come to me also, you,
Swimmers, you Satiaters.'

Then she took the bones into the dinghy to row out to the spot she had caught it and reverently returned them to the water.

As they headed south in the last week of the holiday, riding the waves put up by the northwest winds which took them back to Westview in a series of exhilarating sails, she began to feel her personal freedom diminish day by day. As they relaxed that last Saturday evening at Annette Bay watching the family of otter playing in the sea she thought of Andrew's written description of the anchorage that Mr Dixon had asked him to read to the class.

ANNETTE BAY

By Andrew Barlow

'Annette Bay on the north side of Prevost Island is long and thin with its centre waist and mud bottom, and is not only a safe anchorage but beautiful. Here, you can watch the cormorants airing their wet wings in the leafless trees, made so by their own white crap. Here, the cormorants leave as the eagle settles in the tree. Here, you can watch a family of otter frolic in the sea and on the shore. Here, the peace is disturbed by the ravens angry at the arrival of the turkey vultures whose slow crawl across the sky with out-stretched feathered wings of black and grey swoop into a tree top holding their wings open. Here, you can see the family farm with cows and sheep. Here, you will be studied by the steady gaze of the seals floating in the current, their grey bodies stretched out in lazy sunbathing or blowing their noses in surfacing or spanking their tails on the water. Here, a great blue heron stands statuesque, infinitesimal movements of its head, eyes on the surface of the sea; the fish interpreting driftwood are swallowed alive. This bay, you will tell the world is a poor anchorage to keep it private for us.'

On the ferry next evening John gave her a cheque for $60.00 which he had made out to her.

"You have been far more help than I could have imagined."

He handed her the cheque with an extra twenty dollar bill.

As John's car came nearer to home she felt the tension of conflict in the pit of her stomach. They sorted out their tote bags and she helped unpack the car and bring his gear into the house. She would have liked to fling her arms around John, tell him how much the holiday had meant to her and linger over one last evening with them. Her reticence would not allow it.

"Alexandra, are you going to stay over tonight?"

"No, Doctor Barlow, I had better go home, my mother and father will be expecting me."

She went to Andrew's room to wish him a good stay with his grandmother. She lingered some time in his room, thinking of John and making up a presentation of her feeling for him. She closed her eyes thinking back to the fights over who would get breakfast, to Laura Cove, Walsh Cove, Matilpi and Smuggler Cove remembering small details of his face, eyes and youthful body and the fun of swimming together on those hot mornings.

She went to say good-bye, feeling her mouth become dry and her face change, the outward sadness and the inward frustration.

CHAPTER 5

The Price of Assertiveness

"You've changed, Alex," her mother said as she stood in the kitchen.

"Yes, and I have had my first period."

There was an edge to her voice and her mother looked ruffled. They went together to the front room to see her father. She approached his chair, bent forward and kissed his cheek.

"Has Doctor Barlow paid you then?"

"Yes, I have a cheque from him and he also gave me an extra twenty dollars, a bonus he said for my help."

"Give me the cheque and money," he said with his usual authority.

"No, Father, please give me the passbook and I will put it in the bank myself." She could see his red faced anger start to rise from his neck as he raised himself out of his chair and knew he was about to order her to her room. She forestalled him by quietly adding, "I found and read the principal's letter."

It took a moment for the meaning of her statement to register. As he eased back in his chair she was reminded of a balloon whose air is slowly released. She had won the first battle. Her mother, who looked aghast when Alex crossed her father, did not understand the significance of her statement that had so deflated her authoritarian husband.

Her mother accompanied her to the bank the following week. The account was transferred to her and she found a not untidy sum accrued over the last fourteen years. She had no intention of squandering her money but did take pleasure in keeping some cash for herself. She discussed with her mother some improvements that she would like in her room to make it more feminine and attractive. She did not change her bed, she was more comfortable on a hard bed. She did not allow the rope ties to be removed from her bedrail, hoping they would act as a steely reminder to her father whenever he saw them.

When she went to the church on the following Sunday the minister remarked to her father on her appearance. Alex loved the church and its services with its haunting tuneful music. When she started going to adult services she had followed her prayer book with genuine interest. She did not resent the family attendance at church and had her own strong faith. A distinct faith which had not been extinguished by the harsh discipline and spartan life at home. She did not blame God for her father, she prayed for her father and mother and in her meditation during the service felt that God wanted her to become strong in her individuality. Her God agreed with her that an apology was due to her from her father and she was going to get it.

She went to the kitchen to help get the Sunday dinner. She took a knife out of the drawer to prepare the vegetables.

"You don't need to do that, Alex," she said, "go and join your father in the front room."

"I need to learn to cook, Mother, I'm a woman now," she smiled at her, "I want you to teach me."

After grace she continued to talk with her mother about the holiday.

"I'll hear the Collect for the day, Alex," her father said when lunch was finished. Alex stayed in the kitchen to help wash up.

She continued to ignore anything that he said to her. She found she was fortified a little more each time she refused to listen to him. She knew she was right and was going to get her apology.

"Why are you not speaking to your father, Alex?" her mother asked her during the week.

"Because he owes me an apology."

She told her mother about the letter from the principal.

She did not know if her mother asked out of curiosity or because he had requested it. Certainly it had not been an easy time for him and his apology to her must have been difficult for so proud a man. He must have felt the irony of her reply rather than the sincerity with which it was meant, "May God forgive you, Father."

Her father had a study in the basement of the house. The stained cedar panelling and small high windows, which did not open, added to its airless atmosphere. Its darkness combined with the central pillar made it seem smaller than its size. He spent much of his time away from the rest of the house and seemed to be brooding and surly with her which she attributed to his forced apology.

When she attended the first volleyball practice only six girls in grade eight turned out and at five feet nine inches she towered above them. Initially she held an advantage and was able to spike and block the ball because of her height so that she seemed to outshine the other girls but that turned to disadvantage in defence when required to dig and roll with her gangling body. After the first practice in spite of the sore muscles of her shoulders, back and thighs and the bruising of her knees and hips she felt exhilarated to be once more involved with a team sport.

With her natural athleticism combined with determination she soon caught the eye of her coach. She did not make it into the first string before Christmas but with her increasingly powerful and accurate spike she was being substituted across the front row on a regular basis. She was not popular with the others, resented by the more senior girls whom she displaced as she improved. She had no experience with girls as friends except for Jessica and found it difficult to gain acceptance. She was more physically aggressive towards them, treating them as boys which they in turn found disconcerting. As her skills improved she became a leader and if not liked was certainly respected for her play. No girl displaced Andrew as her friend, brother and confidant.

The cruise with Alex that summer had been marvellous for Andrew. She was everything he had wanted in a sister and even managed to irritate him like Jessica did Jim. Most of all she had made John look happier than he could remember since his mother died. Waking in the morning he would listen to their laughter over their fights to get breakfast or if hot, hear them splashing in the water having a morning swim.

At Junior High together he helped her train for the volleyball team honing her defensive skills and joining her father in the stands during the games to lead the cheering. Since the cruise she had become outgoing and less subject to periods of silent anger. She never invited him into her home and would not allow any discussion of the subject.

On the evening that Flora would stay home to have supper with him, he wondered where John was eating his meal. Eventually, curiosity demanded inquiry and they were at supper one evening following his absence the previous night.

"Where were you last night?" Andrew asked John.

"Having dinner with a friend."

"Who was he?"

"She, Andrew," he replied feeling a little embarrassed. "We meet quite often, enjoy each other's company."

"Are you going to marry her?"

"Neither of us wants that."

Andrew turned a grave face on John.

"Do you, you know...?" he asked, his interest pricked by their summer talks.

John smiled at him and chuckled.

"We do, you know, Andrew." He had always promised himself that he would be honest with him.

"Will you bring her home, to meet me?"

"No," he answered, "nor will I tell you her name."

Andrew wanted to ask what his mother would think, whether she would consider this as his promise kept; looking after him in a way. He stayed quiet and planned to discuss it with Alex the following Friday.

Alex's inclusion onto the volleyball team made her father lose some of his antagonism towards her. She asked him to come and watch a match one Thursday evening. When she had been substituted into the front row, he began to be interested in the power and skill required of the good player. He started to attend regularly and with his Welsh lilt she could hear him urging the team on. After the games her father would be enthusiastic and he started to put his arm on her shoulders as they walked across the gym. She felt the pleasure of his company and a closeness with him for the first time. She would turn towards him putting her arms around his neck and embrace him. She wanted a relationship with her father that was akin to John and Andrew with its trust and regard for individuality; she wanted their ceremonies of affection.

In the New Year she became a regular starter for the team and her father's pride in her became ever more vocal from the stands. He would meet Andrew in the stands and the two of them would urge the team on. It was evening, Alex had showered and was dressed ready for bed.

"You never ask Andrew here," he said, "he's a nice boyfriend."

"He's not a boyfriend."

"Why ever not, Alex?"

"I don't want to attract him that way."

"Because you're taller. I suppose you prefer someone tall like me."

He took her in his arms to kiss her cheek, hugging her to him. She felt his hands run down her back over her bottom.

"You're very attractive," he said, holding her away from him, "and desirable."

"Thank you, Father," she said, genuinely pleased that there was a developing affection between them.

"Good night."

"Would you like me to tuck you in?" he asked, smiling at her.

"That would be nice."

She was in bed and heard his footsteps on the stairs. He sat on the edge of her bed.

"You are doing well in school," he said to her, "have you thought about university?"

His hand rested on her thigh.

"I'd like to go," she answered, and feeling his hand slide up the inside of her thigh, shifted her position, "if you let me."

"Of course I will." He raised his hand to her chin, placed a lingering kiss gently on her lips, "sleep well."

He got up and left her room, leaving her feeling warm at the new found intimacy between them.

Alex would spend time with her father talking, and she would get his evening drink for him and join him with hers, no longer sitting in the kitchen alone. On Saturdays they would meet for lunch and he would take her shopping. As their intimacy and closeness allowed more physical contact, he started to buy her gifts. She would watch TV sitting with him, his arm nonchalantly on her shoulder encouraging her to rest her head on his shoulder. He regularly came to her room at night to kiss her goodnight, his hands lingering on her breast so subtle in his movement that she did not heed the warning.

She remembered awakening at some time in the night aware that she was not alone. The naked outline of her father sitting on her bed holding his head in his hands. His hand moving slowly towards her, she felt the comforter slip down over her body and feigning sleep she waited. His hand went lightly down her body reaching the hem of her night-dress which he gently lifted, exposing her stomach.

"No, Father," she said quietly.

"Sh!" he said as he exposed her breasts and his hand stroked down her stomach.

"No, Father," she said more urgently, "or I'll cry out."

"Quiet now."

He put his hand over her mouth pushing her head back into the pillow holding her so she could not move or cry out, his hand between her legs prying, his naked body heaving on her as he sought to enter her. She struggled to get away, praying to God to make him stop. As if answered, she heard her mother call out to him, he disengaged and left her room. She wondered if it had been a dream but the semen between her thighs told her otherwise. She wondered if she was still a virgin; she could not remember pain.

She knew that her father was in the wrong but wondered whether she had been partly responsible.

'Did I seduce him?' she questioned herself.

As other questions came she answered them to herself and knew she had been violated totally and unwillingly. Her old hatred for him returned as she understood his obsequious wooing of her; a courtship for a courtesan.

In the morning before school she joined her mother in the kitchen for breakfast.

"Father tried to sleep with me last night." She said it simply.

"What did you say, Alex?"

Her mother stared at her in disbelief.

"He came to my room in the night and I awoke to find him sitting naked on my bed taking up my night-dress. When I said I would cry out he put his hand over my face muffling my cries and forced himself on me. I don't know if he succeeded. Anyway, I have my period."

"You must have been dreaming, Alex, your father would never do such a thing."

She was shaking her head and Alex watched doubt creep into her mother's face.

"It's true, Mother."

As she walked to school she felt that her mother did not believe her. When she arrived back from school her father's car stood in the driveway. She entered from the back and heard her mother in the kitchen before she realised that the door behind her had been shut by her father. He looked pale and his angry eyes were narrowed into slits.

"What is this latest accusation, Alex?"

She found herself tongue-tied by the imminent danger.

"So you have nothing to say for yourself," he said and turned to her mother, "what did I tell you."

"Alex, how could you be so vicious?" her mother asked.

Alex, feeling trapped like a rabbit in a snake's gaze, said nothing.

"She must be punished," he said, agreement written on her mother's face, "take her down to my study."

Alex stumbled, legs numbed with fear, ahead of her mother. Once in his study she saw a short leather whip in his hands which made the fight in her return. As he tried to take both hands together to tether her to the central post she kicked at his groin, just missing but making him viciously angry. He knocked her to the ground kneeling on her chest as he tied her hands. He stood up and jerked her roughly to her feet and tied her to the post. She felt her mother lift her clothes above her head, now in darkness, an eternity of waiting.

"Get out of here," he told her mother roughly.

The door closed and she heard her mother's footsteps on the stairs.

She heard the first whiplash coming, the wind knocked out of her and then nothing for a second followed by pain like a red hot wire held against her back. Again and again the pain, at first resisted by her, mounted until it was impossible not to scream at him to stop. As the pain reached its peak she felt as if her life was slipping away and she fainted, becoming limp against the pillar.

When she recovered consciousness she was lying on the floor, her top clothing removed, her feet bare, the room strangely quiet, the door locked and no window to release her from her captivity. The residual pain in her back and the recollection of her tied arms and dark world were clear but the physical pain induced by the whipping was strangely absent from her memory. She felt cowed and frightened by the silence of the house as the night moved in and darkness fell. She was cold as she took a cushion onto the hard floor and slept fitfully through the night. Early in the dawn she heard footsteps on the stairs, the lock slide back and as her terror mounted she heard the stairs creak as the person left. She tried the door feeling relief when it opened.

She climbed the basement stairs to the kitchen, her bare feet noiseless on the steps. The house was eerily quiet, the kitchen tidy with no evidence of recent use and a blanket of warm air closed around her naked upper body. As she moved slowly out of the kitchen into the corridor leading to the stairs she watched for him to appear out of the shadows to menace her, making each step a challenge of will against terror. She listened outside their bedroom and hearing no sound of their presence started to relax. She slipped into the bathroom using the mirror to try to see the damage to her back, becoming dizzy again, she sat on the toilet to recover. From what she had been able to see in the mirror her back did not look too bad and there was no sign of blood from the wounds. She washed her hands and face, brushed her teeth and tidied her hair and put on her father's bathrobe which was hanging on the back of the door.

She looked out into the carport to find the car had gone and climbed the stairs to her room, confident now that they had left, and as she entered her room the usual feeling of welcome solitude was replaced by utter loneliness.

When she took off the bathrobe she inspected it for blood and finding none stepped into the shower. As the hot water hit her back she felt dizzy with the pain and had to sit in the tub to avoid fainting. She was unable to rub her back dry, instead, she replaced the bathrobe and allowed the back to dry itself. In her room she dressed in a T-shirt and jeans, finding she was unable to wear a brassiere. When she put her coat on it made her back too sore to tolerate. With a wry smile to herself she took out the top of the thermal underwear and wore it under the T-shirt protecting her back.

She packed her tote bag with a clean T-shirt, bathrobe, night attire and washing things in preparation for staying overnight with Andrew. She wondered where her parents had gone and, as she left the house locking the door behind her, started to walk towards Andrew's house to tell them what had happened. Half way to the house she changed her mind, resolving instead to seek out the school nurse and show her.

As she approached the school she felt her resolve melt and decided to wait and tell Andrew. As they walked to his house full of good intentions, once more she was mute and left with the frustration at her inability to tell her story. As they entered the house they were greeted by Flora.

"You're stuck with me for supper tonight," she said adding, "John's been asked out to dinner."

She assumed their amused smiles were for the pleasure of her company at supper.

After supper they settled to their assignment spreading their books and papers over the table. Flora left them to it and it was late as they were finishing writing their reports. Alex finished first.

"Are you going to order pizza?"

"I'll do that now," he said picking up the phone and ordering one with everything.

"There's something else, Andrew," she looked at him, her face a blank.

"Let me finish this report first, Alex," he appealed.

'The moment has gone,' she thought to herself, 'will I have the courage again?'

The pizza arrived as he finished writing. They sat smiling at one another as they munched.

"Good eh!" he said.

"H'm."

"What was it you wanted, Alex?"

"John's home, it can wait."

As John came through the door she felt her dry mouth and knew she could not tell him.

"Good dinner, Dad?" Andrew said, nudging Alex as obviously as possible.

"Yes, steak."

"and dessert?"

"Bastard."

John was looking a little embarrassed, not knowing whether Alex appreciated this exchange.

"Really, Dad!"

"Do you want a shower first, Andrew?" she inquired.

"Yes, I'll go now," he said, indicating to Alex that he had better get out of his dad's line of fire.

"So, Alexandra, did you understand that little exchange?"

"Was it worth the price of dinner, Doctor Barlow?" she said laughing at him.

"No secrets between you two."

She watched him, a slow blush covering his face as he busied himself in the kitchen. She thought of him at Laura Cove, wondering whether his friend of the evening had also admired the sight of him.

She saw Andrew heading from the shower to his room with the towel around his waist. She knew if she hurried to get the tea towel she might 'get him a good one' before he was in his pyjamas. She opened his door, saw the target and scored.

"Alex, you beast, I'll get you for that."

She undressed and went to the bathroom in her bathrobe only, leaving the door visibly just open she slipped her bathrobe off her shoulders. She did not wait long for Andrew to seek revenge. In her naiveté and not having seen the wounded state of her own back, she had not expected to cause such a terrible reaction. She knelt beside him as he vomited into the toilet, each retch tearing at her ineptitude. Even as she went with John to the bedroom she could feel her dry mouth return and as she sat on the bed that wave of anger, her self-pity exposed in those great crying sobs.

As Andrew gently exposed her back to show John, she looked up to see the incredulity on John's face turn to a twisted look of hatred directed at her and she asked herself fearfully, 'have I lost their love forever?'

CHAPTER 6

Douglas Takes A Case

I followed Alex into the spare room where she slept when she stayed overnight. I sat in the chair and she on the bed. She looked demure in the white bathrobe which contrasted with her sandy hair but she seemed to be struggling for words. Then, as that mask drew over her face she started to shake, only a little shiver at first and then violently. I had never seen her cry before, however much the pain, but now she lay face down on the bed and was incoherent with sobbing. Andrew, now composed again, came into the room and whilst Alex continued to sob he gently lifted the bathrobe down her back turning away so he would not have to see it again.

"Her father whipped her."

I had seen many ugly sights in my professional capacity. None could have prepared me for this. Purple weals criss-crossed her back mounting one upon another, but remarkably no blood from the wounds in the skin. I felt shock at the sight of her; the anger and hatred for the man who did this was written in my face. I sat beside her on the bed, put my hand on her shoulder and stayed quiet for some time unable to look her in the eyes.

"When?" I asked.

"Last night."

"Why?"

"It's a long story."

"Can you tell it now?"

"No, not now, tomorrow, maybe."

"Do you need something for the pain?"

"No, it's not too bad. Would you read to me?"

By the time I had finished reading *'Mink's search for a wife'* she was asleep. I looked down at her, touched her head and turned out the light.

Jessica answered the phone, and I asked if Douglas was at home. Our friendship had not extended beyond the sea and I did not know his name was spelled Macleod.

"Yes he is, John, I'll get him for you."

"Hello, John, it's unusual to hear from you."

"I need professional advice from you."

"You sound upset?"

"Very."

"Why?"

"Could I bring Alex to see you tomorrow morning or whenever."

"Alex, why Alex?"

"Child abuse."

"You must be kidding," I heard a change of tone in his voice.

"Tell me about it."

"Doug, not now, not over the phone."

"What about ten in the morning?"

"Thanks, Doug."

I remember Andrew getting up and going to bed too upset to say good night. I heard him go into the spare room and when eventually I went to check him he was not in his own room but had taken his comforter and pillows to the spare room, sleeping on the floor next to Alex's bed. An act of kindness, knowing how she used to like his company when she first stayed over. I knelt to touch Andrew's head and did the same for Alexandra.

In the morning, I heard Alex get up, always the early riser. She was sitting on a kitchen stool.

"Is it very painful?"

"I have learned never to give him the pleasure of observing me in pain," she said bitterly.

"This has happened before!" She nodded. "Alexandra, could you not have told me?"

The mask dropped over her face.

"It's nice out this morning, Doctor Barlow," she said with a rueful smile, "shall I cook you breakfast?"

The doctor in me still required a post mortem. I busied myself helping her to get a breakfast of bacon and eggs, trying to make my questions recede into the background, 'what, where or when' had I missed the clues; those signs and symptoms of a disease.

A missed diagnosis for a doctor requires careful self-conscious scanning of the brain, seeking for the flaws in reason which lead to mistakes or misjudgements. Every good doctor applies the method to himself; the gnawing of personal competency. Alex was asking too much of me and by the time the plates were cleared I could no longer contain my curiosity.

"If I asked you a series of questions would you answer yes or no?"

"All right," she replied her serene face accepting the challenge as if it were a game.

"Did he cause those bruised wrists?"

"Yes."

"Did you have a cold when your ear drum was perforated?"

"No."

"Was this the first time he whipped you?"

"Yes."

"Did he spank you?"

"Yes."

"Often?"

"Yes."

"Is that what you were hiding at Laura Cove?"

"Yes."

"Has he sexually assaulted you?"

A conspiratorial whisper.

"Yes."

"When I went to slap your face, why didn't you duck?"

"I can't answer yes or no to that!"

I watched her drinking her coffee, her mask replaced. Then she turned her gaze on me.

"Was that the last question?"

"No. How can I help you?"

"No more questions. Please."

As I drove Alex into Vancouver we were quiet for some time. The silence was broken by her.

"I have upset Andrew."

"That's not true, Alex, I think Andrew is deeply upset for you not for himself. He made a Freudian slip the other day when I heard him say Alexandra, my sister!"

"Andrew called me Alexandra?"

"He usually calls you Alexandra now. I guess you are no longer one of the boys." I said, trying to humour her.

"I love Andrew, Doctor Barlow, like a brother. I had a nightmare last night and when I awoke Andrew was beside me sitting on the bed. He held my hand and stroked my hair, soothing me back to sleep," she said, looking at me, not wanting to be misunderstood. "Nothing else happened."

"Did you mind my contacting Douglas without asking you first?"

"I am glad you did, I can talk to Anne easily if she will let me."

"I'm sure she will."

As we walked up the path to their front door, Douglas came out to meet us.

"I told Jim and Jessica to get lost for a few hours," he told Alex, who looked visibly relieved. As we walked to the door Anne appeared, with her open smile of greeting.

"Lovely to see you again, Alex," she said warmly, "Doug thinks that you might want to come with me first and talk."

"I hoped so too."

Doug took me into the sitting room. I told him what had happened the evening before and what I had seen when Andrew drew back her bathrobe. I had written a medical report on the state of her back which I took out of my pocket and gave to him.

"Do you remember the swim at Laura Cove?"

"Yes, I do," he said with a smile.

"Did you notice Alex's odd behaviour?"

"Not really, why?"

"She had faced me whilst she undressed, leaving her clothes where they lay and jumped sideways into the water. She was never untidy like that. On shore she kept herself a bit away from us and was face up on the rocks."

"I remember that because you remarked on her modesty."

"Why would she not let us see at that time and so break her secrecy?"

"I never understand why children protect their parents. I don't know whether it is loyalty or fear of consequence. I know I did the same myself."

"This happened to you?"

"I remember feeling ashamed for them and wanting to keep it as a secret in the family; my only recourse was to run away. I had no one I could turn to. I went to crew on a boat with a skipper who treated me like a son; he was my saviour."

"Douglas, I have not seen worse," Anne said, as she returned to join us, her head shaking a little between her hands on her cheeks, "and so much worse when it's a friend not a client. I have asked her to give me a minute to tell you and for her to get her story together. I asked her to decide if she wanted John present when she talks to you."

Alex came into the room.

"Would you like John to stay?" Douglas asked.

"No, I think I have already hurt him enough," Alex said, not able to look at me.

I felt relief that I would not have to endure the bitterness of what I considered to have been my own negligence. As Anne showed me out she suggested that I give them two hours before returning. I drove out to the university campus and passed the time in contemplation in the Japanese garden. The tranquil gardens did not prevent that cold gripping fear as my self conscious scanned for memories of other patients, raising questions; which of all the other perforated ear drums caused by abusive trauma had I passed off as just another cold? In how many childhood fractures or dislocations had I missed the cause? How many times had I covertly prevented a child from telling me of some grim truth in their lives?

A doctor does not like to think badly of the families he cares for. Was I guilty of 'Human kind cannot stand too much reality'? All these questions were echoing in my mind as I walked along the paths of the moss strewn gardens. 'What inner strength in Alexandra made her contemplate the feelings of others before her own?'

Anne took me aside when I returned to their house to suggest that Alex would need medical help in case of infection or ulceration of the skin.

"Anne thinks you should see your doctor," I said to her, driving back home. "Who looks after you?"

"Could you look after it for me?" she pleaded, "I don't want to have to tell anyone else what happened."

We stopped at the drug store to pick up some dressings, antibiotic ointment and antiseptic soap. Almost as soon as we sat down for lunch, Andrew sounded in a panic.

"You will stay with us won't you, Alex. Won't she, Dad?"

"I don't know, Andrew," and she turned to me but not with her eyes saying, "Anne said she would phone you later this afternoon."

When Alex left us to go to the washroom, Andrew persisted, and I told him testily to keep quiet until I had talked to Anne.

"John, it's a horrible story," Anne said, over the phone.

"Yes, what I know of it. Alex does not want to reveal it to Andrew and me."

"She says she feels that she has hurt you," she answered, "do you understand why?"

"I think so. Anne, is there any way that I can help?"

"I asked her if she would like to stay here with us since I did not know where she intended to live. It would not be fair to make her go home but she seemed upset by the question."

"Did she say anything?"

"No, so I asked her where she would like to go. She would not answer, do you think she is waiting for you to ask her?"

"Surely she knows she is welcome here; Andrew has been bugging her with the same question and I said I wanted to speak to you first."

"John, have you asked Alex yourself?''

"No, why?"

"She thinks she has hurt you and can't ask you, don't you think?"

"Bless you, Anne."

They were in his room, Andrew black as thunder and Alex with her mask; a death sentence hanging over them.

"Alexandra, Anne tells me you would like to stay with us."

"How did she know, John?" she grinned and corrected herself, "Doctor Barlow!"

"Probably because you would not answer her question and she knew I was too stupid to understand you would need to be asked."

"Would you let me?" she said, still keeping her eyes averted.

"My mother says you cannot trust a person who does not look you in the eyes."

She came close to me, put her head near my shoulder and whispered in my ear.

"I was frightened... frightened you wouldn't want me now."

"Well you were wrong," I said, gently pushing her back. She seemed suspended in time.

"What about me, sister, out here all alone," Andrew said, not one to allow a cloying sentiment to last and pretending to look lost and forlorn.

She opened her arms towards Andrew like a romantic Hollywood movie and as his arms went out to receive her I saw a cunning look spread over her face as she stopped suddenly and punched him in his unprotected stomach.

"Got you!"

"You little vixen, you wait."

I phoned back to let them know the outcome of our conversation.

"That's good news," Douglas said, "I'm sure that it is genuinely what Alexandra wanted."

"Douglas, is it awkward for you; would you prefer to transfer the case to a colleague?"

"No, but if she wants to be placed with you by the court there are two things which we need to discuss. First, the lack of a mother in your house. Judges are reluctant to place children in single parent homes, particularly a girl like Alex who has been sexually abused, to a home where the single parent is male."

"But I wouldn't..." He cut me off.

"Stop being subjective, John," he said sharply, "put yourself in the judge's position making objective decisions. Secondly, I think it would be best to ask for an independent assessment. What do you think?"

"Yes, it makes good sense."

"Have you reported the incident to the police in Richmond yet?"

"No I haven't, should I do so before the weekend?"

"Yes, the sooner the better. Let them know that I will be acting for her and that arrangements are being made for a medical assessment. Now, could I speak to Alexandra to see if she would agree - and by the way, Anne says would you all come to dinner tomorrow evening?"

"We'd like that. I'll get Alex for you."

When she took the phone, I saw her listen intently, and make a face of 'do I have to'.

"Yes I will, thank you, Douglas," and after a short pause, "Hi Jessica, how are you?"

"On Sunday evening?" Her face went blank. "Thanks Jessica," and she was smiling again.

"Why the mask when you were talking to Jessica?" I asked her, recognising the set of her face and its meaning.

"Jessica said that Jim couldn't wait to hear all the gory details on Sunday. She was teasing me and then promised that the subject would be off limits unless I said anything."

"Doctor Barlow, I hope you will forgive my use of your gift," she said, preparing for me to dress her back pulling the thermal underwear over her head and lying down on the bed. I saw what Anne meant; since the previous evening the deep bruising under the skin had coalesced into a continuous hematoma. The skin was not broken but there were areas in the skin where the damage might lead to necrosis which would allow infection into the hematoma. I cleaned the skin as gently as possible with the antiseptic solution, dried it and applied antibiotic netting. Alexandra was quiet and still until I was applying the dressing.

"Will there be permanent scarring, John?"

"I can't say at this time, Alexandra," I replied, not quite certain whether the skin would stay intact.

"You mean you don't know, Doctor Barlow." She sounded testy.

"If the skin stays intact it will be fine. There are one or two places where the skin might give way. Shall I get you a mirror?"

"I was only teasing you, John!"

An RCMP constable came to see us soon after I had finished dressing her back.

"Could you tell me when you last saw your parents?" he asked Alex.

"When they took me to the basement."

"Not since then?"

"No. I heard someone come down to unlock the door but neither saw nor heard anyone in the house after that."

"Did you go back to the house to look?"

"No. I was too scared."

The constable turned to me.

"I have been unable to contact them, no answer at the house and nobody has seen them at his workplace. They left no messages with anyone I can find, Doctor. Do you have a key to the house, Alexandra?"

"Yes."

"Would you come with me to search the house?"

"Yes."

"Would you come with us, Doctor?"

Alex looked pleadingly at me to say no, and seeing this the constable addressed her.

"I may need a witness, Alex, I must not take the risk."

"I'll stay in the background, Alex, unless I'm needed, I won't intrude unless necessary."

We went to the house through the back door and into the kitchen. I told them I would remain here unless needed and she took him to search the house but found nobody and then they went downstairs to the study.

"Did you lock the door?"

"No I'm sure I didn't."

"Could you come down, Doctor. I would like you to confirm that the door is locked. Do you have a key, Alex?"

"No," she said, "and I don't know where he kept it, the study was out of bounds to me."

"I'll need a warrant to search any further," he said, as we headed to leave from the back door. "Anything you need?" he asked her, "I will have to close the house until I can search it."

She shook her head.

"Not even clothes?"

She changed her mind and went upstairs with him to get things from her room.

As she came down I noticed she had a stack of jeans and T-shirts mixed up with socks, underwear and another pair of runners, all surmounted by two books, her Bible and her Prayer Book. She had a suit or dress covered in dark plastic on a coat hanger which I took from her to help carry back to the house. When I went to her room that night to wish her a good sleep I noticed the two books on her bedside table.

"Are you comfortable?"

"The bed is soft," she answered, like a politician evading the question. I made a mental note remembering that she liked to sleep on the hard floor.

"Good night, Alex."

Alex was already in the kitchen when the sun woke me in the morning. She was dressed formally in a trouser suit and was drinking her coffee.

"Couldn't you sleep?" I asked her.

"I slept well, thanks."

"What are you up so early for?"

She was wearing a hat with her long hair hidden inside it.

"I could ask the same question."

"I woke and it's a lovely morning," I told her and it was then that I saw the prayer book. "Off to church?"

"I thought I would go to early communion," she answered and revealed her reason, "it's not well attended."

"Would you like my company?"

"I didn't think you went to church. Andrew says he never goes."

"I'd be happy to go in your company, Miss Jones," I teased her, "and you would not have to walk."

There were a few cars outside the church as we parked, left the car and walked into the church. We sat near the front with the handful of other worshippers. It was Trinity Sunday and as the epistle ended 'for thou has created all things, and for thy pleasure they are and were created' I wondered how her back must have felt. 'The wind bloweth where it listeth' I heard with some amusement being a sailor, but watching Alex in her sincerity I knew I must be careful not to mock those things I did not believe. I wondered bitterly if Mr Jones had trusted in his own righteousness each time he approached the communion rail. Alex, not yet confirmed, did not take communion. The Reverend Roberts gave the blessing and walked to the door of the church. Alex sat back in the pew, sighed and gave me a nervous smile.

"Alex, how are you?" Mr Roberts asked as he greeted us at the church door, "your father and mother not with you today?"

"They're away," she said, her eyes willing me to say nothing, "I brought Doctor Barlow with me. Doctor Barlow, this is the Reverend Roberts."

Back in the kitchen she busied herself getting breakfast for me.

"You don't believe in God do you, Doctor Barlow?" she challenged, having noted that I had not said the creed or responses; silence prevailed for a short while.

"No, Alexandra, but that must be irrelevant to you. I will come to church with you each Sunday, but will never try to convince you of my belief if you never proselytise for my soul."

"What is proselytise?"

"Try to convert me to your belief."

"Why did you come to church with me then?"

"Because I want to encourage you to be an individual who makes her own choices and decisions. I also thought you might like company; I will be happy to come to church with you as often as you wish so long as sitting next to a non-believer does not make you uncomfortable."

"What do you want me to get you for lunch?"

"You got my breakfast for me, you are not the maid, Alexandra. I will get lunch around one."

"What time does Andrew get up?"

"Late, unless his sister decides to wake him."

"Could I?"

A mischievous look on her face.

"If you promise not to say I sent you. Although he will probably sense a conspiracy between us."

"I promise."

I did not see them until lunch although I heard their laughter coming from Andrew's room. After lunch, Brian and David were in the field for a game of baseball. Watching them through the window they were just as rough with her as ever which made me feel I should go out to defend her but thought better of it. The right decision, as I was to discover later, when we were driving into Vancouver.

"You're very quiet," I ventured.

"Alex is a bit worried," Andrew said, sitting in the front with me, "about meeting Jim and Jessica."

"Shut up!" she said from the back of the car, thumping him firmly on the head, making sure he understood that he had betrayed a confidence.

Andrew and Alex joined the twins in the family room and I went with Douglas to the sitting room. Settled with our drinks, he started to discuss the program for Alex the next day.

"Could you take her to see a paediatrician on the north shore tomorrow?"

"Peter, you mean?" I said.

He was a known expert in problems involving child abuse.

"Yes, we usually use him if he's available and he would see Alex tomorrow at one-thirty."

"I'll take time off work. The others will understand."

When we were at dinner, Alex indicated that Jim and Jessica had been models of discretion in not prying into her affairs.

"Do you know the story of the man who lost both of his ears, Alex?" Doug asked, and she shook her head.

"He was extremely sensitive about them and got very upset with anyone who mentioned anything to do with ears. There was one old friend who had not seen him since the accident but had been warned about his touchiness and was quite nervous. They were in a hotel at the time with one of those large staircases. He saw his earless friend coming down the stairs towards him and in trying to avoid the touchy subject blurted. 'Good to see you Joe, but I notice you're not wearing your glasses'!"

When she laughed with us the egg shells on which we had been treading were swept aside and the conversation became uninhibited.

I noticed that her sense of fun, one of her endearing features, had come back since punching Andrew in the stomach. As we were clearing the meal away that evening, they had the tea towels in their hands with no thought of leniency for her and none asked.

"Andrew! Stop doing that to Alex," I said, as the towel caught her on her back.

"Don't be such a softy, John," she interjected, laughing at me.

"Yeah, Dad, this new sister of mine is not made of all things nice."

On Monday morning going downstairs to get my coffee I found Alex was already in the kitchen making it. I felt irritated by the disturbance to my routine of silent drifting in the kitchen slowly bringing order out of sleep. Andrew always abed at this time, conversation had been with myself or superfluous.

"Shall I cook you breakfast?"

"I just have coffee before I leave for work." I said it abruptly.

"You have breakfast on the boat and weekends," she continued, undaunted by my mood.

"That's different."

"What does Andrew do?"

"I don't know, he's never up by the time I leave at seven. I've always expected him to look after himself for breakfast. I think Flora gets cereal for him."

"So bacon and eggs is weekends only!"

"Quite, are you disappointed? What do you usually have?"

"Porridge," she said making a face, "I will never have porridge again."

"What would you like in the mornings?"

"I'll try just coffee and toast until I decide."

On the trip from Richmond to the university every morning, the route so familiar, driving becomes automatic leaving the mind free to tussle with problems. Long conversations with foe, friend or self roll off the silent tongue. 'Why did Alex irritate me being in the kitchen as if she were violating my space? You're in a rut, an old stick in the mud. Partly, but also pique at Andrew for landing me with difficulties I don't need. Not fair, he needs friends. We only have a few close ones in our lifetime. Why Alex? Why a girl? Trying to replace Steph? No, you had things you couldn't talk to your Dad about! You talked to Mary, she would know. Fear of the eternal triangle perhaps? Alex taking Andrew away from me? Leaving me alone and jealous? I'm not the jealous type. Selfish? Oh yes, a selfish old bugger, aren't we all? Steph wasn't, she would have opened her arms, to hell with the consequences. What's one more, I can hear you Steph, no trouble expected, no trouble; Andrew's like you, bless him. Jessica seen manipulating Doug? She sure does, but Alex on the boat for six weeks, you liked her, always bright, cheerful and more sail John! Direct and good company, she'd punch you, not manipulate you. Worrying about a teenage girl? H'm, thirteen a difficult age. You noticed her at Blind Bay, a bit ashamed; scared of yourself, finding her desirable like her father? No, couldn't work at the clinic if I was like that. Her developing femininity could be looked at and enjoyed. Same for Andrew asking if he will attract, assessing his looks and body. What about Alex? If she finds she has an irritable guardian, my God, guardian, shuffling antisocially around the kitchen this morning! Uncertainty? Yes, the two of us so certain, our days predictable, actions predictable and I can read his face, no masking of expression. Will she be happy, awkward, awakened by Andrew, or want to go back to her parents?' The last making me shiver as I drove into the parkade.

When I walked into the clinic at 7.30am I phoned home and she answered.

"Alex, I haven't told Flora that you will be staying with us. Do you want to talk to her yourself?"

"I could come home at lunch time," she said, but I could hear the inconvenience.

"I'll phone her, Alex, and let her know that you will be with us this week while your parents are away."

"Okay," she said, "I'll talk to Flora after school tomorrow to let her know it is more permanent. What time will you pick me up at school?"

"About 12.15 I hope."

"What will he want to do, John?" she asked as we drove to see the paediatrician.

"He will want to assess the evidence that you were beaten and may want to take a photograph of your back," I said hoping that was all she wanted to know, already taking on the mantle of father, and wanting to protect her from the unseemly.

"Anything else?"

"He will want to examine you for evidence of sexual interference," I said evasively, and not looking at her.

"How will he do that, John?"

"He will ask you to undress and put you on the examining table so that with your legs apart he can examine the entrance to your vagina and anal area for signs of interference." I said it half hoping she would understand without further queries, still embarrassed to make eye contact with her.

"What did your mother say about eye to eye?" she asked, and I looked at her to see her laughing at me, "just teasing you 'to see if you would be honest with me'," she mimicked me. "Anne told me on Sunday about the examination and said she would come with me but I told her I would be okay."

She spent about an hour with Peter before he brought her into his reception, suggesting she wait a moment while he spoke to me. In the privacy of his office he said he would make out his report and send it to Douglas.

"Alexandra has asked me not to discuss my report with anyone other than the officers of the court," he said, looking embarrassed.

"I had expected that would be her wish, Peter."

"How long have you known her?"

"Since she entered Grade 7 with Andrew, about a year and a half. Andrew brought her sailing." Peter's eyes lit up, a keen sailor himself. "They behave like brothers and Andrew and his friends say she is 'one of the boys'. I got to know her when she crewed for us on our trip to Queen Charlotte Straits last summer."

"She told me she had her first period on the boat!"

"Don't remind me!" I laughed, remembering the ordeal for both of us. "I made them tell me stories in the evening after I had read them one of the Kwakiutl legends. Alex told a story, which I now realise was an allegory, but I was too stupid to see it or read the symptoms of her abuse."

"I think she will tell you when she is ready, which may be some time. When she does she will need a good listener. Is she staying with you temporarily?"

"At the moment, but I think she would like the court to accept our invitation to stay permanently."

"That's brave of you."

"I don't know, the disruption will be good for Andrew and me; we were getting too stuck in our ways. Thank you for seeing her, Peter, she'll appreciate your confidence."

I shook hands with him and as we left his waiting room he said good-bye to Alex.

"I hope you are not ashamed of something that is not your fault," I said, as we drove home.

"I feel stupid not to have realised that my home life was different to others, but I don't feel any blame now."

She was sitting back with her eyes closed, looking older than thirteen.

"The sailing last year was so different. When I did things that were punishable at home, you all laughed," she gave a chuckle, "it was confusing. By the end of the holiday I knew I would not ... would not." She looked at me and grimaced.

I thought that I understood as I finished the sentence for her, '... would not forget the kindness and companionship' or words to that effect. However I had stopped taking statements from patients at face value or finishing their sentences because experience had taught me that months or years later I would be presented with the real meaning.

As we circled the airport a plane landed and must have triggered a thought.

"I hear your mother is coming to stay," Alex said.

"I don't think so."

"Hasn't Andrew told you that he phoned her and asked her to come?"

"No, Alex, he hasn't!"

"Maybe I shouldn't have said anything, John."

I could imagine him twisting her round his little finger with 'Dad needs you, Grandma, so do I'.

"What's she like?"

"She's a tyrant!"

"Andrew always says she's great when I ask him."

"She used to chase after me with a wooden spoon to discipline me, if she could catch me." I was laughing when suddenly thinking this a taboo subject said, "Whoops! Sorry, Alexandra."

"I should tell Andrew to cancel her visit, Doctor Barlow."

"She's all right, Alex; she never caught me and scolded me with words as she chased."

"Did she reason with you?" she mimicked me again.

A social worker from the family court phoned during the late afternoon and came to see her. She started to ask Alex to give her story again so I left the room. I heard later from Alex that she managed to persuade the social worker to wait for the report from the paediatrician and from Douglas to save her repeating it. She showed the social worker that she had indeed been physically abused, allowing her to lift up the dressing, so that the police might lay charges against her parents. The social worker told Alex that she would support her in remaining in our home and that she would contact me at work. Flora had already left by the time the social worker came and Alex had not told Flora what had happened.

The next morning the coffee was ready in the pot. My ritual complete and ready to leave I went up to Alex's room and knocked on her door. She was sitting at her desk reading, an empty coffee cup at her right hand. The room was spotless and tidy; the opposite of Andrew's room.

"Thank you for the coffee, Alex."

"That's okay," she said cheerfully.

"Did you have work to do?"

"No. I sensed that I was an intruder and Andrew said you liked to be by yourself in the mornings."

"May I sit down?"

"Why do you ask? It's your house!"

"Andrew and I did not ask you to be a lodger. It's your house too - a place to call home; a room of your own. I've become irritable and grumpy with myself in the mornings as I wake up; you may have to tolerate that but it's your kitchen too."

When I arrived home from work that evening I found Flora in the kitchen with Alex. Andrew was sitting with the evening newspaper spread out on the table from which he was reading them titbits.

"I decided I would stay and have supper with you if that's all right," Flora said, her face turned to the stove, concentrating on the food. "Andrew says you like a pick-me-up before supper."

"Can you break free and join me?" I said to Flora.

"Yes she can!" said emphatically, even stubbornly from Alex. As Flora left the stove she turned to me, raising her eyebrows in resignation.

When Flora was settled with scotch and water and I with a martini she smiled at me.

"I don't think I am needed here this week!"

"Ugh!"

"Alex seemed determined, insisting on helping with supper," she said with amusement and no dismay in her voice. "When she came in from school she said she was going to help me so that she could learn to cook for you on the weekends."

"How do you get on?"

"She's a nice wee girl."

"Has she talked about herself at all?"

"She said that her parents had gone away and that she hoped to be staying here for a few weeks."

"Did she tell you why?"

"No," she said puzzled, "and I haven't been able to get Andrew alone to ask him."

"Be patient, Flora," I said, just as Andrew came in, carrying the evening paper.

"Flora, Alex asked if you would help her," he said, and Flora finished her drink, taking both glasses with her.

"Did you have a good day, Andrew?"

"Well."

He started into one of his more florid diatribes of the agonies of a grade eight teenager. He reminded me of Stephanie when she would half act and half rail, describing her less than satisfactory experiences of her nursing day before settling into the more pleasant life for her of homemaking. Andrew was not able to leave his thoughts unsaid and his sixth sense had detected my own regret at the disruption of our comfortable relationship.

"She won't come between us, Dad," he said, "I would never let that happen."

Supper finished, I wondered how to get Andrew alone with Flora.

"Alex, I'll dress your back for you, unless you would like Flora to do it for you."

"No!" she said sharply, a dagger look of fury as she turned her eyes on me.

I removed the old dressing; the hematoma was turning purple, the skin intact and no oozing.

"No sign of infection, Alex," I said, "How does it feel? Any throbbing?"

"No, I can hardly feel it now." She had her face turned to the side, her eyes searching my face. "I can't tell Flora. I tried twice but couldn't start."

"That's all right, Alex, I think Andrew will have given her the gist by now." I had a look of triumph on my face.

"I could have killed you asking if I would like Flora to do this for me." Her fury returned to her eyes momentarily. "You are devious!"

Back downstairs I found Flora getting prepared to leave.

"Stay and have coffee with me?" I asked.

By her countenance I guessed Andrew had told her.

"All right, John," she said, and settled back with her coffee. "Poor wee girl, Andrew told me what he had seen. What a terrible thing to do to a child."

"Alexandra does not like to be pitied I suspect, Flora; she tried to tell you herself this afternoon but couldn't."

I told Flora that Alex only wanted us to know this much and both Andrew and I were prepared to accept her without prying further. I explained about the court and Alex's choice to live here if she were allowed to, leading up to the question I feared to ask in case the answer was negative.

"Would you come and be a live in housekeeper and surrogate for her?"

"I'll need to think about that," she said, getting ready to return to her home.

My mother arrived next day from Toronto; Andrew and I went to the airport to meet her. I was still miffed with Andrew about her visit and would have preferred to cope first and then have her come to see the results of my decision. As Andrew bubbled on to her about Alex and how pleased he was to have an adopted sister I could feel her antagonism build. So long had I known and loved my mother, never having to view her with objectivity, I had ignored her barbs of enmity to those outside her tribe. She took an absolute dislike to Alex even before they had met. Flora was to tell me later that she saw it instantly and this had weighed in her decision to come and live in with the family.

Whilst Flora was a housekeeper I could never consider her as less than a close friend. There were to be times when the arrangement seem to be misunderstood by some people, making me stumblingly apologise to her for not being able to extend our relationship beyond friendship.

"I like you as a friend, John; och you'd be impossible as a lover." She allowed our jesting relationship to continue intact, and later she said in front of Andrew and Alex.

"You'll not have to tell me now when you've been asked to dinner!" A chorus of laughter rang out from all three at my expense.

CHAPTER 7

Birthdays

After the first Sunday when John said that Alex could wake Andrew she was still dressed for church. She went to her room to change, feeling more comfortable in her jeans and T-shirt.

She saw him lying asleep on his stomach and approached the bed. A smile crossed her face as she stood beside his bed, just prior to jumping onto him, landing with a thump. A muffled roar of disapproval came from under her. He struggled to turn over to see the offender, recognising her face.

"Dad sent you I suppose."

The reek of morning breath made her retreat and sitting beside him on top of the covers she grinned at him.

"Do you want some breakfast?"

"What time is it, Alex?"

"About nine-thirty, far too late for being in bed."

"You know I never get up before eleven on weekends, Alex." He turned back onto his stomach and settled for more sleep.

"Why not?" she asked, suddenly getting off the bed, carrying all the bed clothes.

"Ooh! Sorry, Andrew, I didn't realise."

He lay clamped to the bed on his stomach unable to move with her standing looking at his naked body.

"Pass me my dressing gown at least!"

She picked it up and held it against her.

"Come and get it," she said, ogling him, and then advanced towards him, laying it over him.

"Would you like some coffee, Andrew?"

"Yes, anything to get you out of my way so I can have the room to myself."

Andrew got up as she headed for the door and he went to the bathroom and cleaned his teeth. She returned from the kitchen with his coffee as he left the bathroom. He opened the door and let her into his room. She set the cup on his bedside table and was straightening up as he grabbed her from behind with his arm across her neck, pressing her back against him. He was aware of a momentary grimace of pain as he released her.

"I'm sorry, Alex," he said, mortified by what he had done.

"It's not your fault, softy," she answered, "I deserved it anyway for waking you."

"Tell me what happened?" he asked, taking her by surprise.

"Please," she sighed, "I'll tell you when I'm ready. Promise you won't ask again."

She reached towards his head taking a clump of his hair in her hand and pulled.

"Promise?" she said again, jerking her hand.

"All right," he answered and she released his hair, "what about Jim and Jessica?"

"Jessica said they wouldn't ask unless I wanted to tell them."

"Did you believe her?"

She looked at him, raised her eyebrows and shrugged her shoulders, a sourness on her face telling him of her worry for that evening.

Mr Roberts greeted John and Alex at the church door looking at her with quizzical concern. Back at the house in the kitchen John needled her.

"You're going to have to tell him."

"I know, I know," she replied, "I will... soon."

"Perfect love casteth out fear, Alex."

"So you do listen," she said, turning to punch him on the chest, "you... you old heathen."

Later, John heard her phoning Mr Roberts to make a time to talk to him.

"I'll drive you to the rectory."

"No, I'll walk down. It will give me time to think how to tell him."

"You mean how much to tell him, Alex!"

She rang the door bell and heard footsteps, felt her face become sullen, wondering if she could muster the courage to say anything. She need not have worried, he made it easy for her.

"I'm living with the Barlows at the moment," she said, "Dr Barlow sent me to explain."

"Alex," he said gently, "your father has written to me."

"Did he tell you what happened?"

"I don't know; would you like to read his letter?"

He went to his desk to pick up a single sheet of white note paper and handed it to her.

Dear Reverend Roberts,

My wife and I have left Richmond leaving Alex to continue school. I think she will be staying with Dr Barlow for the present.

What I did is too terrible to write, and I doubt I can be forgiven. Watch over Alex for us.

yours sincerely

Art

There was no address or date, just this simple statement. She looked up at him, his eyes expecting an explanation.

"What happened, Alex?"

"Please, please don't ask me; I can't even tell Andrew or John, Dr Barlow I mean." She looked at the letter on her lap. "I have been to the lawyer, doctor, social worker and police."

"You don't have to tell me."

"Thank you, Reverend."

They talked about her staying with John and Andrew. She assured him that it was her choice, explaining to him the bond that had developed over the two years she had been friends with Andrew.

"Is he your boyfriend?"

She looked at him a smile breaking.

"I'm one of the boys," she replied, "Andrew is like a brother."

She told him about their relationship, hinted at the oddity of her raising and let the conversation drift into the present. As she was going through his front door she turned to say good-bye.

"I will pray for you, Alex."

"You don't need to pray for me!"

"Who then?"

She gave him a withering look of anger.

"Them!"

And she bounded down the steps onto the street, not turning to look back.

The summer was disrupted by the decisions made on her behalf so that they spent only weekends on the boat, missing a long cruise. There was agreement that she could remain with the Barlows, and Flora agreed to move into the house as surrogate for Alex. They cleared the small bedroom of accumulated junk and brought her bedroom furniture from her house. She felt comfortable on the hard bed again, relieving the austerity of the chairs with cushions to match the drapes made by her with Flora's help. It was a cosy pleasant room but unlike her old home she only went there to sleep or study, preferring Andrew's company, solitude no longer necessary for the flowering of her personality.

She finished Grade 8, doing well in spite of her upheaval. Hidden under her natural sunny personality was a developing seething anger at the action of her parents, their desertion and disappearance. She wanted them made to face their iniquity in the courts and jails of society, her fury induced by unrequited revenge. The police seemed unable to find them, making her paranoid that their efforts were purposefully failing. Alone in bed her vengeful spirit would conjure up visions of them hanging hand tied and squirming, an eye for an eye, a tooth for a tooth retaliation; or standing in an imaginary dock, at the time of their sentence, the judge in black-capped splendour.

At other times she would envisage her parents at home or church almost as if she was missing them, a duplicity she could not fathom. She was still unable to open out her story to Andrew or John, making her brooding and sullen silences a mystery for both of them.

She took it out on Andrew by waking him in the morning and meanly turning him out of his bed, removing his comforter so that he had to move to cover his nakedness. A pest and a pestilence on his head, she would pound him with her fists if he said anything she did not like. When he was silent with her she would fight him to the ground and pin him by his arms, wanting to spit in his face, the intensity of her anger taken out on the only person she could trust to understand. She was hoisted on her own petard of secrecy, still unable to tell Andrew her story or tell him why she felt so angry and frustrated. Andrew kept his promise and never asked again.

In late July, Andrew told John that he had discovered that it was Alex's birthday the following weekend. Next morning in the kitchen having coffee, she started to leave for her room.

"Please don't go, Alexandra."

"What do you want, Doctor Barlow?" she said with hostility.

"I've missed your company in the mornings. Except on Sundays you have been deserting me."

"I thought that's what you liked!"

"I have decided to take a day off this Friday and spend a few extra days next week on the boat. Would you like to come?"

"Can we?" she brightened, "I miss the boat."

Friday night at Montague Harbour on a mooring buoy was peaceful in spite of summer; Saturday afternoon brought a large number of boats into the bay, making it noisy. Alex's tolerance was being eroded by the hour until at about three in the afternoon she could no longer stand it.

"John, couldn't we get out of here?"

"Where would we go this late in the day, Alex?"

"Anywhere, Annette Bay even, couldn't we?" she begged. "Please, John."

"You might have said something sooner, Alex. It will take some time in this light wind."

She released the boat from the mooring buoy, her mood improving with the activity.

"Anyway," she sulked when she got back to the cockpit, "it should be my choice today."

"Why so?"

"I'm fourteen today."

"Why didn't you say something before, Alex?" he said, sounding cross and testy.

The sail across Trincomali Channel refreshed her and she began to think that there was something contrived about John's reluctance to leave for Annette Bay but dismissed it. As they entered the bay it was nearly six o'clock.

"Can we go to the inside bay, John?"

"Since it's your birthday you may choose," he answered, and as she guided them through the waist of the bay she saw *Heron* at anchor.

"What's *Heron* doing here?" she asked John.

"Must be another Lapworth 36."

As they approached she could be fooled no more, Jim and Jessica appearing to help tie them alongside. Suddenly pitched into her own birthday party, she realised that it was planned. The happy hour, the birthday greetings and presents which materialised out of hideaways made her the focus of the evening. As her bitterness dissolved her mood rose in the company of gruff Douglas and welcoming Anne.

She opened Andrew's present first; her own book on pacific coast birds.

"How did you manage to keep a straight face?"

Her accusation was made with a handful of his hair tugged hard towards her. Blushing a little as she saw the hair brush from Jim and Jessica, a teasing note saying that it fitted Jim's hand perfectly. Douglas and Anne's present continued her education in feminine attraction, just a T-shirt, but in hooped shades of green to make her less gangly and bring out the beauty of her hair colour. John's in a small box opened to reveal an Indian barrette, a Kwakiutl motif killer whale carved into the silver, nestling in the satin.

"Quick, Anne, put it on for me," she said, her excitement initially hiding her shame; then as she remembered her sullen treatment of him feeling the prickle of tears, thinking to herself 'I can't be seen, I must get away' for she could never allow such sentiment to be shown in public.

"I must see it in a mirror," she said, hurrying to the cabin where she could be hidden from them in *Heron*'s bathroom until she could control herself and return to thank him. She went over to John turned to show him and then jabbed him lightly in his chest.

"Thank you."

After supper, looking at Jim, she willed him to take her ashore to sit and talk to him and perhaps steal another kiss.

Back in the cockpits of the boats, segregated into young and old, she sipped her hot chocolate and snuggled against Jim's warm body, a contentment not experienced for a whole year. They watched in the cool starlight night the shooting stars of August.

"Time to turn in," she heard Anne say.

"That's my decision!" she replied with authority, staying outside, puckishly refusing to let Jim obey his mother, no longer feeling sullen.

The next morning she went ashore with Jim and as they walked she was able to tell him about her discontent.

"I feel so angry with them for deserting me," she told him angrily. "They deserve to be punished and now the police say they can't find them."

"What did they do to you?" he asked, wanting to understand her anger.

"Jim, I can't," she hesitated, dismayed by her continuing secrecy, "I can't even talk to Andrew. As soon as I try to, I feel my jaws lock."

"Do you love Andrew, Alex?"

"I'm a friend, brother to Andrew; he's the only person I have been able to tell some of my secrets. Why did you ask?" looking at his dog eared expression, "you're jealous!"

"Alex," he replied, his pained expression giving him away, "yes I am."

She reached her arms up around his neck, pulling his mouth towards her and kissed.

"I've never kissed Andrew, never even wanted to."

She watched him, intent on his eyes until his face relaxed and his big arms tightened around her.

When Anne talked to Alex about her anger she realised that Jim must have been the source. While Jim was to learn never to betray another of her confidences, just as Andrew had, there was comfort in the way Anne questioned her during a walk together without pushing her to answer, as if Anne understood that the answers unsaid were more important than those spoken. It was the continuation of the friendship carried over from the previous year.

"I find it so hard to talk about it. I can't even tell Andrew."

"H'm, Alex, be patient, it will come."

"Do you remember Octopus Islands in the forest together?"

"Yes, you almost told me then."

"Did I? What I really wanted to do was this," she turned to her, took her in her arms with her head over Anne's shoulder, "and tell you how much I had enjoyed your company, your friendship. If I had, then I agree I would have been able to tell you."

"How are you getting on with John?"

"I've been horrible to him," she replied, her hand reaching behind her head and touching the barrette, "I did not deserve this."

"Perhaps I should send you to Douglas."

Alex knew that Anne was joking, but she was unable to let it pass.

"No man will ever do that to me again!"

In church the following Sunday, she wondered if the thirteenth after Trinity was unlucky. She sat back to listen to the Gospel.

Alex accused her God after the reading of the parable of the good Samaritan.

"You always do this to me, my good Samaritan sitting by me; a non-believer too."

"You have not treated them kindly this last few weeks," he replied.

"What must I do?"

"Alex, you know the answer to that question!"

She was silent as John drove her home and remained so as she got his breakfast.

"John," she said tentatively, the last drips of coffee going through the filter.

"Yes, Alex."

Serving him some coffee, she paused to find the phrase. "I'm sorry."

"What for?"

"I haven't... haven't been nice."

"It's hardly your fault."

"Don't excuse me," she answered, able to look at him now, "Anne's right, I must not make them," the word sneered, "the excuse for being angry or unkind to the very people who least deserve it."

"I accept your apology, Alexandra."

"Thank you, Doctor Barlow."

She made fresh coffee later taking a cup to Andrew, put it beside him on the bedside table and sat on the bed alongside him. She took a clump of his hair in her hand and pulled gently.

"Coffee for my brother."

"Why do I deserve such gentleness from my sister?"

With her apologies she experienced absolution, a weight lifted from her shoulders, even before she had learned about it from confirmation.

Alex, now in Grade 9, performed like a successful automaton in a world of machines whose cogs well greased worked with accurate efficiency. Always sunny in the companionship of Andrew and his boy friends, competitive in her school work, ever striving to be the best. She threw herself into the volleyball program with a desire to win that gained respect without regard from her team mates who still found her cold and unfriendly. She drove herself and her team-mates with intensity; one afternoon she overheard them.

"I wish Alex would go play with herself!" coming from one girl.

"She wouldn't know how," from another, a rejoinder that was accompanied by guttural laughter.

Andrew, the philosopher, raconteur and bookworm would marvel at her energy and tease her for her innocence.

"What did she mean, Andrew, go play with herself?"

"Masturbate," he said, looking at her puzzled face.

"What's that?"

"Look it up," he said, passing her the Oxford dictionary.

"It says self-abuse."

"Is that all it says, Alex?" He got off his bed to look over her shoulder. "A better definition would be to excite yourself to orgasm. No, don't ask, Alex, look it up."

"Violent excitement, rage, paroxysm; height of venereal excitement in coition." She read aloud, still unenlightened.

"Sex, Alex," he said, "orgasm happens when the sperm is put into you, it's fun, feels good and you can make it happen without someone else there and that's masturbation."

Even though Alex had now understood, she asked innocently.

"Andrew, I still don't see, would you show me?"

The friendship grew with the days, Andrew, needing the good listener for his extrovert nature, found his sister, and Alex, needing to create a home for herself and a 'girlfriend' relationship, found instead her brother to whom she could reveal all. They irritated, fought, loved and hated each other with sibling intensity, becoming tolerant and inseparable. She was able to discuss any topic with him and even able to let him trespass on her emotions so long as they involved her life after leaving her home. The school year passed quickly, her bitterness diminishing, even though there was no news of her parents and the summer break was suddenly there.

Alex had planned to find a quiet time on the boat when she would pluck up the courage to tell them her story. She had the courage to tell Andrew now, but she always saw John's twisted face when daydreaming his listening to her. She knew she would not tell Andrew alone, she had to tell them both together. They were a week away from their cruise when Alex was stricken with appendicitis and admitted to hospital for an operation. The confinement in hospital, the pain on waking, the reduction in her activities were nothing to her in comparison with losing her anticipated cruise. She would think of it as the wasted summer, unfulfilled and with only one highlight to remember.

The boat, her symbol for security, freedom and change, took them one weekend to the Butchart Gardens. The anticipation of another birthday, the slight uncertainty that they may have forgotten but determined not to remind them. Watching John's nonchalance and waiting for Andrew to give their pretence away until they arrived at Brentwood.

They were joined by *Heron* and anchored near the small float giving access to the gardens. They walked around the paths viewing the multicoloured show of flowers, feeling the tranquillity of the sunken garden with its pond and huge fountain. It was her fifteenth birthday.

John arranged to take them all to the Garden Restaurant for supper; her uncertainty growing as they walked to the restaurant, no mention of her birthday at happy hour and no evidence of presents. The waiter showed them to their table, the gifts surrounding her place setting. Their happy faces knowing they had fooled her again, but making her feel the centre of the universe!

The huge book from Andrew and the twins together on Totem Poles and Kwakiutl masks, shoes from Anne and Douglas to go with her new church suit and last but not least another little box; Kwakiutl salmon motif silver earrings.

The dinner was help-yourself-style piled on her plate and the chance to return for more. There was a sudden silence in the room as the cake alight with fifteen candles was set before her, the singing of happy birthday from all around the room. After leaving the restaurant, they walked to the outdoor theatre to watch the variety show with its Australian humour and slapstick ballet.

By the end of the show, darkness covered the gardens and they walked the paths admiring the illuminations set to pick out clumps of flowers or a tree. In the sunken garden, trees and shrubs overhung the still pond reflecting these images turning the gardens into a magical theatrical set. Andrew led Jessica by the hand to the observation rail to admire the display.

"What a set for our play," he said to Alex, who had helped build the set for their school production of *'A Midsummer Nights Dream'*, in which Andrew had played Oberon. He looked across at the border of flowers, ever the actor.

"It fell upon a little western flower, before milk-white now purple with love's wound. Maidens call it love-in-idleness. Fetch me that flower; the herb I showed thee once: the juice of it on sleeping eyelids laid will make or man or woman madly dote upon the next live creature that it sees."

Taking Alex's hand Jim pulled her along the path widdershins to the others so that they could fall behind. He turned her to him, gently closed her eyes with his lips so that he could flower-streak them and make her see him first.

Arriving back at the float, Anne was waiting and chiding them with match-making eyes for taking so long rowed them back to the boats. Sitting in the cockpit with hot drinks for a warm night, Jim was irradiating memories of summers past, for once wishing the others were not there. In her innocent naiveté she suggested that Jim change bunks with Andrew, Jim's keenness showing in his red face.

"Can we, John?" she asked eagerly, and as John shook his head, "you said I could make my own decisions!"

"You can Alex," he was laughing, "but not Andrew's."

"Quick thinking, John."

Anne's voice from the corner of the cockpit.

"Worried what Andrew might do to Jessica, eh?"

Alex was beginning to see the funny side.

"No, what Jessica might to Andrew!"

When, in the solitude of her attic room, she had created a home for herself in her daydreamt imagination, Andrew was always her brother. Sitting on his bed now watching him read at his desk, 'what is the attraction; he is small, a runt', smiling at the thought, 'and yet such imaginative games and stories come from the small frame, pictures painted in words chosen for their shades'. Shaking her head now 'he listens to me intently and with interest. He watches me, seems to know when I need him'. At night lying in bed her thoughts intense before sleep 'Flora too, a real mother, ally in the battle of the sexes, worrying like the hen with two chicks, a little afraid of the cock?' leering at her double entendre, 'the evening meal at six, inviolable, Flora punctual, sitting at the table inquiring about our day's activities; belonging.' Walking back from school with Andrew in trouble with another teacher not appreciating one of his smart arsed remarks. That evening leaving him with John, 'I always know when Andrew needs his father', retiring from them to let them talk, 'no jealousy of their special love for one another. I have no denial of attention, breakfast with John, cooking with Flora and Andrew's door never closed against me'. Sitting in her pew on Sunday chatting with her God about John, 'I always dreamt of a father like him, one who would give me freedom to expand and yet believing in his quotation, Alex, he would say "there is no freedom without self discipline". He supports my aspirations, proud I talk about medical school, comes to watch me play volleyball, my only wish that he were more vocal'. When she hurt John's feelings she would know by his silence accompanied by some of his more sombre classical music. Her love for him grew undiminished. 'Perhaps, it was like Andrew's love for Anne which he had admitted to her as his ideal of a wife for his own children'. Before sleep one night, 'Why am I frightened to touch John or hug him goodnight like Andrew?' The wind outside disturbing the drapes simulating with its shadows a human presence, she sat up gripped by momentary fear, lying back ashamed of her silly self; 'did I think it was my father again, am I frightened John would do the same?'

He was usually even tempered with both of them, the demon skipper of the boat rising to the surface on a few occasions when her behaviour was antisocial; particularly when that behaviour was directed at or affected Flora. She had lately become sassy with Flora, starting to take her for granted, a house fixture for her convenience, like her mother.

The first occasion came when the volleyball team meeting was followed by a spontaneous party making her an hour late for supper. The evening meal time, important to them as a demonstration of family unity, was always at six. She had not bothered to phone Flora to tell her that she would be late. When she got home she found Flora upset and anxious for her. John called her in to the front room to account for herself.

"That was unkind of you, Alex, Flora has been worried about you."

"I'm only one hour late," she replied in a 'so what' tone of voice.

"Flora feels responsible for you in this house like a mother and she is always ready with our meal at six."

"Well she's not my mother!" she said pouting at him.

"You forget that Flora is fond of you, even loves you, Alex. I hope you will apologise to her."

"Certainly not, I've done nothing wrong."

"Then go to your room," he snapped.

Alex squirmed in her bowels, fear followed by fright, the cramping sensation stealing its way up into her chest the fright that her father had made her feel with the same order.

"And think about it," she heard as she flew from the room.

She didn't go to her room but into the bathroom and sitting on the toilet, empty now, slowly recovered her composure. Then she sought Andrew in his room. He was sitting at his desk reading when she entered. He looked up at her.

"So you have returned," he inquired, "and in some shit I expect."

"What's all the fuss?" she asked, exasperated by him.

"Dad said he was upset because of Flora."

"He says I should apologise to Flora. Told me to go to my room and think about it," she said sullenly, adding, "what do you think, Andrew?"

"Certainly you should."

"You can't mean that, I was only an hour late."

"I was anxious about you, my sister, for that hour, imagining all sorts of horrible fates." He said it seriously, but seeing Alex's pained expression, "I was preparing to rescue you from Dsonqua!" She stepped forwards and punched him in her frustration, turned, and went downstairs into the kitchen.

"Flora, I'm sorry, I didn't mean to upset you."

"What a fuss about nothing," she replied adding, "now you're safe."

At breakfast next morning she made her peace with John.

"I apologised to Flora."

"Yes, she told me."

"Am I grounded?"

"Do you deserve to be?"

"Yes," she answered, watching his bemused expression.

"For how long?"

"That's for you to say."

"One month."

Suddenly she realised that that included the evening they had been asked to stay with Jim and Jessica.

"But that means..." she started to say. She was now being teased and knew it.

One evening, Andrew out at a rehearsal, they were sitting together after supper.

"Don't you ever feel the need to rail against your world, Alex?"

"Not like Andrew."

"Don't you feel anger or frustration?"

"John, please," she appealed.

"Sorry, Alex."

Hearing the sad music a few minutes later she knew she had hurt his feelings.

It had not been an easy year trying to break free from her secretiveness but the year of living together had been happy as she slowly allowed her own personality to break out and some of her feelings be reflected on her face. So much of her mood related to her previous home life which still held her under a tight rein.

They were late going on their cruise that year. She was missing *Heron*'s company and her sixteenth birthday was on the second day in August. The weather was hot and sultry with no wind to sail. They powered to Silva Bay for Saturday night and hoped for good weather to cross the Gulf disparaging a northwest wind which might prevent their objective. They left Silva Bay in the late morning to take the incoming tide.

"So we made it," she said to John as she steered them through the narrow entrance into Smuggler Cove.

"Go to the far bay, Alex," he said, going forward to prepare the anchor. She headed for the narrow channel between the two cottages built on the low rocks.

"*Heron*!" she shouted, taken by surprise. "How did you get Andrew to keep that secret?"

"With difficulty and threats of..." John checked himself and looked pained.

"A dozen lashes; softy," she said and laughed at him.

It was early evening when they tied alongside. There were Happy birthday greetings and kisses all around as they settled down for happy hour and gift opening. She opened Andrew's present first and saw the hard cover book *'The Winthrop Woman'* by Anya Seton.

"What's it about, Andrew?"

"It's historical fiction about a puritan family leaving England for the New World. She reminded me of you, your sort of spirit and I kept seeing your face as I read it."

She thanked him and put it on one side going on to open her other presents coming to another little box. This time a watch lying on the satin with a note attached 'No excuses for being late for supper!'.

Her birthday meal appeared with planned magic from Anne's galley completing her pleasure, almost. The washing up done, she looked at Jim expectantly.

"Want a walk ashore?"

"Yes," he said, turning to everyone else with a deadpan mask, "who's coming for an evening stroll?"

She could have killed him and knew her face showed it. So little opportunity to be alone with him.

"Yes, let's all go ashore!" they exclaimed in unison. She surveyed their deadpan faces coming to Andrew's, always the first to let them down, and as they laughed at her, she blushed with embarrassment.

"You might have told me," she said, punching Jim's solar plexus, half wanting to wind him.

"Careful," Jim told her, "or you might find yourself swimming again." He took her hand and assisted her into the dinghy.

They walked to Halfmoon Bay along the path through the swamp. She felt the warmth of his hand, the question and answer of their intertwined fingers, as they chatted their way along the path. They sat on the rocks of the isolated bay looking out to Merry Island the setting sun imparting pink borders to the fluffy white clouds. They sought each other's warmth, his kisses making her pleasure complete.

The cool evening air made her suggest returning, an excuse for the truth, finding the anxiety of her rising desire unsettling.

She wished that *Heron* did not have to leave them in the morning; Jim's company would have added enjoyment to her holiday. Sitting in the cockpit that evening she teased John.

"Can Jim exchange bunks with Andrew?"

"Certainly not!" she heard, not John but Andrew. "I must be the protector of your chastity, my sister."

He did not sound altogether humorous.

A system approaching the coast had given them wind for a fast passage. Soon after anchoring at Hardy Island, the clouds rolled in and the rain started to fall, huge drops bouncing off the saline sea. After supper, no chance of going ashore without being soaked. Andrew took *'The Winthrop Woman'* and started the first chapter. Andrew liked to sit forward at the table with his head over the book concentrating on the words and phrases. He read well, his acting voice giving distinction to the characters. John liked to close his eyes appearing almost asleep and Alex sat up watching her extrovert brother. Andrew kept his eyes down until the end of the chapter, just after Elizabeth had whispered 'I'll never forget it'. He looked up from the book at Alex's face, tears coursing down her cheeks. He was about to tease her when he sensed that something unusual had caused it. He reached across for her hands, took them in his, drawing her towards him. He brought her hands up to his lips.

"What's happened, Alex?" he asked gently, "this is not like my sister."

"I'll never forget it, either."

Then as if a floodgate had been opened, the story came tumbling out of her, a catharsis of a constipated mind, on and on until it was empty of every detail she could remember of her weird childhood up to the time he broke her, the spoken version albeit edited for John's listening, omitting some of her father's excesses against her.

"The gripping nausea of fear not knowing what to expect," she said nearing the finish, "at first trying to resist showing him my pain and then screaming for him to stop. Waking up half-naked and alone in the room feeling cold and hungry, the fear mounting in the silence of the house. Then those footsteps on the stairs, I expected to be killed." She paused and started to chuckle.

"All that silly runt could do was vomit!" she said, pointing to his tear-stained face. "I remember looking up at you, John, the hate in your eyes seemed to be directed at me as you looked at my back."

"My hate was not directed at you, Alex."

"I know that now!"

Then, as if to leave the whole episode behind her, Alex's chuckle expanded into one of her infectious giggles.

"Doctor Barlow, I will never forget the first weekend on this boat. You completed my education."

John appeared puzzled, his eyes open.

"After breakfast looking at the chart, I saw the dressing gown fall from your body revealing, the first time for me, an adult male's naughty bits!"

Andrew recovered his humour.

"When was the second time?"

"Yours at Laura Cove, not much to them either!"

Finished now, she went over to Andrew and sought comfort on his shoulder to rest her head, feeling utterly exhausted. Andrew kissed the top of her head and gently eased it down to his lap, stroking her hair to comfort her. There was a long silence.

"Put on the kettle for hot chocolate, Dad," Andrew said and added hopefully, "are we old enough now to have brandy in ours?" Alex buried her head in his lap to hide her mirth, knowing that Andrew had always pilfered John's brandy for his nightly chocolate.

The next morning, a light rain still falling, John suggested to Alex that they stay over another night. Alex, tight-lipped, was bent on getting beyond Desolation Sound. Knowing the tide would not be favourable until near midday she got Andrew his breakfast earlier than he wanted in order to walk ashore with him. They were on the path to the farm house.

"Andrew. Where would you really like to go?"

"Mamalilaculla, but I don't think John will agree."

"If we work on him together we could insist on beyond the rapids; then who knows, the weather might cooperate."

Returning to *Never Satisfied* the turn of the tide an hour away, she went to the cabin and prepared sandwiches for the trip.

"What are you planning, Alexandra?"

"Well, Doctor Barlow, I'm making sandwiches for the passage to Westview."

"You don't want to stay here."

"Nope."

"I suppose you want to go beyond Desolation Sound."

"Yes, to Mamalilaculla or die!"

"And if I refuse?"

"I'll ask for a democratic vote."

"Already rigged, is it?"

"Yes, and I'll bet that's what you really want too."

"How much?"

"A dollar to a pinch of sh..."

"Tch Tch, Alex."

They all went in the dinghy to Mamalilaculla, walking along the path past the salmonberry bushes, the fruit long gone and into the mint meadow. They checked the seawolves, regretting their slow deterioration and continued on to look at the one remaining Totem pole. Then down to the clam shell beach to walk back, Alex going up to the rock at the end of the beach.

"This is Big Figure," she said smiling at John. "The whale came onto the beach just below the fish net huts."

They rowed John back to the boat and continued on to the east end of the bay. They entered the forest and strolled amongst the big trees.

"Can you feel the spirits, Alex?"

"Like a graveyard?"

"No, like people coming to the Transformer to ask a favour. No single almighty God lording over it with heavenly discipline, just a happy band of spirits awaiting their next life."

"That's silly!"

"No more silly than you telling me that you talk to your God."

"That's different."

"How?"

"I believe in God; I know he's there."

"Ah!"

"Heathen, just like your father."

"He's your father too!"

"No, Andrew, he's not."

"Well, I'm your brother."

"You can choose a brother; a father's a package deal." She said sourly, "I didn't tell you everything at Hardy Island." She frowned at Andrew. "I did not want to upset John."

"Explain, Alex."

"He didn't spank me anymore after I was ten."

"That's nice!"

"No it wasn't."

She started into a graphic description of her beatings. As she told him of her waiting fear, humiliation and pain, Andrew in his heart wanting to shout 'stop Alex', but knowing she must expunge herself of these memories, stayed quiet and listened. He could not hide his discomfort although he was determined to show it as little as possible.

"My little runt of a brother," she said, hoping to relieve him of his uneasiness, "I sometimes wonder what would have happened if I had not joined you in the field and become your friend. I may never have gone on the cruise that changed me."

"I needed a sister."

"Not as much as I needed a brother and then couldn't tell you once I had you. Why did you need a sister?"

"There were things I couldn't tell John. Jim and Jessica would talk to each other about them. I thought I could ask Anne but it was the same as with John. Then there you were in the field 'one of the boys' but you were not a boy. Hard to explain why, but there was something of Anne about you."

He put his hands out asking for hers, but wanting to break his soppy mood, she gave them a hard slap, crinkling her nose at him with disaffection. He persisted and took her hands pulling her towards him to hug her to him.

"Don't always push me away."

"Are you changing, Andrew?"

"How do mean?"

"Am I becoming attractive to you?"

"It's not like that," he said looking embarrassed, for once stuck for words.

"It's not like what?"

"Well you know you say 'my little runt'. Oh Alex, I don't want to go on with this."

"Go on, Andrew."

"I don't think of you as sexually attractive."

"What do you think of me as, then?"

"My 'giraffe'," he answered, looking up at her, "but I adore you, as my sister."

"Game to Burnett, 15-13, Burnett now leads two games to none, change ends." The announcement from the officials; the girls lined up on the service line started to change ends, the Burnett squad lead by Alex.

"She's hot tonight, Dad," Andrew said to John and turning away shouted, "Alex; Alex," in two four time and the chant was taken up by her supporters. John sat quietly cheering Alex on in his mind. She was now the respected captain of the team even almost liked by her four contemporaries left on the team with her. Andrew's enthusiasm increased as the Burnett team ran away with the final game.

"Don't wait for me, Dad."

"Where are you off to?"

"I said I would walk Wendy home."

"Where's Andrew, John?" Alex asked as she walked across the gym from the locker room door.

"Wendy took him off, Alexandra."

"His latest passion, Doctor Barlow," she said, smiling at him and shaking her head, "such a lusty lad as Flora would say."

"Jealous?" he asked, still not quite believing that she was just the professed sister they both affirmed. She gave him that 'you must be joking' look.

There were things, personal things that Alex would ask Andrew about. There were times when Andrew did not know and she was too shy to ask John. She could ask Anne but so seldom saw her during the winter. She entered the kitchen to find Flora alone, hoping for an answer to her latest thing.

"What are you cooking, Flora?"

"Pot roast tonight, should fill you up."

"Can I help you?"

"Too late. I have just put the vegetables into the pot; shall I get you a snack?"

Flora had once told her a snack would spoil her appetite but had since learned of Alex's hollow legs.

"No, I'll wait," Alex said, staying in the kitchen and hovering.

"Go sit down, Alex, you make me nervous standing over me like that," she said, looking at Alex whose face was flushed, "is there something else you want?"

"Can I ask you a private question?" Flora nodded. "Do you abuse yourself?"

She hoped Flora would understand the dictionary definition and so avoid using the embarrassing word.

"What do you mean, Alex?" she said looking perplexed.

"You know, mastu..." the word sticking in her throat, "masturbate."

"Alex! What a thing to ask now! You should be ashamed of yourself." Flora's outburst was accompanied by both embarrassment and anger, and Alex got up and fled from the kitchen.

John found Alex lying on her bed looking sullen. She sat up as he sat down.

"Alexandra, why not ask me your question?"

She was silent, but obviously working on her reply. "Because, Doctor B... Barlow, I know the answer for you. Andrew says all boys and men masturbate." She was angry. "I want to know about women and hoped Flora would understand."

Her sullen countenance gave way to a grin as she made eye contact with John.

"I guess she didn't!"

She started to giggle.

"If Flora does, she may be embarrassed by her behaviour, and if she doesn't, embarrassed by her ignorance," he said gently, her giggle infecting him. "Even a mother might find such a private topic difficult to discuss with her daughter; even though masturbation is normal human sexual behaviour."

"How can I find out if not by asking?"

"Come with me."

He lead her to the bookcase and handed her the first volume of *The Psychology of Sex* by Havelock Ellis.

"You will find some answers in this book."

"It's a big book."

"Yes, and it's only the first volume," he said pointing to the other five on the shelf, "and do me a favour, Alex, go and apologise to Flora, will you?"

It was not until a week or more later, driving home from church, that Alex leaned forward from the back seat.

"Flora," she said stumbling a bit, John could see her embarrassed face in the mirror, "I want to apologise for upsetting you with the 'M' word."

Flora accepted her apology with a smile, remembering her own touchiness.

"The Collect got to you, 'the spirit to think and do always such things as be rightful'?" John inquired of her.

"No, my God told me that there was nothing wrong with the word, just my insensitivity to how Flora might feel."

John watched them getting breakfast together, the harmony of mother and daughter between them. Flora, firm and critical of her always forgiving in the end, had become very fond of 'our Alex'. There was an easy intimacy, that of two women in conflict with their men, tenderness that would show in a nightly embrace or a kissed cheek.

"Did you enjoy the service?"

"Yes," Alex said, turning to the stove to attend to the eggs, "but this word 'fornication' keeps recurring. What does it mean?"

"I don't know, Alex," he replied, winking at Flora's flushed face, "go get the dictionary and look it up; Flora will take over the eggs."

As Alex left, Flora turned to speak. He put his finger to his lips.

"Shush, Flora," he whispered.

Alex returning with the dictionary opened it and searched for the word.

"Fornication; Ah here it is... voluntary sexual int..." Momentarily flustered she went over to Flora, buried her head against her neck, he could hear the giggle start and saw it spread to Flora's face.

"When's the plane due?" Andrew asked, excited at the prospect of seeing his cousins from Toronto.

"Phone Air Canada and ask when flight 105 will arrive," John said.

"It's late; arriving at 11.30, what time will we leave for the airport?"

"Be ready at eleven."

"Can Alex come?"

"Where is she?"

"In her room."

She was reading in her room, totally engrossed in her book.

"Do you want to come to the airport, Alex?"

"You take Andrew, I'll stay here." There was no resentment in her reply. "It will be too crowded in the car if I come too." Her room was as tidy as ever, but the rest of the house was a lived in shambles.

Mary left university when John was in second year. She moved to Toronto after completing her degree in commerce to work at the Toronto Dominion Bank. She met Ted soon after starting at the bank, he too was just starting his career. Less volatile than John she was courted by frugal Ted, who the family found staid, even dull as a companion. They entered a long careful courtship; sense before passion. By the time John had finished medical school, their daughter Ann was born followed by David two years later.

They saw Mary first at the carousel with them, well dressed, straight toothed and modelling their best behaviour. Each with their own baggage they walked towards John, faces wreathed in smiles of greeting.

"Aren't they small!" Andrew said, watching Ann and David coming towards him, "Alex will look like a giant to them."

Andrew was already showing some anxiety about her reception in the family.

Mary, just five-three, and Ted not five-six, their children's small size was not surprising. Formal greetings over, they drove back to the house swapping family trivia as reserve slowly melted.

They had moved Alex out of her room into Flora's double bed to sleep with Ann. David would sleep with Andrew and John moved to Alex's room to make way for Ted and Mary. Flora with Alex's help had prepared quantities of food for the freezer planned to cover most of their meals.

"Alex, it will be a bit crowded, will you mind Ann in the same bed?" John had asked her.

"I'd prefer Andrew!" she said, trying to goad him.

"No longer one of the boys, eh!"

"Four years and you are still trying to marry me off to Andrew and that other matchmaker to Jim." She was jovial but with a sting in her speech, "at least Jim is taller than me." All these changes hurriedly made in the previous two days had caused the shambles.

As they came into the house with Mary, Ted and the children organising their luggage, John was struck by the tidiness. All that mess cleared away, lunch laid on the dining room table leaving nothing for him to do except to offer festive refreshment before eating. Alex, introduced all round, seemed to meld into the background, running the house as if she were Flora.

Meals for adults, games with the children, decorating the house, organising the tree on Christmas Eve and arranging most of the meals, Alex was looking tired by Christmas morning. John heard her getting up just after six so went down to see if he could help. He noticed the prayer book in her hand which betrayed her real purpose.

"Why not wait until the later service, Alex?"

"I thought I would get it out of the way."

"I want to come with you and the family service would be fun for all of us."

"Is everyone coming to church?" she asked, her tiredness lifting and pleasure radiating from her face. "Even Andrew?"

"Last night after you went to bed, Mary asked me what could we all do for Alex. I said that Alex would like the family to attend church with her. Was I correct, Alexandra?"

She turned, looked at him, advanced towards him. He thought she was going to embrace him and got his arms ready to receive her, but she stopped short, knowing she had fooled him like she did Andrew and punched him lightly in the paunch.

"Right on, Doctor Barlow."

Mr and Mrs Barlow senior were at the church when they arrived and took up a long pew. The family sung the Christmas music with hearty enthusiasm and when leaving the church Alex introduced all of them to Mr Roberts in turn, her face full of pride in her family. The turning point year when Alex, no more the outsider, brought Andrew and John into her life, no more secrets to overcome. Back home she accepted help in the kitchen from Mary and Mrs Barlow making sure to include Ann in the preparation of the meal. After the meal she settled the grandparents in front of the fire for a nap and organised the rest of the family in a raucous game of Pit. Ann and David, tired from their long day, came to say good night.

After Alex and Andrew had changed into their night attire so as not to disturb their room-mates coming to bed, they said goodnight to Ann and David and went through the dining room where Andrew stole the brandy bottle into the kitchen. They made hot chocolate.

"Do you want brandy in yours, Alex?" he asked as he poured a generous dollop into his cup.

"Does John know about it?" she looked at Andrew, grinned and held out her mug, "just like the boat."

"Did you hear John tell Ted that he was thinking of getting a bigger boat?"

"Really! What size did he say?"

"No, we'll wheedle it out of him when they have all gone back to Toronto."

"Let's join them," she said, putting her cup into the sink.

"Wait, Alexandra," he said taking her hand, "no, don't pull away or punch me," putting her hand to his lips, "my adorable sister."

They joined them in the sitting room, Alex chatting to Mary, Andrew to Ted and John, time passing with Alex almost asleep. She got up leant down to kiss Mary, went over to Ted said goodnight and taking Andrew's arm walked across the room to the door allowing Andrew to go before her she turned towards John and waved goodnight.

"Why did she not include you, John?" Mary asked.

"I don't know, but she never does and I never ask why."

Alex drew back the drapes letting the moonlight flood into the room and slid into bed alongside Ann careful not to waken her. She looked down at the sleeping form wondering if she appreciated the ease of her young existence. Remembering the magic of last Christmas comparing it to the joy of this one she thought of her Christmases past, their austerity, the "pagan" tree forbidden by her father, no presents or gaiety just the religious celebration of Jesus' birth dinned into her with Gradgrind method; no giving or receiving, no feasting, humour or apparent love. Another meal taken by three seated at the usual table and eaten in silence. Contrasts, no wonder artists stressed contrasts. She smiled as she thought of John's mother who had allowed Alex to embrace her when leaving to go home.

The day such a success, the attendance at church as a family, returning home to open presents; home, even a present from Santa under the tree, it wasn't the present, but the presence of Santa Claus that feeling of belonging to 'my' family a sense of identity making her know she was a real person. Not just an animal walking down the street but 'there goes Alex, John's girl, such a lovely family'.

CHAPTER 8

Jim

John went to the bow to weigh the anchor whilst Alex started the diesel of *Never Satisfied II*; 1976, their first summer cruise in their new boat. So much bigger with its 32 feet, centre cockpit and diesel power which transported them with delight on those hot sultry windless days of summer. The 10 foot beam gave a feeling of space wanting in a 25 foot boat.

"Which way, John?" Alex asked.

"Whitebeach Passage out of Farewell Harbour."

She turned to the western exit of the harbour watching the display on the depth sounder.

"Quite a deep harbour," she said, "any obstructions ahead?"

"Leave the islands to port, mid channel and into Whitebeach Passage," he said, showing her the chart.

Another lovely morning with a light westerly breeze promised a lazy sail to Robson Bight. She steered out of the passage into Blackfish Sound and with the current headed for Blackney Passage, another of those current induced turbulent spots, a favourite of fishermen who, moving in the circular action of the waters, cast for the big one of their dreams.

"How far is Boat Bay?" she asked.

"With this current, shouldn't take much more than two hours. I'll get the spinnaker ready."

"We will be there before eleven. Do you want the main up?"

"No, let's be lazy," John said, never having been in the Robson Bight section of the Johnstone Straits, "then we can admire the view."

Passing Swaine Point, John took down the spinnaker and they headed behind the islets into Boat Bay. It was still early by Andrew's reckoning as he came up on deck just after wakening. It was unusual for him to be impressed this early in the day but looking across to the Tsitika Valley, the river rising quickly into the hills, the whole scene an amphitheatre to the mud flats of the river.

"What a magnificent sight," he said, "The eagle soars in the summit of heaven, the hunter with his dogs pursues his circuit," he quoted.

"What was that?" Alex inquired.

"Eliot: The Rocks." he replied, "I'll read it to you after lunch. What a place to be buried," he continued, "I could almost believe in Mr Eliot's God."

"We are making progress," Alex teased, "preparation or premonition?"

"Neither," he said, making for the head.

While John made lunch, Alex rowed ashore to investigate the campers whose tents were pitched for the view of the straits. Andrew, washed and awake, waited expectantly for his coffee.

"Where does she get the energy and strength from, Dad?" he asked, seeing Alex reach the shore.

"She is certainly not like you in the morning," John answered.

"Do I detect criticism or praise?"

"Praise I think. Two individuals from the same family but so different. If you had been an early morning person I don't think that I would know Alexandra nearly so well."

"Do you love her?" Andrew had a habit of asking the most personal questions when least expected, "as my sister?"

"No. I am very fond of her, as Alex. The feeling is different to my love for you. She is everything I could wish for in a daughter but she is not my daughter."

"But do you love her?" Andrew persisted, looking so directly at John that he felt caught in a trap, not explainable at the moment.

"Coffee's ready, shall I get you a cup?" John asked.

"I'm glad," he said. "No, I will."

Alex returned and over lunch told them that the tents belonged to a group of students who were studying the killer whales that returned to Robson Bight in the summer to breed. When lunch was finished Andrew read the opening stanza of "The Rocks" as he promised earlier in the morning.

'Where is the life we have lost in living?
Where is the knowledge we have lost in information?
The cycles of Heaven in twenty centuries
Bring us farther from God and nearer to the dust.'

"I think I've made my first convert, John!"

They had tried to persuade John to stay in Boat Bay for the night, but he had wanted to explore Forward Bay knowing that they would have to start back home the next day.

"Why would the cartographers want to confuse us with Forward Bay and Forward Harbour within 25 miles of each other?" Andrew, still protesting that they had not stayed in Boat Bay. "Very forward of Mr Forward to name these places after himself."

"*H.M.S. Forward* was a gunboat up here in the nineteenth century," John informed him, and Alex sniggered.

They anchored inside the Bush Islets out of the northwest wind with a stern line to shore. Alex and Andrew took the line when they went for a walk on the beach in the bay.

"Dad was right, this is worth exploring," Andrew said as they were standing on the point looking south to the Adams River, "everywhere you look is majestic."

"Challenge," she said, "no slang. Seagull."

"Shit!"

"No slang."

"All right, faeces."

"Sewer."

"Drainage."

"Swamp."

"Grass," Andrew said, to change the direction.

"Lawn."

"Pathway."

"Pavement."

"Sidewalk."

"Two words."

"It's not.

"Okay, cloister."

Her challenge had given her time to find this word.

"Walker."

"Frame."

"I challenge that, what do you mean, frame?" Andrew said.

"You know, in old people's homes you see the ladies with a frame in front of them; it's called a walker."

She said it convincingly, and Andrew shrugged.

"Picture."

"Painting."

"Water-colour."

"Yellow."

"Piss."

"Slang."

She challenged.

"Pce."

"Slang." She challenged again.

"Urine then."

"At bat," she said with a cunning look.

"Two words, Alex."

"So's you're in."

"Ho Ho Ho; try again." He laughed.

"Bladder."

"Bowel."

"Twixt," she cried and looking at each other they burst in unison, "interposed!" Taken from the Shakespeare sketch in 'Beyond the Fringe' which they both loved. Their laughter continuing they collapsed together on the rock seat. Close to each other now.

"Andrew," she said, "I'm sad though, this could be our last summer together."

"Why do you say that?"

"We'll be at university next year and have to work in the summer to pay our fees."

"We'll still get out for some time in the summer."

"Yes, but there won't be time to get up here," she protested, "I love these trips together. The memory of that first trip is so clear in my mind."

"Do you love Dad?" the same query asked of John, "as a father?"

"No, not as a father. I don't love my father. John's just a friend."

"You can love friends," he said, but seeing her mask knew he was striking deep into her.

"Do you love Jim then?"

"I'm very fond of Jim; I enjoy and look forward to his company," she said pensively, quiet for a minute, "Jim loves me I know, he's told me so many times."

She put her arms around his shoulder, pulled him towards her putting her head on his shoulder so he could not see her face. "I don't know, I don't know, Andrew. Every time he says it, I feel him wounded by my inability to say so back. Yet I can't pretend, just to make him look happy. I love his attention, I think I could make love to him and enjoy it. Maybe I just don't know what love is."

Feeling the wetness trickle onto his neck he gently eased her head away from his shoulder.

"So Alex, you're not Dsonqua's daughter - or maybe you are, and I'm going to be rich!"

"Oh shut up, Andrew!"

They stayed overnight at Big Bay to shower and launder. Next morning, leaving with the last hour of the flood tide, they were swept down the Yucultas like a shot out of a barrel.

"Where shall we go tonight, Alex?" John asked.

Nobody had mentioned her birthday and she was concerned it had been overlooked.

"Squirrel Cove," Andrew said belligerently.

"No. Walsh Cove," she said, "it's going to be hot and I like to swim there more than Squirrel." Watching Andrew's attempt at sulkiness and the bemused look on John's face, she thought 'they have remembered,' "Anyway, Andrew, *Heron* will be there." And put her tongue out at him.

"How did you know? I thought I was acting pretty well."

"John's face told me."

The afternoon sun heated the granite rocks to a foot burning temperature, the water attracting them time and again to cool their burning skin. Laying her towel on the hot rock, Alex, removing the top of her swim suit, lay down to sun her back. Remembering the wish to sleep the night away the time she had lain there five years before, her eyes closed in sleep. The others let her sleep, then remembering how easily her skin would burn felt they should wake her. Andrew leant over to whisper in Jim's ear, a smile spread across their faces as he got up, he filled his pop tin with cold water. Poised over her back, Andrew ready with his camera, he poured the contents over Alex's back. She awoke with a start, sat up coincident with the click of Andrew's camera. Recovering her top, she chased Jim into the sea, catching him by his foot she pulled him towards her ducking his head.

They came out of the water hand in hand, the dance of laughter in each other's eyes as Alex chided him for his obscenity. As they approached Andrew she put her arms around Jim's neck pulling his face towards her, kissed him and brought his body close. Letting her hands stray down his back her head looking over his shoulder she saw Andrew raise his camera, a message passed between them at the minimal shake of her head making Andrew delay. Suddenly without warning Jim was standing with swim trunks around his ankles exposed to the unshuttered lens. Not waiting for his reaction Alex dashed into the sea swimming back to the boats, Jim in hot pursuit delayed enough by his legs tangled in his shorts that she made it to the boats before he could catch her.

Happy hour putting Alex front and centre, hidden gifts appeared, her excitement soothed by the wine and food, she opened her presents. The book from Andrew, the make-up case from Jessica, the ink pen from Jim, clothes from Doug and Anne and as ever another little box. This little box was noticeably bigger, in which lay a Haida Indian silver bracelet enhanced with the wolf design.

The happy hour became ribald as beer and wine were liberally dispensed by John and Doug. The bathroom humour of yesteryear was replaced by what the movie censor describes as 'suggestive scenes'. Andrew telling the story of the descent of Jim's swim trunks with outrageous embellishment.

"I have never seen swim trunks removed so adroitly," he said all eyes on Jim's blushing face, "and I thought that was unpadded Alex until this afternoon." He pointed at her bosom, earning himself a swift punch on the shoulder.

The ceremony of finding *Heron* as if by accident and the anticipation of time alone with Jim had become her tradition but there would be no leg pulling this year. She announced after dinner.

"Jim and I are going ashore, alone!"

All shared merriment in the remembered teasing of previous years.

"Do you remember the first cruise here?" Alex asked Jim; they were coming out of the water on the island.

"I remember hearing the splash as you went into the water and seeing all the phosphorescence as you treaded water."

"What a hot night."

"There was a huge moon wasn't there?"

"Yes, and it really showed off the colour of the water. You ran your fingers down my bare back." She shivered at the remembrance. "I felt the strangest feeling."

"What feeling?"

"Desire, I didn't know it then," she said, moving closer to him.

"I fell in love with you that summer, Alex."

"I know," she said it almost imperceptibly, "I did not understand then."

"I haven't changed, you know that?"

He was looking at her willing an answer from her. She didn't want to reply feeling no such commitment; instead took his face in her hands and kissed him. He brought his body close to her, his hands running down her back and feeling her response, their lips parted and he slipped the straps off her shoulders, exploring her breasts with his lips. As her excitement increased he laid her back on the smooth rock, her anxiety rising with his urgency, the tree shadows taking on human form robbing the night of privacy as her excuse to stop him. Later that night in the forward cabin she confided in Andrew her almost irresistible desire for Jim.

"Come for a walk, John?" Alex said.

"Sure," he replied, recognising her 'need for advice' voice. Alex rowed them ashore looking back at *Never Satisfied II*. "She looks as big as *Heron* even though a few feet shorter, I guess it's her beam."

John looked back at her high freeboard, the two stern cabin ports and name in bold red lettering and thought that her awkwardness was diminishing as familiarity with her lines grew on him; from stern quarter-deck to bow she was taking on the look of a sedate Bentley.

"Are you pleased with her?"

"So far," he said, as he took the painter and secured the dinghy to the rock shore.

The paths of the island, still drenched from a wet summer's rain, they chose to walk to Kanaka light rather than cross the island. The long weekend in early August, a certainty for good weather, Alex was relaxed after celebrating her nineteenth birthday the previous evening.

"Are you on call next long weekend?"

A manipulative question, the answer known.

"Yes, why?"

"Would you let us have the boat for that weekend?"

"You and Andrew?"

"Jim and Jessica too."

They had reached the path along the rocky shore allowing John to play for time whilst pretending to make heavy going of the climb up the path.

"Worried we might damage the boat?"

"There's that too," he said turning to give her a hand up. "What sleeping arrangements?"

"Andrew and Jessica forward, Jim and I the stern." She said it simply and naturally, "jealous Dr Bartolo?"

They had seen 'The Barber of Seville' in the winter when she had identified with the heroine, occasionally teasing John with Dr Bartolo.

"You've no dowry, Rosina," he mused aloud as she went ahead of him along the path.

"I'll have to become a Lydian pro and earn my own marriage portion," she said, turning and laughing. Knowing she was on the last volume of Havelock Ellis and quoting Herodotus, he understood.

"Have any coins fallen into your lap yet?"

"Not yet, not quite!"

He observed her tall athletic body, neat hair in a single braid and strong shoulders clothed in her uniform of T-shirt and cut-off jeans. He thought back to Blind Bay when he first noticed her femininity and now seeing her grow more desirable, he quelled his proclivity with guardian reserve, but was never able to remain unmoved by the undulation of her walking ahead or the bouncy flow of her hair in the wind of movement, or watching her closer, the apricot colour of her skin, eyelids of moth-wing pallor offsetting the blue stars bright in her face or the left side of her upper lip which would first show the white teeth of her developing lopsided smile. Just as his rapture approached completion she would destroy it with an outrageous remark or physical jab.

"Do I need to worry?"

A loaded inquiry.

"I thought you would know I had been to the clinic," she said genuinely surprised, not knowing that the doctors would see each other's children never revealing the fact by tacit agreement.

"No, I would never ask or look in your medical record unless you were coming to see me."

"I don't think I'm ready yet," she said as they sat on the bank near Kanaka light, a ferry silhouetted in the sun's reflection on the shimmered sea. "I like him close, to be caressed and kissed, but I shrink from him if he tries to get closer."

She stopped suddenly and with an anxious voice, "John, does it bother you for me to talk with such candour?"

"No," he answered untruthfully; then sensing a need for honesty, "Yes, Alex, it does as your father. It's a private matter, but I can change like a chameleon and act as your doctor."

"You're not my father."

There was an edge to her speech and then she turned to look him in the eyes. "Is it my reluctance or what he did to me? I enjoy the physical contact of our bodies, his exploring me as an outsider but stop short of allowing him inside. Poor Jim, I know he's longing to find out if he has the knack!"

"Was the examination painful?" he asked, wondering whether pain, or fear of it, was a factor for her reluctance.

"No, I was surprised."

"Do you think about that night with your father?"

"When I'm with Jim?" she asked and he nodded, "No, that never enters my head."

"Perhaps you're not sure of him."

"Of monogamous Jim!" She looked surprised and got up to start the walk back to the boats, "I've been sure of him since that first cruise. It's me I'm not sure of."

When they reached Royal Cove John started to get the dinghy ready to return to the boats. He felt her hand on his arm. "Thanks, John."

She reached towards his face and brushed his cheek with her lips. John was surprised by her, it was the first time she had allowed intimate contact with him.

As they approached the boats she saw Doug turn to watch their approach, his square-cut features breaking into welcome as he took the dinghy's bow holding it while they got aboard *Heron*.

"Good walk?" Doug inquired.

"We went to Kanaka and back. Still wet in the centre from the rain," she said as she climbed down to the cabin to help Anne with the meal.

She felt comfortable with Anne, able to banter always bordering on the outrageous. Her birthday was celebrated with just the four of them since Jessica was working, Andrew away to visit his grandmother and Jim still in the interior planting trees.

"John says we can have the boat the next long weekend."

"Who's we?" Anne asked.

"Jim, Jessica, Andrew."

"Who will be with you?"

"Just the four of us."

"No chaperon?"

"Anne, from the supreme match maker, I'm surprised at you!"

"Does John know that Jim and Jessica are going with you?"

"No," she teased, putting a finger to her lips, "what father doesn't know he can't grieve over."

But John, sitting in the cockpit overheard them.

"Don't believe the little vixen, Anne," John said, surprised this time by her paternal reference.

Evening now, the hot sun was setting into the cockpit. As it fell behind the hills the chill of the clear summer night required a change to long jeans and sweaters. She sat back, her head against the cabin sole and thought back to the party after their examinations. Jim had taken her into his friend's bedroom, locked the door and both shyly undressed getting together under the comforter. His excitement, not seen before, the anticipation of his exploring gentle fingers and lips and the shimmering warmth of pleasure rising and falling to spent relaxation and yet unable to let him atop; instead, touching that velvet smooth skin and watching his eyes pucker, his nostrils dilate, even his ears moved forward as the picture of erupting joy dissipated into the contented pleasure on his close eyed face. They lay still.

"Why did you stop me, Alex?"

She was unable to confess the truth of her own fantasy as her pleasure peaked, John's slender naked body standing in front of her before she jumped sideways into the water. How could she explain to Jim such a betrayal?

"I'm not ready just yet," she said limply.

"Is it what your father did?"

"Yes," Alex said with honesty. Only she appreciated the ambiguity of his question.

Still awake in her bunk now, the others asleep, she thought about a breakfast conversation with John when she was still reading Havelock Ellis.

"Have you been surprised by the extraordinary variety of human sexual behaviour?" he had asked her.

"Yes."

"I didn't read about sex until after becoming a doctor, so I always assumed that everyone was like me. I had the usual stereotypes of the women in my practice who were either good girls or bad girls."

"What am I?"

"Good."

"How do you know?" She looked at him and frowned. "You don't know if I've done it."

"That's my point; goodness or badness cannot be measured by assessing your sexual behaviour. You are not good because you are chaste. I don't think that a celibate priest is good just because he is not sexually active. As your father, I would not think ill of you because you made love to someone."

"Go on with you! I bet you would not be pleased if you found me in bed with someone!"

"Like Jim?" he inquired and she blushed.

"Yes," she said going on the attack to cover up her embarrassment, "and you found us in bed together."

"I'd ask you both three questions."

"What three questions?" she replied truculently.

"Will you get pregnant?"

"And." Her face a sneer.

"What would you like for breakfast?"

"Porridge! And."

"Did you enjoy yourselves?"

"Oh yes, I'm sure," she had said sarcastically.

She had felt confusion one morning in the autumn when he asked her what contraception she would use, remembering Walsh Cove and knowing only too well that the need was approaching. Since then she had been careful to restrict her time alone with Jim as his protestations of love became more compelling.

"Do you know about morning after contraception?" he had asked.

"At the clinic?"

"Yes."

"They gave us a handout and it was mentioned."

"It is just another of life's decisions, Alexandra, and the time's at hand."

"Yes, Doctor Barlow," she replied, getting out of the hot kitchen to think in the privacy of her room.

The boat moved to a wave which slapped the side of the hull. She got up to look through the open hatch to check the reason and then slid back under the covers. 'I believed John the weekend that Jessica stayed overnight', she thought.

"Shall I take Jessica some coffee?" Alex had asked John at breakfast.

"Where's Andrew?"

"In his room."

She noticed a brief smile and shake of the head as she took the cup from him and went up to her room. Jessica was reading with Andrew fast asleep beside her. She put her finger to her lips and seeing Alex's stunned countenance she had slipped out of the bed to join them in the kitchen.

"Did you enjoy yourself?" he teased Jessica. "What do you want for breakfast?"

The third question unnecessary since he looked after Jessica at the clinic.

Alex recovered quickly from her discomfort, appreciating the relaxed banter between Jessica and John.

"What about the third question, John?"

"I don't need to ask it, Alex," he said, a glance of intrigue at Jessica.

She had longed to ask Jessica 'what's it like' but it was too private and she was no invader. Now, with her experience with Jim she would like to ask Jessica whether she had had similar visions of Doug in her early lovemaking with Andrew. 'Too private' she thought, shivered 'just too private', wondering whether she had reached another roadblock of secretiveness. She relived their afternoon walk sensing that her candour had been painful remembering the look on

John's face just before she brushed his cheek with her lips, that same expression of pain she had seen before.

She remembered the doctor in the clinic ask, "Is it what you want or he wants?"

"What he wants," she had replied, "me too I think."

"Better be sure!"

Projecting herself to the next long weekend and talking to herself she said, 'I shall lose my virginity next long weekend,' and started to giggle at herself.

As the long weekend approached she became certain that she wanted Jim or maybe certain she wanted the experience still uncertain she wanted Jim. In her muddled thinking she wondered whether it might mean more to him in commitment than she was prepared to give, the opposite of what she had heard about a woman's attitude; 'still one of the boys, eh!' she would think and grin to herself.

Jim returned from the interior just before their planned weekend. The time had dragged in the heat of August, but at last they were on the ferry together talking about their summer experiences.

They were walking up the hill at Otter Bay, a starlight night, the clarity not often seen in Vancouver with the halfmoon lighting their way down the hill. The sweet smelling freshness of the islands pervaded the air. Bob checked them in as they approached the gangway onto the dock. John had said that Andrew was to be skipper and to obey him. He oversaw the stowage of supplies and then sitting together with their hot chocolate and brandy made light conversation. Alex wondered whether Jim could think of anything else.

With their cocoon cabin enclosed around them she explored him and then lay back awaiting her experience. He had the knack, such a short word. She lay on her side, her head propped on her hand watching him asleep thinking 'all the anticipation for this; so much nicer when I had not allowed him inside.'

Up early she filled the kettle, put it on a low burner and went forward to the head. She slipped off her dressing gown and slid into the bunk alongside him. Pulling his drowsy form onto his back she mounted him. As he opened his eyes he looked trapped. Feeling him respond, she inquired.

"So, that was why you used to give way when I sat astride you!" she said and he smiled at her, moving his body to try and enter her.

"Oh no," she whispered, lying beside him now, "we know you have the knack, now make love to me."

"Satisfied?" he whispered, looking down at her. 'I love you' he mouthed and saw her frown.

"Coffee?" she said changing tempo, "kettle's on, I'll get it." Turning the comforter aside, she reached to put on her dressing gown, his hindering hands seeking to make her stay.

Making the coffee, the elation of its aroma, the kettle's bubbling droplets hissed as they caught the hot burner, echoing her own duplicity.

Andrew got up that morning, Jessica already in the head, and he pushed past Alex in the galley to relieve himself into the sea.

"That's better," he said, smiling his good morning to Alex and taking his toothbrush from his pocket he cleaned his teeth into the galley sink.

"Sleep well?" she asked mischievously, flicking his backside with the tea towel. Andrew was unable to answer with his toothbrush in his mouth, his laughing eyes told of his intended revenge. He spat some bloody saliva into the sink.

"Must be something wrong with my gums."

"When did that start, Andrew?"

"Last week, but it just doesn't want to stop. I'll ask Dad when I get home."

Alex, looking at Andrew, saw his pale face, 'paler than usual?' she queried, and felt a portent of something horrible. She was right.

CHAPTER 9

The Transformer

John's perspective.

"Would you let us have *Never Satisfied* if Douglas and Anne will let you stay with them on *Heron*?" Andrew asked me on the ferry.

"You've already made the arrangement with them."

"Yes," he said smiling at me, "they said they'd enjoy your company."

We all came over to Otter Bay on Good Friday morning in the pouring rain which stopped mid afternoon. The warm front made the cockpit pleasant, albeit with adequate clothes.

"Thank you for asking me to be with you, Doug." I said, accepting their invitation gladly feeling the need for their company. "We didn't ask you, Andrew ordered Anne to take you!" he chided Andrew. "I hope he can't wheedle Jessica as easily as he does Anne."

We went to Bedwell Harbour on Saturday morning and tied up to a mooring buoy for the night. After supper on *Heron* the kids left for the pub on shore and we sat back at peace.

"How's Andrew doing?" Douglas asked.

"He seems to be in remission at present. His attitude is remarkable. He talks about his brush with cancer."

"What's the prognosis John?" Anne asking with her usual frankness.

"With his type of leukaemia, fifty-fifty, who knows," I replied, still feeling the desperation from the sight of him during his chemotherapy, "he looks better than at Christmas time, he's gained weight and got his hair back. He's even finished second year university and says he did well."

The period through the fall starting his chemotherapy attended by twenty four hours of racking nausea and vomiting had made life wretched once a week, leaving him exhausted for a day or two so that just as he felt better the next round was approaching.

"I don't know what I would have done without Alex," my eyes pricking at the memories, "I'm sorry."

The tears of exhaustion were remembered and repeated.

"Don't be," Anne replied, "it's good for you to let go."

"Only for a woman," I said, "it seems to do nothing for me. Better when I'm in control."

Sitting quietly, I thought of Alex who had been constantly with Andrew during those post-chemotherapy days.

"She would, Alex that is," I said to Anne, "would bath him when he was too sick to help himself. He became so light she could lift him and after helping him undress would lower him into the tub or onto the toilet. One time approaching the bathroom to see if she needed my help I heard her say to Andrew, 'you naughty boy,' Andrew replied, 'I can't help it, Alex,' then I heard her say so gently, 'Well close your eyes and think of Jessica.' I retreated, feeling an interloper."

"No longer one of the boys?" Douglas asked.

"Alex and Jim you mean?"

"No I didn't."

"I don't think so Doug. I used to worry about it but whenever I tested Alex she would give me that 'you must be kidding' look and she has been so candid with me about Jim. When I asked her she said she was being both practical and kind to her brother." Although I didn't say it she had added, 'the oversexed little runt.'

"How is Jim?"

"He seems to be doing really well, he intends to apply in third year and thinks he stands a good chance if his results remain as good. I detected some frustration when he was unable to be with Alex as much as he would have liked." He looked thoughtful for a moment. "He told Anne he wanted to marry Alex; he's too young."

"I was married and a father at nineteen!"

"That's different," he said, "contraception has changed relationships. Marriage seems an intention to conceive rather than a licence to sleep together as in our days."

"Alex once referred to him as monogamous Jim," I said smiling at Douglas, and turning to Anne. "Has Alex ever talked to you about him?"

"Yes, she has."

Douglas looked at her with surprise. "What did she say?"

"That is confidential," she replied, "because she came to see me professionally and made an appointment after asking if she was allowed to, saying she was going to pay me."

"Did she pay you?" Doug asked.

"She paid my secretary in cash before she saw me so that I was unable to argue."

"I knew about it," I said to Anne, "when I asked Alex why she had seen you she told me it was none of my business. Very nicely mind you, but also firmly."

I had assumed it was to do with her father which may have been upsetting for her and needed another woman to counsel her.

"With Andrew I feel I have a right to know as his father. With Alex I think she has the right to conceal from her guardian. If ever I indicate that I'm her father or she's my daughter she gets snappy with me. Although recently she has stopped doing it. How's Jessica doing?"

"Very well at university. She says she wants to go into Law after finishing a degree in Political Science. She hated it when Andrew was so sick and found visiting him so upsetting. I didn't know how to advise her, it seemed to me that she was withdrawing from him as if already dead so as not to hurt so much. Perhaps we all do that?"

"I found myself doing that as a doctor until I read Kubler-Ross," I replied, then in despair. "I think I have already grieved for Andrew."

Four weeks after Easter, Andrew's gums started to bleed again and on the Friday I took him down for blood tests which showed a serious deficiency of platelets as well as recurrence of the leukaemia. He was booked into the hospital on Monday for a platelet transfusion and to start another course of therapy. I had phoned Alex the previous evening to warn her and she decided to return for the weekend at least. That night she took her pillow and comforter into his room to sleep near him in case he needed her help in the night.

Alex woke me in the night shaking my shoulder.

"John, come quickly, I can't waken him and his breathing sounds funny."

She hurried back to his room. He was unconscious, his stertorous breathing telling me the truth. I called the ambulance, getting him ready for transportation to hospital, knowing it was the end.

"He will be all right after his chemo?"

I knew my honesty would be crushing.

"Alex, be brave."

She looked at me, desperation in her face, started to reach out for me, then putting her face in her hands sat beside him, perched on the bed resigned like a lost and trapped dog, ears back with head between its paws.

"Do you want to come with me or go in the ambulance?"

"Ambulance," she said, "I must stay with him."

At the hospital, my impression that he had had a massive brain haemorrhage confirmed, I asked that there be no heroic measures. We sat keeping watch over him until he died late that morning. Even then she seemed reluctant to leave him. I remembered back to his initial illness when I had done my grieving. One afternoon when we were alone I had discussed some of his wishes.

"Cremation and into the sea at Robson Bight, if it comes to it."

I remembered the cracking of fear in his voice.

"You should make a will, Andrew," I said.

"What happens if I don't?"

"The money from your life insurance will come to me."

A policy bought with the money Stephanie had left.

"Would you be upset if I left it to Alex?"

"Why do you think I suggested it?"

"How do I make a will, will I need a lawyer?" He started to laugh. "Sounds like that sonnet by Shakespeare."

"It would be best."

"Have you made your will, Dad?"

"Yes, and updated it last year to make some allowance for your sister."

"You're not my father!" he mimicked Alex, and smiled at me. "You're struck on that girl."

"Shall I contact my lawyer?" I said, leaving his remark unchallenged.

"No, I would like to contact Douglas to act for me; is that the correct way to put it?"

The next day he phoned himself to arrange it, Douglas coming to the house to have it signed and witnessed by Flora. Alex was not around at the time and I did not know whether Andrew had told her.

I made arrangements at the local funeral home for a short memorial service, asking the Reverend Roberts to officiate more for Alex's sake than my own.

Alex, at times inconsolable, protested to both myself and Flora, "I feel as if my home has been taken away from me again."

"But your home is still here," Flora told her and I remained silent.

"You just don't understand, Flora," she said hastening out of the room again, unable to be seen with tears in public.

When she was angry at us or at times talking about him I felt confident she would survive, but when she was silent for long periods I was worried she might take her own life, knowing the brittleness of youth in despair. My own grief was overshadowed by my concern for her.

On the Friday of the funeral service she seemed composed, accepting some of the responsibility when our consoling friends returned to the house for the reception. She chatted with Jim and Jessica, talked at some length with Anne and even appeared to console Andrew's friends of youth, Brian and David.

"Does Alex know about the will?" I asked Douglas.

"I have not said anything, John," he answered, "I'll take her aside before we leave."

"Thank you, Doug."

I watched him out of the corner of my eye as he slowly made his way towards Alex, chatting with others on his passage. He took her a little away from the others so that they were isolated. I saw Alex's face and knew that Andrew had not said anything to her. She nodded at him, turned and left; so unlike her to leave with guests still in the house.

Flora and I cleared the debris away, tidied the house and I went to her room. I knocked on her door and in spite of no invitation to enter, wanted to check that she was alive. She sat motionless in her chair staring at the wall, did not move as I started towards her.

"Go away," she said angrily and I obeyed.

Up early Sunday morning for breakfast she joined me as usual.

"Which service are we going to?" I asked.

"I'm not going to church," she said sullenly, "I'll return to the interior this afternoon and go to work tomorrow."

"Will you resign?"

"Why would I do that?" she put on her mask that he had not seen for many years.

"I hoped you would come with me to Robson Bight at the end of June to do as Andrew asked."

She was silently eyeing me with blankness.

"Oh, Alex, come here to me, please."

I waited as she turned to me, half hoping she would punch me as I took her in my arms. She was stiff, unyielding and hiding her face from me. I knew she was crying because she was shaking and to notice it would make her angry.

"I felt desperate like you after Stephanie died, for days I couldn't talk to anyone and just wanted to be alone. It was Andrew saying, we have each other, that snapped me out of it." I felt her shaking lessen and yet she still hung onto me tightly. "Andrew would want us to go on living, fully."

"I don't want his money, I want Andrew," she hissed.

"Don't be ungrateful Alex, he didn't often think of anyone but himself, you were always the exception."

She eased herself away and left the kitchen for her room. At lunch with Flora she was more at ease, chatting with her about the tree planting, complaining about the food.

"When will you start up to Robson Bight?" Alex asked.

"Best if I go the last week in June first in July."

"Can I come with you?"

"If you're a good girl!"

I hoped there was light at the end of the tunnel. The left side of her upper lip lifted revealing her teeth.

"Yeth, Daddy!" she said sarcastically.

She left with Jim in his car in the early afternoon and immediately the house felt empty. I went up to her room and seeing the full wastepaper basket picked it up to take downstairs. It felt heavier than the apparent paper it contained and as I emptied it I saw that she had put both her Bible and Prayer Book in it for disposal. I took them out and put them in the book case in my room.

Her letter arrived seven days later:

The Forest,
B.C.

Dear Dr Barlow,
I have arranged to leave work here the last Friday in June. Jim will drive me down late on Friday, stay the night with us and drive us to the ferry next morning (if you wish) before returning to continue working. I think I have enough saved to see me through the next year at university. My employer has been understanding and offered both of us a job next summer. He says he is pleased with us as a team and keeps telling us "we carry a suffolk punch", although neither of us understands what he means and we are too shy to show our ignorance.
I feel sorry for Jim, who, in providing a shoulder of support for the past two weeks, has been more than kind. I realise I have not been easy to live with. It did occur to me to try and join Andrew and I should not have been so snappy with you. I only meant that no amount of money could compensate the loss. I look forward to the cruise and your companionship.
Give my love to Flora, forgive the briefness of this letter and regards to my guardian!

yours
Alexandra

In planning the trip up to Robson Bight I knew that I had to be back in two weeks if possible, three at the most so we pushed the boat to get to Forward Harbour in five days, hoping for luck with the weather for the Johnstone Straits. Each evening we would sit in the cockpit in the dying sun. I listened to her tell stories from previous summers, some familiar and some new to me. Each evening I was aware of her veil of grief lifting and by the time we were in Forward Harbour she laughed as she told me about his stealing my brandy.

"The Haida," I told her, "hold their potlatch for the departed only when they can speak of them with humour."

"What time do we leave?"

"I'll wake you at four thirty with coffee and leave at five before the westerly wind gets up."

There was no wind, just the endless sea of the straits like a sheet of ice ahead. Under power, a half knot current against us we made the Broken Islands by late morning and arrived in Forward Bay at noon. A light westerly kept the boat cool as we anchored behind the Bush Islets, lunched and caught up on our sleep. We took the dinghy ashore, Alex insisting she take Andrew, as she referred to his ashes, to show him the majestic view. I stayed on the beach looking at *Never Satisfied* from a seat of warm rocks. Alex walked towards the promontory to view the straits.

I heard her voice cry out 'seagull', saw her standing, and only heard her when she turned towards me. I caught other words like 'yellow' and then distinctly 'bladder, bowel, twixt and interposed' followed by great gales of laughter. I saw her sitting with his ashes on her knees and I wondered if she was going mad, but she got up suddenly and disappeared beyond the promontory.

I noticed her come up onto the promontory and watched as she scrambled down to the beach to join me. She sat close to me on the rock, a huge smile of happiness putting her arms around my neck pulled me towards her and rested her head on my shoulder.

"I'm over my grief," she said simply, "Andrew is everywhere, it's an uncanny feeling. Thank you, John, for making me come."

Next morning Alex was up early, had made the coffee by the time I dressed and was cooking the breakfast. I felt a return to the old routine as she chatted about the trip up and prospects for the ceremony of committing Andrew's ashes. We powered out of Forward Bay timing our departure to catch the last hour of the ebb current intending to return to Forward Harbour on the flood current. We lined up the centre of the Tsitika Valley heading towards the river delta. She turned and indicated she was ready. I put the motor in reverse and as soon as the boat motion was stopped turned off the diesel. She hesitated a minute or more and then let the ashes drop over the bow standing in silence for a minute. Her silent vigil was broken by the blowing sound of whales and looking astern of the boat a pod of five whales surfaced. Four of them had tall straight fins with one of them a distinct notch in the middle of the trailing edge. The fifth whale was smaller with a fin curved backwards shaped like an eagle's beak. They seemed suspended in time on the surface of the glassy sea. Alex hurried to get her camera but by the time she was ready they were too far away for an effective photograph.

It was only ten o'clock by the time we had completed our ceremony, a light northwest wind beginning to ripple the surface of the sea. I leant down to start the motor and as my hand went out to the key she held it.

"No, John, peace before speed," she said, "it's a spinnaker day."

She was right, the gentle breeze picked up, the current helping, we made the 25 miles to Forward Harbour by late afternoon.

"It's Saturday isn't it?"

"Yes," I replied. "Why?"

"Is there a church near here?"

"No, that's why the Anglicans ran the MV Columbia."

I had taken her Bible and Prayer book from my bookcase stowing it with my luggage hoping over time she would find her God again.

I recollected standing in front of Andrew's books, my eyes drawn to a small volume of poetry. I bought a card and inscribed a quotation from Blake, a poet I had not read before. Now was the time to return it to her.

"I thought you might need these," I said, handing her the two books, "they were in your room as you know, I thought you were just miffed at him so I recovered them."

She took them in her hand, then noticing the card, read the inscription aloud.

> *'Think not thou canst sigh a sigh*
> *And thy maker is not by;*
> *Think not thou canst weep a tear*
> *And thy maker is not near.*
>
> *O! he gives to us his joy*
> *That our grief he may destroy;*
> *Till our grief is fled & gone*
> *He doth sit by us and moan.'*

"I feel so ashamed."

She got up and came towards me arms open to hug me and there was my chance, a swift dig into her solar plexus.

"Got you!" I said, savouring the sweet pleasure of my action.

"There was an old Indian at Forward Bay who asked what I was doing," she said quietly. "I told him I was angry at my God for taking Andrew from me. He looked at me as if I were stupid saying that God can only receive not take anyone away. I put Andrew next to him and took their photograph together. I will have an enlargement made and framed to remind me of my lack of faith."

As I drove to work I admitted to the misery of missing Andrew trying to cover up the added fear of losing Alex to Jim as well. Together they behaved like a married couple, working together, planning ahead to next year's tree planting and both heading for medical school, albeit with Jim trying to get in a year ahead of her. My mood during the morning not helped by the dull, dragged out day at work. I was glad to be driving home, anticipation of a long weekend of warm weather and compatible company cheering me.

Provisions stowed, lots cast for bunks I left the cubs to settle and went to *Heron* with my gear. They joined us in *Heron*'s cockpit for a night cap. Jessica's David was self assured and slowly insinuated himself into the family chatter. David, already friends with Douglas and Anne, was careful to keep Andrew out of the conversation and the talk turned naturally to the next day's destination.

"I want to show David Portland Island," Jessica said firmly.

"Have you been to Butchart Gardens, David?" I asked.

"No," he replied, "I've heard a lot about them from my grandmother, an amateur but serious gardener."

"That would make a pleasant round trip," Anne said, speaking from the galley, "Butchart Saturday and Portland Sunday."

"What time will we leave, John?" Alex said, from out of Jim's shoulder.

"When's low tide, Doug?"

"Eleven thirty."

"Should leave about eleven then."

"Early morning walk, Anne?" Alex inquired.

"Yes, come for early coffee here first."

Sitting in the early morning sun at Otter Bay sipping coffee, one of those distinct pleasures, I saw Alex approach. She came aboard sat next to me, kissed my cheek and accepted her coffee from Anne.

"Where shall we walk?" I asked.

"Girl talk," Anne said, "you're excluded."

"Can't talk about you, John," Alex said apologetically, "when you're there."

"Can you sail *Never Satisfied* with Jim and the others?"

"You'd trust me?"

"No, Jim I do though!" I replied, waiting for my shoulder to hurt.

We sailed into Brentwood Bay mid-afternoon, a splendid time to visit the gardens. Laziness encouraged us to book for dinner at the restaurant, giving us more time to explore. In the sunken gardens Jim lead me away to climb the centre monadnock.

"I asked Alex if she would live with me, did you know?"

"No, she has said nothing yet," I answered, "I wouldn't try to stop or persuade her against it."

"You know I want to marry her," he said, "would you approve?"

"Yes, I knew that from Anne." I evaded an answer to his question.

"She says she will only agree if and when she can look me in the face and say she loves me. I find it so frustrating."

David and Jessica were coming up the path to join us and he let the subject drop. David joined Jim and I was walking with Jessica. "Do you mind?"

"Having David with us, do you mean?" She nodded. "No, Andrew would expect you to live your life fully."

"I don't think I would have married Andrew," she said, "we were too alike."

"Andrew was still too selfish to marry. I suspected he lusted after you more than loved you, Jessica."

"He was capable of love. He loved Alex..." she added, looking up at me, "totally and unselfishly."

"You mean they slept together?" I asked, shocked by her remark.

"Heavens no! Their love was spiritual, unsullied but total. I once criticised Alex, I was jealous of her I suppose, and he nearly parted my neck from my body," she was laughing at the memory, "he told me I had no reason to be jealous of her, he thought her physically unattractive and anyway she was his sister. Alex would tell Andrew all about her feelings for Jim. They discussed books, science, films, TV and everything including sex. After Alex told you about her home life when she was sixteen, she would tell Andrew about things in horrible detail, upsetting him for days. But he sensed that he was the only person she could tell with complete honesty. Andrew would come and tell me to get it off his mind."

"What sort of detail, Jessica?"

"Has Alex told you how her father would punish her?"

"Slapping her face and spanking her you mean?" But Jessica was shaking her head, starting to tell me, which prompted again the nausea of hate against her father making me plead with her.

"Stop, Jessica."

"Alex was right, she always told Andrew that you were too sensitive to hear the details. That's why you only heard the edited version."

"Is Alex as sensitive and thoughtful about others as she is with me, Jessica?"

"I think so," she answered, "she was so kind to David, she took him aside and promised she would not compare him with Andrew more than once every five minutes. Her teasing made him relax."

We were all together looking out over the quarry to the fountain sitting on the garden chairs when Alex gathered us all together asking a Japanese tourist to take the photograph for her. It was done with elaborate sign language to get us to produce the 'whisky effect'.

Jessica's engagement to David came remarkably quickly and we were both invited to her engagement dinner party. Alex arrived back from the university later than expected and hurried upstairs to bath and dress. I heard her door close and went to the hall waiting for her to come down the stairs. She was wearing the black dress given to her by Anne, the silver barrette and earrings her only adornments.

"I know I'm stunning," she told, me laughing at her own conceit, "Anne should be pleased with her pupil."

The sight of her made me go upstairs to my room and take Stephanie's string of pearls from the wardrobe. I had intended to give them to her on her twenty-first birthday, now, seeing her, I knew they would compliment her dress as well as give her pleasure. There was pleasure for me, the excitement expected as I put them round her neck.

"Alex, I was going to give you this for your twenty-first birthday, but you look so gorgeous I couldn't wait."

"What is it?"

"Open and see."

"They are beautiful," she said, viewing them lying in their case, "Where did you get them?"

"Here, let me put them on for you," I said, removing them from their case and standing her in front of the mirror, "They were Stephanie's, and when you have worn them a few times the oil in your skin will restore them to their former lustre."

"They do... Oh John, thank you."

Her face flushed with excitement, she turned and kissed my cheek. "Beauty itself doth of itself persuade the eyes of men without an orator," I quoted.

"Where is that from?"

"You would not like the answer!"

Alexandra's perspective.

Alex rowed from *Never Satisfied* to *Heron* to collect John to attend church at Bedwell Harbour. She rowed carefully to avoid spoiling her church clothes with sea water. She dressed as a woman now, preferring trouser suits to skirts but was unmistakably feminine, "Did you have a pleasant evening? What did you talk about?"

"Children; all of you," he said and to reassure her, "Anne was very quiet."

"I'm sure I could tell Anne I had murdered and she would keep my confidence," she replied, "that's why I chose her."

They walked silently now and Alex recollected the way Anne had listened to her.

"You have a problem you want to discuss?"

"It's more a situation than a problem, one in which I am unable to ask John for advice and Andrew says he doesn't know either. I would ask Jessica but it's too... too private. You know how secretive I can be." She sat smiling at Anne, waiting for the lead.

"Go on."

"There are two things really," Alex said, fighting anxiety. "I wouldn't mind leaving right now!" she said limply, while searching her handbag for a kleenex to blow her nose. Then she had looked straight at Anne.

"I can't tell Jim I love him."

'There,' she thought to herself, 'it's out.'

"He keeps saying he loves me, wants me, to marry me. You know that I have made love to him."

Anne's professional mask hid her memory. She remembered the weekend he returned from the boat, he had walked into her kitchen, put his arms around her and told her how much he loved Alex. She remembered her own joy at the success of her matchmaking. Now she stayed quiet, waiting for Alex to continue.

"I enjoy so many things about Jim. His gentleness, quiet confidence in himself, the way he talks and listens to me and now the way he makes love to me."

She thought to herself, 'All her tender limbs with terror shook', still gazing into Anne's eyes, "but I can't look Jim in the eyes and say 'I love you'."

"Do you know why?"

"We went to a party after our exams at one of Jim's friends who lent us his bedroom. The first time I had seen Jim naked in the light since Walsh Cove," both smiling in recollection, "as he made love to me, I climaxed," she said looking at Anne with the uncertainty of children about adult knowledge, "and as I reached that point another person was standing in front of me, naked. I felt it such a betrayal I could not let him inside me. He asked me why and I could not answer. He asked me if it was because of my father and I said yes." She examined Anne's face for understanding, "he didn't deserve such duplicity."

"Not your natural father then," she commented, understanding, to Alex's relief.

"John, standing in front of me just like at Laura Cove offering to put his swim suit on if I was too uncomfortable to skinny dip with you all. I felt so guilty, making love to Jim under false pretences, so conscious of his feelings. Oh, Anne, I don't want to hurt someone so gentle and kind."

"Do you feel guilty about sex?"

"No," Alex's eyes wide with surprise, "I enjoy sexual feeling and make use of it for myself. Did John tell you about Flora and the "M" word?" Seeing Anne smile and nod continued. "I had talked to Andrew, telling him I could give myself pleasure, wanting to know if it was normal for women. He said it was for men but didn't know about women. It was at that time John took me to his bookcase and started me reading Havelock Ellis. All six volumes!"

"Have you really read them all?"

"Yes, but he doesn't say much about fantasy and I got the impression it was normally just part of masturbation. Am I wrong?"

"You are wrong," Anne shifted uncomfortably in her chair, choosing her words carefully, giving Alex a sense of her discomfort, "many women will use fantasy during sex to bring on their climax."

"But do they fantasise about their own fathers?"

"I don't see why not. Most women adore their fathers and tend to marry men like them."

"That's incest," Alex exclaimed.

"What do you think about during masturbation, Alex?"

"Well," Alex's turn to be in the court of embarrassment, "there are many themes," she said evasively, "to do with nature usually."

"Such as."

"I might be in a field of long grass watching an eagle swoop down on me. One time I was in front of a horse that reared up as I climaxed," she said, choosing the least disconcerting and non-human erotic examples she could remember.

"Have you been looking for an eagle or horse to have an affair with? Does it justify my accusing you of bestiality?"

"Of course not."

"Then why do you feel need to be guilty about a human fantasy?" Anne looking straight into her eyes. "You must love John, he's your spiritual father."

"He's not my father," she snapped.

"A raw nerve, Alex," she said frowning, "you have lived together for five years, by all accounts with great harmony and I suggest happiness. You are bound to have feelings towards both John and Andrew."

"How could I love John; he's old enough to be my father, it's ridiculous."

"Many women have loved, even married, men old enough to be their father," Anne paused, "as you say, John is not your father so it is not incestuous for you if you should find you love him."

"What about poor Jim?"

"The session is over, Alex. What I say now is as your friend. I have willed you and Jim to love each other. I'd cast a spell if I thought it would increase the chances."

"Matchmaker!" Alex's bright laughing blue eyes fixed on Anne.

"I admit it. I would love you as my daughter-in-law, but if that's not to be then I will still love you as a friend."

"Is that fair to Jim?"

"Jim needs sex as much as you do, Alex. If being together leads to love as well, so be it, if not so long as you have been honest with each other, the pain will be manageable."

They got up, walked around the desk to each other, embraced and as Alex opened the door she said, "I knew it would be worth the forty dollars!"

The walk to the church was some distance but had passed quickly with this recollection. As she stepped onto the pathway she thought 'last night I told Jim with complete honesty how I felt.' In the church, Alex thought, 'I am to give thanks to my God for restoring my brother to health'. The sheer joy of last evening watching him with Jessica, her old ebullient brother in an intellectual dogfight with Jessica, both proud and humorous before finally tumbling into bed.

As the service progressed she felt at odds with her God. Maybe it was the epistle that set this tone:

'Mortify then your members which are upon the earth; fornication, uncleanness, inordinate affection, evil concupiscence and covetousness which is idolatry.'

She felt his answers to her exuberant spirit seemed cautionary, leaving her with a sour taste in her mouth.

Walking back to the dinghy, she asked John Anne's question of the previous evening.

"What are Andrew's chances?"

"Fifty-fifty," he answered with complete honesty.

As Alex stood on the promontory looking down the straits to the Adams River, she found herself shouting 'seagull' the start of reliving the word game played here with Andrew two years before. She sensed Andrew's replies as the word game reached its conclusion. By the time she reached 'interposed' her grief was gone, replaced by her laughter; an uncanny sense that he was laughing with her. Then she wondered, 'where was that flat rock we sat on', looking around until she identified it. It was occupied, an old Indian sitting on it by himself. She got up taking Andrew and her camera with her. He was quite still, his old leather wood face turned towards her as she approached, crinkling in greeting. She sat beside him on the rock, putting Andrew on her knees.

"What have you?"

"My brother, Andrew," she answered, "or at least his ashes."

"You mocking him up there?" A sternness to his inquiry.

"No, I was reliving a game we played together just two years ago. A remembrance of my love for him."

"I glad for him," crinkling once more, "and now what."

"He asked us to commit him to the sea at Robson Bight so that he could have the majestic view of the Tsitika Valley. I told him he would be transformed into a killer whale. It was a joke between us."

"You believe in Transformer?"

"He is the Kwakiutl God."

"You believe in God?"

"I'm angry at my God for taking Andrew from me."

"Only one God, don't take people away, receive them only," he said contemplating her as if she were simpleminded, "come to people in different ways. Think Andrew like be killer whale?"

"That is what he would tell you if he could," she answered, amused by his interest.

He turned away indicating that the conversation was ended for him. She put Andrew on the rock beside him, took her camera out stepping back to include them both in the picture. She left the Indian sitting there and walked back to the promontory.

Her birthday in early August was her grief's last hurdle. For five years her birthdays had been contrived to surprise her. The struggle on Andrew's face, the smug look on John's after she had made the correct choice of Harbour where she knew she would find *Heron*. More important to find Jim to explore her growing passionate sensuality. Now, her twentieth birthday, she would still number it her seventh of personal freedom, constantly reminded her of her brother's absence. Only John and Flora to watch her open their presents and the delivered ones from Jim, Jessica, Anne and Douglas. Anne, who over the seven years had encouraged her to exploit her femininity, making her take more interest in her appearance and to treasure her ability to attract. The final step, she thought as she saw the little black dress snuggled in its box, the card instructing her to be a mankiller in it, and she knew that when it molded her body offsetting her pallid complexion and sandy hair she would be successful. She looked forward to accompanying Jim to the next party, dreaming of stepping from the wings the reaction of her audience looking up to enjoy the pleasure of triumph on his face. That face transformed from boy to man, mature and beard prickled, the sloping forehead to heavy brows edged in a brown fringe leading onto his straight nose. The strangely round rosebud mouth, the white incisors fluorescent against his ruddy complexion, sensual, demanding contact. Over six feet she could see him now towering above her, her hand on his arm. They would make a striking couple.

Then there was another little box, different this year, smaller and flatter, the exquisite pendant lay on the satin, its Kwakiutl eagle motif carved into the silver, the pendant hanging on a chain of silver links.

"Put it on for me, John."

"There," he said coming around to see her from the front, "just as I had imagined, the eagle nestling between your breasts."

That night she lay back in bed wearing the pendant, seeing the eagle in her cleft, hearing in her mind 'the eagles soars in the summit of heaven.' Looking down she saw the eagle take off and soar into her Tsitika Valley.

"Oh Andrew," she whispered, "I do miss you."

The long weekend before the start of third year university, monogamous Jim returned from tree planting, bursting from self-imposed abstinence, came to stay overnight on the Thursday in preparation for a weekend of boating. Alex, up early as usual to get John his coffee, watched him drift through his morning ritual.

"Sleep well?" he inquired, seeing her eyebrows raise in amusement, remembered that Jim had stayed overnight.

"Did you enjoy yourself?" he asked, turning his head to hide his sour smile.

"He had some catching up to do," she replied with her usual candour to the back of his head.

"I'll try to be back by four-thirty if you will get something to eat so that we can get away by five-thirty."

"Jim says that Jessica is bringing her boyfriend."

He turned, viewing her sadly.

"Andrew would expect all of us to go on living, fully."

He said it more to reason with himself than Alex, who was more generous.

"Poor boy, everyone will be making their comparisons."

They were silent for some minutes.

"Will you be staying on *Heron*?" Alex asked.

"Anne suggested it, saying it would leave the young cubs to play!"

Watching him getting ready to drive to work she knew that she could not accede to Jim's invitation to live together in Vancouver. She wished she could allow herself more tactile intimacy with John to reassure him that she understood his loneliness. She would not desert him, she must fulfil Andrew's promise to Stephanie, but to say so might open a flood gate of emotion that she was not ready to face.

Anne went ahead of her up the gangway from the dock headed for the bathhouse, Alex, sitting on the steps in the sun, waited for her. They were silent walking up the hill, Anne out of breath trying to keep up with the striding Alex. They walked slowly along the road allowing Anne to catch her breath.

Alex told her of the trip to Robson Bight, how her grief had slowly resolved as she began to feel Andrew's presence ever stronger as they approached Forward Bay. She told her about the old Indian, unable to describe any feature of him.

"I was sure I took a photograph of him on the rock seat," she said, "I told John I would make an enlargement and frame it for my room. All that came out were Andrew's ashes on the rock. Did John tell you about the pod of killer whales near the boat just after I had committed Andrew to the sea?"

"Yes," Anne replied, he told us last night. "How's he doing, Alex?"

"Shrivelled, lonely," she answered, "his face looks strained, sometimes sour, I think he's lost weight and appears two inches shorter. Flora remarked the other day that everything seemed an effort for him."

"What do you think of David?"

"I like him," Alex replied, "not like Andrew, more like Douglas," she said, a glance of conspiracy between them. "And when away from you he has a great sense of humour. Do you like him?"

"Doug does, but I'm not sure."

"Comparing him with Andrew?" Alex asked and seeing Anne turn away, the movement of her shoulders revealing the unseen face, she took Anne in her arms drawing her towards her. "How selfish of me to assume that you were over your grief just because I am."

"We loved each other you know," Anne said, "more than a mother's love. I wanted him and was quite jealous of Jessica at first. When you saw me professionally your questions made me quite uncomfortable."

The confession took Alex by surprise and she pondered the oddity of human loving.

"Jim asked me to live with him; did you know?"

"Yes."

"I told him I could not leave John alone at present. That's not the whole truth as you know." Anne's turn to comfort Alex. "I always feel better after being honest with you."

"Still John?"

"He won't go away; and now he obviously needs my kindness and companionship which is easy to give. I must stay with him, Anne."

After dinner they strolled through the gardens again waiting for dusk to turn dark eventually making their way to the top of the gardens where the Saturday night firework display is held. When the display finished they walked back through the gardens now illuminated with coloured lights. She took Jim's hand and seeing John detached and lonely, took his hand walking between them to draw him inside. Back on board, preparing the hot chocolate, getting the brandy, everything reminded her of Andrew. After she had made love to Jim she would not let him sleep, insisting on talking with him to expunge the memories and exorcise his spirit.

"Not the most relaxed weekend."

"No, everyone seemed a little strained. Do you like David?"

"Yes, I do. Why?"

"Think he will make a pleasant brother-in-law?"

"That serious already?"

"Oh yes, she's bowled over. She came to seek me out after their first date and told me David would be her husband."

"Has he popped the question?"

"No. I don't think so, I don't think David knows yet."

"He'll probably be the last to know," she chuckled, and seeing his eyes closing pushed Jim over on his side, "go on, go to sleep." Almost immediately she heard the steady rhythm of his breathing. Looking at him, she was still not used to the ease with which he could drop off.

CHAPTER 10

B 10 of the B Pod

Alex had first met Allison Johns in the genetics course in fourth year. The close proximity of their names had brought them together as lab-partners. They recognised each other from previous classes but had never talked to each other before and the co-operation in their labs started their friendship. Allison had spent three years in residences at the university and had made many acquaintances without close friendships. She was shorter than Alex but equally as strong physically. She played basketball for a league club in Vancouver, not wanting to try out for the university in order to find some social life outside off campus. Their paths had not crossed in the Memorial Gymnasium where Alex had played volleyball with the UBC team. Their friendship blossomed quickly and before the end of October, Allison had spent the first weekend of many with them in Richmond.

Allison was shorter, wiry with dark hair and black brown eyes. Her face round and pugnacious, her skin coarser than Alex's and she kept her hair shorter, almost boyish. She replaced Andrew as the person in whom Alex was able to confide. They worked together, talked and argued in a similar style in their easy companionship. Alex who still preferred the company of men, not for their sexuality but for their beery companionship, still met Andrew's and Jim's old friends. Soon, Allison became a regular with them although noticeably, like Alex, seemed impervious to pairing off with one of them.

The second weekend staying with them they had been up late working, Alex now using Andrew's bigger room into which she had moved her bed. During her affair with Jim she had stopped wearing night clothes and still preferred the freedom without. She liked to read before sleep, the comforter covering up to her waist and Allison had come to say good night sitting on her bed chatting.

"Do you have a boyfriend?" Allison asked her.

"Not at present," she replied, "since I was fourteen I thought of Jim as my boyfriend."

"Big Jim at the pub the other night?"

"Yes, that's him, I broke off with him after this summer when we returned from tree planting."

"Why?"

"It's a long story, I may tell you one day," she said. "What about you?"

She watched Allison shake her head, turn away and thought she was going to end the conversation.

"I'm not for men," she said, "except for company like the other night."

Alex kept quiet, a long pause ensued, then she looked her in the eyes.

"Can I sleep with you, Alex?" she asked, leaning over, putting her hand on Alex's breast, her face towards her allowing her lips to lightly kiss Alex's mouth. Alex shifted away from her. "I'm sorry, Alex, I've offended you."

"Not offended, just surprised me," she said, lifting the comforter, "you'll get cold."

Alex would always remember her face at that moment, the expectation of rejection turned to incredulity at her calm acceptance of Allison's nature. She slipped in beside her, turned towards her on her side, looking suddenly uncomfortable.

"My God, this is the most awful bed, Alex!"

"It's my anti-seduction bed," she said, dissolving into gales of laughter.

"Will you come to my bed?"

"I need time to think about that, Allison."

She asked John about homosexuality over breakfast the following Sunday and whether he had ever been propositioned.

"Of course," he replied, looking surprised at her question, "I declined for myself but took no offence at the offer; what did you say?"

"None of your business," said with a nervous laugh, but quickly recovering her composure. "I told her I needed time to think about it although she doesn't know I would discuss it with you. You won't say anything to her will you?"

"I would imagine that it would be pleasant for women, at least they would understand what is pleasurable," he said musingly, "and you do tend to communicate more directly than men."

Alex did not want this friendship to end, she genuinely enjoyed Allison's company and was intellectually stimulated by her. Yet when she challenged herself she was not interested in a sexual relationship. The parallel was her love for Andrew, a person who she found comforting and comfortable, but without need for lust.

When Alex started medical school and Allison was in first year of graduate studies, at Alex's urging, John invited Allison to live with them. The friendship had deepened in spite of its asexuality.

Alex drove down the hill into Horseshoe Bay, pleased to see so short a line-up for the ferry. She had chosen to travel on a Thursday to avoid the aggravation of a one or two sailing wait to cross to Nanaimo on Vancouver Island. It was early June 1982 at the end of second year medical school, the year that medical students are relieved to have under their belts. She was looking forward to the next four weeks in rural practice attached to some doctors in the small coastal town of Port McNeill. The program was designed to give her hands-on experience in a community she remembered from their sailing holidays. She was also excited at the prospect of visiting Allison and joining John to cruise with him to round off the last summer with holidays away from medical studies. She thought back to 1976 the last trip the three of them had taken in the summer before attending first year university. The year they made their intended destination, Blunden Harbour, followed by the glorious sail across Queen Charlotte Straits to Port McNeill in *Never Satisfied II*, her maiden cruise. With a strong northwest wind on their quarter they had sailed off their anchor in Blunden Harbour and averaged their hull speed of seven knots into the small harbour at Port McNeill.

She was looking forward to visiting Allison at Boat Bay in the Johnstone Straits where she was involved with the killer whale researchers who congregate there for the summer breeding season. It would be four years since she had visited this area and that sad occasion when she and John had sprinkled Andrew's ashes into the sea off Robson Bight as requested for his final burial.

Once a week Doctor Ferguson would visit the Indian communities at Nimmo Bay in McKenzie Sound and Kingcome Inlet. He asked if

Alex would like to go with him in his float plane and she gladly accepted.

They were blessed with a glorious crystal clear day as they crossed the Queen Charlotte Straits into Wells Passage flying Visual Flight Rules about 1000 feet off the sea. Looking into Tracey Harbour, the seclusion of Napier Bay at its head bringing back memories of the last trip John, Andrew and she had made together, this had been their jumping off point for Blunden Harbour. They turned eastward into McKenzie Sound, looking into the narrows of Kenneth passage, a mountain peak rising massive out of the water. Saint Mary's heights and then the peak on her left and the glistening sea below passing quickly until they turned towards the peak again and into Nimmo Bay.

"Lucky there is no wind today," he said, "sometimes it's tricky getting down here if the westerly is blowing and we have to land outside and taxi in."

The Indian village at the head of the bay looked insignificant under the mountain. They drew up alongside the float and were welcomed by an old Indian who accompanied them up to the clinic room where several families were gathered to see the doctor. Alex made herself useful taking out some stitches whilst the doctor was seeing a family.

"Would you take a cast off for me, Alex?" he said, indicating the left arm of the old Indian who had led them up from the plane. "You will find a pair of cast cutters in my bag."

"Do you still tell stories for the children?" Alex asked as she chipped away at the cast.

"Yes, I do."

"Which do you like to tell the best?"

"Transformer ones."

"Do you believe in him?"

She stopped temporarily and looked at his craggy face which was assembled into a crinkled grin.

"Of course. There would be no life here without him!"

"Have you ever met him?"

"Sure."

"What's he like?"

"He's only sort of there," he said quietly, "real but not there; a spirit you see."

"Is there any way of knowing he is the Transformer?"

"Not at the time."

"How do you mean?"

"A day later you just don't remember what you saw." He stopped and was silent for a minute or more. "I have never been able to describe him."

"Why don't you take a photograph?"

"I said he's not there, he wouldn't come out."

Her face flushed with embarrassment and she was saved by the cast which now lay in her hands.

"There; how does it feel?"

"Light," he said, with a smile, "but there!"

'Had she seen the Transformer in Forward Bay when holding Andrew's ashes?' she asked herself. She took the photograph which she thought had not come out. She tried to remember his appearance, but like the photograph he was not there. 'Why do I keep saying he?' she thought and could not remember any feature, not even the voice.

The float plane banked to its left at Boat Bay to land against the light northwest wind and taxied towards the beach. She could see Allison in a small boat waiting for them to stop in the sheltered area of the bay. The pilot helped Alex down onto the float with her gear as Allison came alongside. The transfer made, the pilot looked out of his window and waved to them before taking off.

As soon as they reached shore, Allison told her that there was a pod of whales not far out between the camp and the Tsitika river delta.

"I can't come with you," she said, "why don't you take the boat out and try to get near them?"

The wind rippled the water reminiscent of the day she parted with Andrew's remains. She saw the pod and counted six fins which were travelling towards her. Alex stopped the outboard allowing the boat to drift watching the majestic backs and fins of the whales now heading across her bow. She had the strangest feeling of time standing still, then felt a light touch against the starboard side of the boat. She looked for the offending drift wood reluctant to take her eyes off the whales and then saw the black shape slowly rise beside her, a small fin appeared gently brushing the boat. Strangely unafraid of the large muscular shape, the small blow hole issuing a fishy halitosis, she put her hand on the fin.

As her hand came in contact with the whale, she had an intense feeling of Andrew, no hallucination or materialisation, just an awareness of him. The feeling she had in church talking to God but intensified to the point of real two sided conversation. No clicks, no squeals, but communication as surely as she knew she was talking to Andrew.

"Is that you, Andrew?" she asked, still puzzled by the intensity of the sensation of his presence.

"Yes, Alex. Are you well?"

"Andrew, really Andrew?" The pricking in her eyes causing her embarrassment.

"Alex, you have tears in your eyes!"

"Oh shut up, Andrew."

"Same old Alex, angry at her own emotions."

"Where have you been all these years?"

"With my family here and up the coast, always glad to be back to see 'the eagle soar in the summit of Heaven'."

"This is... this is... tell me, just keep telling me."

"The last time I saw you was at the point I entered the water at Robson Bight over there. I had been with you at home, I remember a long tunnel with a source of light at its end. I travelled along the tube and as I emerged I seemed to be suspended above you as you rushed to John. In the ambulance and hospital looking down at myself I noticed a fine thread attaching me to my body which severed as my body stopped breathing. I wanted to tell you to stop mourning me, instead to rejoice, believe and be Alexandra, my sister that I knew, whose company I love. You blocked me out, refused to see me; same with John, frustrating all my efforts at communication. You're so naive still aren't you, Alex." She could sense his teasing laughter. "As we came up the coast together you began to lose your severity and I felt you begin to allow me close to you again. Then you played our word game at Forward Bay, I knew you had accepted me back. You told John that I was everywhere, but of course he didn't understand. Then you handed me to the Transformer who arranged my new existence."

"I feel so peaceful, Andrew."

"Nice of John to bring your Bible and Prayer Book; I managed to persuade him to find the Blake poetry for you. I've seen him each year when he comes north and watch over him."

"Have you seen him this year yet?"

"Not yet, why?"

"He is on his way up and is due to pick me up from here. I just wondered."

"If I see him I'll jump for him. How's Jim?"

"We broke up but we're still good friends and he has a passionate friend with prospects. I like her and think we will be friends."

"You're going to have to deal with your father soon, Alex."

"What do you mean, Andrew?"

"You'll see. Can you hear my family call me?"

"No."

"I must leave now."

As Alex lost contact with the fin she sensed Andrew had gone and the whale sank under the water gently distancing itself from the boat. About ten feet away she saw his snout rise out of the water as he skyhopped his farewell. She did not start the outboard for some time but lay back and savoured the aroma of her experience before drinking its significance.

"I was watching you through the binoculars as that whale skyhopped close to your boat," Allison said.

"Wasn't I lucky?" Alex replied.

"Did you take a photograph?"

"No I was too busy watching, I forgot I had the camera," she lied, now with Allison's observation she knew that it had been real and not imagined.

"I expect the whale belongs to the B Pod," Allison told her, "we identified the four males from their fins this morning. The big male had a notch in the leading edge of its fin. If we are correct the little whale that skyhopped would be B-10."

"Do you know when he was born?"

"We think in 1979; why did you say he?"

"Only a male would skyhop for a single girl in a boat," she said lightly and to tease Allison added, "unless it was you in the boat."

As the time approached for John's expected arrival she would see the wind on the sea knowing it would funnel down to Sunderland

Channel making the trip up to Boat Bay impossible. She imagined the collection of boats in Forward Harbour anchored in Douglas Bay champing at the delay and praying for the north-westerly to abate so they could make an early morning dash to get past the rough area.

The weather forecast changed on the sixth day and she knew that John would appear the next day. Hot chocolate with the mandatory brandy to keep them warm, Alex's face not trying to hide her anticipation.

"Don't forget to give me the car keys, Alex," Allison said, having offered to drive her car back to Vancouver, allowing her to stay with John and sail to Otter Bay with him.

"Better get them for you now," she said going back to the tent to find them. Coming back to Allison, her unrestrained joy radiated from her.

"You're behaving as if your lover is returning from the sea," Allison said acidly.

"He is," she replied, immediately regretting her slip of the tongue.

"Really," taken by surprise and seeing the look of dismay on Alex's face, "or were you being facetious?"

Alex sipped her chocolate and silently planned her story. "It's difficult to start," she said, "Anne is the only person who knows how I feel and since I told her in a professional capacity I know she will never say anything."

"Tell him, you mean?" she said and in her funny voice, "Hi, John, Alex loves you. Are you implying that I might?"

"Allison, I didn't mean it like that," accompanied by a jab to her shoulder, "I couldn't even talk to Andrew about it. Although at the time it was more like a crush on John and I steered clear of intimacy not trusting myself. I have talked to him about so many things, but to talk to him about this I find too... too... Ugh!"

"When did you start to feel this way about him?"

"You sound like a therapist," she commented with a giggle, "it's hard to be precise. I was aware of him since the first cruise, a sort of crush, on Saturday mornings when I stayed over before Andrew got up, we had long discussions over breakfast about medicine, oh I don't know just everything. I used to think, 'to have a father like John'," she hugged herself and continued, "when my parents deserted me he was looking at my back, I thought the look of hatred was for me, only later discovering it was directed at my father."

"What do you mean looking at your back?"

She told her about her father's cruelty to her, which ended with John looking at her back.

"John's acceptance of me in his home must have been difficult because I lionised Andrew, he was the only person I could take my bitterness, frustration and anger out on and still know he would remain my loyal friend and confidant. I was horrible that first summer, brooding, dark, rude and ungrateful. John seemed to wait patiently for me to come out of it and assisted with uncanny perception. Did I tell you about my birthdays?"

"No, never."

"Those five birthdays, a fundamental rebirth, I didn't know that John knew my birthdate. To see *Heron* at anchor and suddenly find myself the centre was symbolic of being in the family. Later that night I felt ashamed of my bloody minded behaviour of the previous weeks. John was never obsequious and they had such obvious fun fooling me or embarrassing me. The celebration was for all of us not just for me. Nothing could break my friendship with Andrew, but in the background was a developing deep affection between John and me. Our Sunday morning discussions after church, he came with me although a professed non-believer, were between two adults as we argued about belief and religion. I never allowed a reference to being his daughter or he my father without refuting it, usually quite snappily and Andrew would tease me by mimicking me. I would observe their natural intimacy not able to bring myself to copy it. On the cruise I was still frightened of Douglas and leery of John, not able to accept his offered hug. During the time I had the terrible crush on him my gooey feelings and erotic imagination always centred on John. To this day I find it hard to touch him or hug him. I feel my whole body stiffen at the thought of rejection."

"He sounds too good to be true!" Allison commented.

"He has his deeply sinister side, too private and brooding. Secretive about how he really feels and when he can't get what he wants he is manipulative. When that fails he gets chippy and selfishly direct. There were times early on when I knew I was in his home on sufferance, I was breaking into the neat cocoon of his dialogue with Andrew. I could feel his resentment when I tried to get through the outer shell and into his inner thoughts. Strange but as I became so difficult that first summer his resentment diminished. He expected me to be like Andrew and rail against the day's misfortunes. He would listen to Andrew and say nothing even when he swore or turned his anger against him. Andrew said it was his therapy session. After telling them about my father's cruelty I too was able to do the same, only I wanted him to respond with advice. I did not like his 'bloody silence'. Now I find his quest for solitude disturbing, wondering whether there is room for anyone in his life again. There is a passive aggressive side to him when you feel he should react but doesn't. Like many doctors he can be obsessional about his life and living. No, he's not perfect but who ever loved perfection!"

Allison sat gazing at her face, tears rolling down Alex's cheeks and for once she did not hide from Allison.

"You're privileged, Allison," she said trying to smile, "I never let anyone see me like this. You have become a very spiritual friend," and reached out to her, hugging her tightly to her body.

"Now," Alex continued, "I am terrified to tell John how I feel, fearing his rejection, not able to read through his private outer shell. He's old enough to be my father and deep down I fear he could only love me as a daughter. I wish my sensitivity threshold was as good as my pain threshold then I might be able to start telling him. I feel like a child trying to keep its hand in front of a hot fire, it only has to feel warm and I take it away. I get jealous when he's asked out to dinner!"

"What do you mean?"

"Haven't you twigged! His assignation when John or his lady friend need sexual comfort."

"Who is she?"

"I don't know," she replied, "Andrew never did find out for all his efforts."

As Alex and John passed the two islands to enter into the Matilpi anchorage there were no other boats. They tucked themselves behind the islands out of the wind but still in the sun and showered on the foredeck. They sat in the sun until another boat disturbed their privacy, making them scuttle into the cabin to dress. Happy hour and supper passed, the wind dropped and the evening was warm from the hot day, as they finished their coffee.

"It's hard to believe that it is four years since we were up here together," John said.

"That's because it is so clear in my memory."

"What do you remember the most, Alex?"

"Standing at the bow looking up at Tsitika Valley."

"What were you thinking as you were silent. Do you remember?"

"In the beginning was the word and the word was with God and the word was God; and you?"

John stayed silent for a minute or more, then a smile flickered across his lips with a shake of his head.

"I was thinking 'in the beginning was unconsciousness and unconsciousness was with God and unconsciousness was God'; I did not say anything then because you had thrown your Bible away."

"Do we believe the same thing with different words?"

"Probably, except my words are better!"

"The voice of experience," she mimicked him, "you have changed me over the years; did you know?"

"Your father feels complimented! Do you mean changed or clarified?" He looked at her, smiled and mouthed 'you're not my father.'

"Both," she replied ignoring his jibe, "you played a part in bringing me back to belief after Andrew died. You appeared more worried about my grief than your own."

"I was; I feared for your life! I had grieved for him six months before he died so his last months were a bonus together. You were crushed as I was with Steph."

"You telling me about her was the still point for me."

"What may surprise you is that I have been changed by you. I am no longer an Atheist or Agnostic or a Theist. With our discussions after church over the years you have made me meditate. At first I sneered at anything that came from Mr Robert's mouth in prayer, scripture or sermon. Watching you and seeing how important your belief had been and still was to you I felt responsibility to discuss, even argue, with you after each service; do you remember when you said 'you listen you heathen'?"

"Does 'your unconsciousness' leave the body at death?"

"As opposed to?"

"Dying with the body?"

"I don't know, Alexandra; I know what you believe."

"What would it take to convince you, Doctor Barlow."

"A lot!"

"What do you think of after death experiences in those resuscitated back to life?"

"I don't think it proof of anything other than that our self conscious is capable of dreaming and the dreams are similar because the physical stimulus, the loss of blood supply, is the same."

"Don't you feel Andrew here, everywhere as soon as you get up here?"

Thinking here among the whales.

"Of course I do."

Thinking here in Kwakiutl country.

"Doesn't that tell you something?"

"Yes, it tells me that that is what I want to feel. My self-conscious brain drawing on my memories and all the old myths related to life after death; because it's easier to die thinking you won't, a human behaviour passed on in the genes. I could go on and on, Alex."

"Still a heathen!" she sighed.

Inside herself she was stubbornly listing irrefutable evidence that B-10 was Andrew reincarnate. Andrew had told her that he would jump for John. She had recorded it in her diary before asking John if she could read the log, where he recorded the small whale jumping for him off the entrance to Port Neville on his way to pick her up.

It was a Friday afternoon when they anchored in Walsh Cove. They swam ashore to the pool in the islands and lay on the rocks beside each other, the bitter-sweet memories of Jim, missing his tender ministrations. Thinking of her confession to Allison she wanted to take John in her arms, hold him close and tell him. Tonight she thought, tonight I will tell him and claim him. The evening came and went, her mouth too dry for the song of love and her face masked by the dance of rejected desire as they moved to get ready for bed; she felt defeated.

"Do you think we could make Westview today?" she asked as they were having breakfast next morning.

"Why?"

"I would like to go to church tomorrow if possible."

"Have you been that bad?" he asked, amusement in his eyes.

"No," she replied, "to give thanks and have a chat, no confession unless you can give me reason." Her irony lost on John.

They left quickly after deciding and picked up the wind at Sarah Point which took them all the way to Westview. On Sunday morning they went to the Anglican Church for early communion where she talked to her God.

'Is it wrong for me to love him?'

'It would be incest for him.'

'He is not my father.'

'He is your father in his eyes.'

'How can I change him?'

'Is his friendship and companionship so freely given to you not enough, Alexandra?'

'Oh, Doctor God, you can be stern when you are right.'

They arrived in Silva Bay on August 1st after a slow sail from Smuggler Cove. It was too late to get through Gabriola Passage against the tide. Next morning, Alex's birthday, she was quite expecting John to remember at breakfast and felt put out that he said nothing to her. She tried to tell herself it was not important but knew her pride would make her stay mum about it. She went forward to pull up the anchor at eleven, the time the tide turned in the passage. She took the wheel as he lazed in the cockpit enjoying the sun. No wind as they came through the passage and into the top of Pylades Channel. She headed for Ruxton Passage wishing they were staying at Pirates Cove rather than Telegraph Harbour and were past the entrance to the cove.

"Do you want some lunch, Alex?"

"What have you got?"

"Soup and sandwich, it would be easier at anchor, let's go to Pirates for lunch."

She turned the boat back, happy at the chance of persuading him to stay instead of continuing on. She lined up the markers at the entrance concentrating on them and turned into the narrow channel. He came beside her took the wheel and asked her to check the soup on the stove. She did not hear him anchor but was conscious they were still and on going up on deck found that they were tied up alongside *Heron*. He was looking like the cat who stole the cream.

"Happy birthday, Alex."

John had just come into the house, Flora staying for supper and looking forward to spending a quiet weekend with Alex at home, when the phone rang.

"Hello, John here."

"Is Alex in, John?"

He recognised the voice of the Reverend Roberts.

"Not yet, James, I'm expecting her before six. Can I give her a message?"

"I've just had a letter from her father. Her mother died this past week and he asked if I would tell her."

"Do you want me to tell her?"

"I have a letter from him for her."

"Do you want to come round, stay for supper if you like."

"That's kind of you, I'd like that. I'll leave right away."

He told Flora he was an extra and Mr Roberts arrived before Alex returned. John left them alone to talk, giving them a quarter hour before joining them. He saw the mask over her face as he entered the room, a letter spread on her knees. She looked up as he approached her and handed him the letter.

Dear Alex,

Your mother died three weeks ago while I was in hospital. I wanted you to know but I am still unable to face you or phone you. One day I hope I will be able to see you and ask for your forgiveness but until then cannot give you my address.

Please give kind regards to Dr Barlow and may the angels protect you.

your loving father.

"What a sad letter. The postmark says Winnipeg," she said as if she had put it out of her mind. "Let's have supper."

John had the impression that the news had little or no effect on her. She chatted about the hospital to Jim Roberts, trying to put him off his food. The next morning at breakfast she was resilient with good humour going to her room to study. Saturday evening they went to Douglas and Anne for dinner where she was lively and good company. Sunday morning, the nineteenth after Trinity, they went to early communion and during the reading of the epistle heard, 'Let all bitterness, and wrath, and anger, and clamour, and evil speaking, be put away from you with all malice.' Seeing her face he understood the bravado of her behaviour, her true feelings trickling down her cheeks as she mourned the loss of her mother.

She moved silently around the kitchen getting breakfast.

"Do you want me to listen?" John asked her.

"Isn't it strange how there is always something relevant in the service after bad news."

"A well written horoscope?"

"You old cynic," she answered, "I was not upset for my mother; she's in a happier place. My tears were for my father, alone, unable to face the real world, staying in his hiding place. It is time for me to put away 'all malice' and try to work towards forgiveness."

John's expression reflected his cold anger at the idea of forgiveness for one so cruel.

CHAPTER 11

Arthur Jones

At first he was vaguely aware of the movement of shadows across his grey vision. He could hear whispering voices and felt motion. As his mind cleared he saw a pleasant face, a young woman looking into his eyes.

"I think he's coming round," he heard her say. There was a strange ringing noise in his ears overridden by the wail of a siren. He realised he was in an ambulance.

"Where am I?" he questioned, his voice seeming to come from under water.

"In an ambulance. We will soon be at the hospital."

"But where am I?" he persisted.

"Toronto, on your way to Mount Sinai Hospital."

Through the wailing outside and the ringing inside his ears, he started to feel the pain in his body. His face felt numb and painful in a mixture, his hands seemed unable to function and overriding all was the deep nauseating pain in his lower abdomen and groin.

"It's all right, we're almost there," she said, responding to his groan.

"What happened?" he pleaded.

"We found you on the street, you're in bad shape and need the hospital."

He was unable to understand, his pain abolished comprehension.

The doors of the ambulance opened soon after the wailing stopped. He heard a terrified scream as the stretcher was moved, not comprehending that it came from himself. The brightness hurting his eyes making his head ache and throb. His face aware of someone's gentle fingers feeling, words spoken yet not heard. The sickness starting in his groin was reaching into unconsciousness after he vomited. He was on his side now, a cover being removed, pricking pressure in his hip and a warmth developing as the worst pain subsided. He was aware he had slept as once more he was moved. He opened his eyes, the light from a strange cone shaped object in his face, a white shape moving on his left and a clanking noise under his head.

"Try to keep still, Mr Jones," he heard her say through his protesting groan and he faded away again.

When he awoke in his hospital bed he saw the intravenous into his right arm, aware of pain in his bandaged fingers. His face was numb but his ear itched and when he tried to move his left hand to scratch, the pain prevented him. He saw a female face in his limited vision framed by bandaging and heard only the end of a phrase. "... Mrs Jones."

He could not see her but knew that she was on his left side. A chair scraped the ground and her face appeared in his vision. She looked pale, more so than usual, her bland face tear-streaked and then it disappeared. Another white gnome changed the intravenous, now appreciated as a nurse.

Each time he awoke he was more aware of the hospital around him. The large open space with other beds which appeared connected to the wall, masked and hatted white figures moving like new communicants over the floor, 'gliding' he thought at first, all noise excluded by his bandaged head, bandaging that now also covered his ears. The pain again now in his face then his fingers surmounted by that nauseating feeling rising out of his groin, his own groaning the only sound he heard.

He vaguely remembered anxiously walking down Yonge Street and sighting his young girl with relief. As the pain contracted like a light source vanishing into a still point in his groin, sleep came.

Time, he could make no sense of time, the pain slow to diminish each episode of consciousness more revealing. A sense of order returning, snatches of conversation from nurses or doctors as he learned that his face was contused, not fractured, his fingers broken and then a whispered exchange somewhere from his lower body. "Doesn't look good; this may hurt, Sir."

A doctor was doing 'goodness knows what' followed by the nauseating pain rising from his groin.

"Doubt we can save the left. The blood supply to the right looks all right."

Silence was followed by scurried activity, lifting onto the stretcher his scream heard again. The lights in the ceiling passing silently overhead, a small room, green people now.

"Just count to ten, Mr Jones."

Over the ensuing days, the pain subsiding and the pain not remembered, only the fear of renewal of pain, his memory of the dreamt young girl in the street now real; chatting to her, entering her room, the exchange of cash, the tying of wrists and the terrible loss of control.

The police came to see him and before his full memory returned he had described the girl, wishing later he had refused. They said his attackers had broken his fingers, and seriously injured his pelvis, fractured it. His head, they said, was bruised but not badly injured.

'What did they know about heads!'

The surgeon told him in whispers that he had nearly lost both testicles, the saving of one seeming the justification for the excision of the other. The pelvis would heal and once the catheter was removed he could be discharged.

Worse, but far worse his memory was returning, eating at his guilt and justifying his punishment. His hands reached for her neck, the shout for help, the sudden pain in his fingers with the cracking noise of breaking twigs. His naked body held as they executed the crushed castration of his person. His screaming silenced by the blow to his face. After remembering he would tell the police no more.

The police had their informers piecing the story together by fact and conjecture. They traced the young prostitute who said she had only seen him once before.

"When I let him tie my wrists to the bed posts he started to hit me and when his hands reached my neck I yelled for help. They hauled him off me and you know the rest."

The constables had little pity for either procurer of teen sex or the provider and she refused to lay charges. At the hospital as the victim recovered the young constable recognised him as the warden at his church. He checked his records and found the history of his flight from British Columbia, a charge outstanding with little apparent effort to pursue him, the commonness of the name Jones cited by one report as the reason. As the father of two young daughters this sickened him. He went back to the hospital to try to persuade Mr Jones to lay charges.

"No," he replied, "I'll not lay charges."

The constable was irritated by this refusal.

"I think you need help, Mr Jones. I have your records from British Columbia."

A statement greeted by silence.

The constable left the hospital to interview Mrs Jones who was also cited in the charges.

"That's not true, Constable, my daughter was a liar and we couldn't prove it," she answered.

"Has your husband told you where and why he was injured?"

"He says he has no memory."

He told her the circumstances and watched her face change. She knew he was telling her the truth. He left her crumpled, her head in her hands sitting on the chair, but he felt no pity.

The constable, still not satisfied with the outcome, decided to visit the Reverend Hayward at his church telling him of the outstanding charges against Mr Jones and the reason for his present injuries.

"Will it come to court?" Mr Hayward asked.

"He is the injured party, Sir, and will not lay charges. If we lay criminal charges none of them will tell the truth."

"I'll see him tomorrow at the hospital."

"He needs treatment for his sexual problem, Sir."

"Leave it with me, Tom, and I will see if I can persuade him."

Mr Hayward was about to leave for the hospital when the constable phoned to tell him that Mrs Jones had been taken to the hospital DOA. At the hospital he told Art Jones as gently as possible.

"She came to see me last night," he said, "she said the police had been to see her. She asked me if I had lied to her about my daughter. I was honest with her for the first time."

The Reverend Hayward had a problem comforting a woman crying with grief and found it impossible with a man. He left saying he would return next morning at the same time. He did not go back to his church; instead he went to seek his friend Doctor Mayhew at the Clarke Institute, not far from the Mount Sinai Hospital, on the off chance of catching him. Doctor Mayhew, well known for his work with patients with sexual aberrations, arranged for his young colleague to see Art before he was discharged from the hospital.

Back at the hospital next morning he told Art what he had arranged for him giving him no room to refuse. He offered him the sanctuary of his home when he was discharged saying that he would not let this interfere with their previous friendship.

Arthur Jones walked through the doors of the institute for his first appointment. James Hayward accompanied him for support, or 'is it to prevent me from running?' he wondered; he was anxious.

"Well now, Mr Jones," he heard the young psychiatrist say, "Reverend Hayward has told me something of you, but perhaps you could summarise your problem in your own words."

Mr Jones surveyed the office with its couch along the wall and the large desk across which he eyed his opponent; 'that's what he feels like,' he thought.

"Yes, Doctor Williams."

'Is he Welsh too, born in the valley perhaps?' he asked himself.

"Did James, the Reverend Hayward tell you what I had done?"

"That you had assaulted your daughter, yes."

They were looking directly at one another. Mr Jones wondered exactly what he had been told as he broke eye contact. A feeling of helplessness crept over him, the magnification of his inner weakness, his mouth caked with his megaglossal muffled voice exposing him.

"I guess you could say that," the words sticking to his palate.

"Would you like some water?"

"Thank you," he murmured, accepting the glass.

"Better now?"

"A little," he said, less dry the tongue moving across his lips, trying to put down the racing in his chest, "I was hard on her." Realising the double entendre, he smirked, looking at the doctor's expressionless face.

"Did you force her to have sex with you?"

"Yes," he said, thinking back to her return from sailing. He burst out, "why did she have to come back all girlish female? Bloody temptress!" He could hear the words coming out of him in a loud wail of grief. "Why was she a daughter and not the son I wanted, none of this with a son, none."

"Go on."

"I brought her up a son, didn't I; all those years of molding her to be male, physical, obedient and in six short weeks all undone; if she had stayed unkempt, unbeautiful, sexless, I might have been all right. Things were in control until then, I managed to control them, channel them rather. My wife sufficed and, my authority unsullied, Alex was an obedient boy, tough and no threat."

"What did you channel or control?"

"Those fantasies, desires you might say, pulling me to..." He stopped and thinking of the visions of those young women who he raped in his mind ever nearer to enacting the terrible desire. Oh yes, they were sated as he climaxed in intercourse with his wife or masturbation, for years he could control them this way, never seeing his 'son' pictured or suggested. All that changed as she walked into the room, her groomed femininity in place of the scruffy boy, bereft of his authority by her assertiveness, replaced by the fear induced by her appearance in his fantasies of desire.

"I must have her."

He had feared this ever since she was born.

"To what."

"To have her."

"To make love to her?"

"No; to have her!" He turned to the doctor's passive face. "Can't you understand!" he shouted, as if unable to suffer fools gladly and then felt ashamed at his loss of control.

"To have her," he repeated quietly; the doctor's face looked unperturbed.

"Tell me about your daughter, what was her name?"

"Alexandra, although I always knew her as Alex. That made her sexless and I thought of her as a son, treated her as a son."

"When was she born?"

"Alex was born in 1958, two years after we were married. She was a good baby, easy to like although I didn't have much to do with her, too busy at my work, home late, away early and working weekends; not too interested in her until she was about five. It was then that I began to insist that she be dressed and treated like a boy. She could throw a ball, you see, not in a sissy fashion but hard like a boy so I would go into the yard and play with her. When she got to school I encouraged her to play with the boys and she was accepted because she could play ball as hard as they could. She was eight when she made the local baseball team and I was proud of her, made her practise constantly, setting up the back yard to help her. She was a good player and well behaved, she had to be, I saw to that."

"How did you see to that?"

"I punished her if she was naughty or cheeky."

"How did you punish her?"

"I would give her face a good slap if she was sassy and I didn't stand any nonsense, making her take it like a man too."

"How do you mean?"

"No ducking or moving her head. You stay still boyo and take your medicine, I would tell her."

"Was that all?"

"If she was naughty I would put across my knee and tan her bottom."

"Did you make her cry?"

"If she cried I would start again so she learned to be a real little man."

"Did you become sexually aroused?"

"Not when she was little," he replied, hesitating in his answer.

"But you imply that you did so later; tell me about it."

He was silent for some minutes trying to think how to phrase his reply with evasive truth.

"She got too tall to put across my knee so I made her bend over a chair to punish her."

"With your hand?"

There was another long pause as they sat, Art evading the doctor's eye.

"How did you punish her?"

He could see her now, the look on her face, determination not to show him her pain. That tall lithe body bent over the chair. He felt himself stir with desire at the images appearing in his mind.

"With a cane," he answered reluctantly.

"What made you use a cane?"

"It was the same for me as a boy at school in England."

He had been punished so on one occasion as a boy in his private school by the headmaster and when he became a prefect at his senior school had derived sexual pleasure from his own cruel application of the cane.

"How often did you punish her like this?"

"Quite often."

"Once a year?"

"More often."

"Once a week?"

"About that sometimes, but monthly at least."

"Did she not complain to anyone?"

"I told her to ask God's forgiveness and she accepted her correction without complaint."

He started to feel new confidence as he thought of the religious justification for his harsh punishment of Alex. He thought back to the time she had broken her Lenten fast and surely she deserved that caning; the doctor was having some difficulty in maintaining a non-judgmental status; Mr Jones seemed to have become relaxed and confident as if his approach to disciplining his child was quite acceptable.

"Was she not a boy in need of correction? Spare the rod and spoil the child?"

"What did God have to forgive an eleven year old girl for?"

"She gave up candy for lent and broke her vow," he said, "so naturally I punished her."

"Where did you punish her?"

"In her room, I would send her to her room and follow a few minutes later."

"How many minutes?"

"She had to consider and repent how wrong she had been."

"You kept her waiting?"

"Usually."

"For how long?"

"Ten minutes or so."

"Did she never try to run off or tell somebody?"

"She never told anyone; once she tried to run off."

His eyes narrowed at the memory of how he had made her pay.

"What did you do?"

"I doubled her punishment."

"How do you mean?"

"I gave her twelve strokes with the cane instead of six," he said just audibly, appreciating the hostility in the doctor's question.

"Did she not cry out with the pain?"

"No, she knew she would get extra strokes if she did."

"Didn't she try to evade the cane?"

"She knew she must take her punishment like a man," he said and then added in a whisper, "and I helped her."

"How do you mean?"

"To keep still..."

"How, Mr Jones?" he said, knowing it sounded threatening.

"By tying her wrists to the bedrail," he said just audibly.

It was with relief that Doctor Williams closed the session and ushered Art Jones out of the consulting room. He sat back in his chair, closed his eyes and thought of the story he had heard. He was used to stories from pedophiles concerning sexual interference of children or rape of teenagers. These had an academic unreality to them, which he, a male, could not relate to in an experiential way. This reminded him of his fellow schoolchildren who would bereft flies of their wings and legs one at a time. He was physically nauseated by the tale of slow calculating infliction of pain for the sexual gratification of Mr Jones justified by his warped religiosity. He imagined Alex, a cowed little creature without spirit and probably not very intelligent since these men so often took advantage of the mentally handicapped. He could not conceive of a child of normal intelligence protecting her parents for so long, after such cruelty.

Doctor Gareth Williams, born and educated in Canada, despite his name, was the son of a family from a farm in the small southern Ontario town of Clinton. He went into General Practice for five years saving the money to take his specialty training. During the four years of post-graduate work he had become intrigued by the sexual nature of man with its unusual aberrations. He took up his appointment at the Clarke Institute after his residency. In his research he was interested in the unpopular study of the pedophile and he was still inexperienced enough to be shocked by individual cases.

Sitting in his wise senior colleague's office he had expressed his concern over the breakdown of his non-judgmental attitude when he uncovered the sadistic nature of his patient.

"You weren't educated in England. You will find it hard to justify the ease with which they condone the cruelty of corporal punishment," Doctor Mayhew stated.

"But surely you are not condoning his actions against his daughter as justifiable?"

Gareth felt his hostility rise again.

"No, of course not," he reassured, "but you must trace back to the start of these aberrant actions and the sexual nature of them if it exists."

He felt that at least he knew where to steer the next session with his new patient.

"You were born in Wales?"

The doctor's first question of the session.

"Yes, in Cardiff," Art replied, "you must have come from Wales yourself?'

"But a long time back, my grandfather emigrated with his family in 1921, they came from the Rhondda Valley."

"A Valley name."

Art smiled and settled back in his chair.

"Tell me about your parents."

"My father was a lawyer and my mother the daughter of a doctor. We were an upper middle class family, well-to-do you might say."

"Did you have a happy childhood?"

"Sort of, my parents had little to do with my childhood really."

"How do you mean?"

"I had a nanny up to the age of five and after that a governess until I went to boarding school at the age of eight. I only saw my parents on special occasions like Christmas and birthdays, except when sent by Nanny."

"Was she kind to you?"

"You could never be right with Nanny."

"How did they punish you?"

"They sent me to my father."

"What action did he take?"

"He spanked me with a hair brush."

"Did you feel ill-treated?"

"No, it was the same or worse for other kids, or so I found out when I went to boarding school."

"Did you enjoy boarding school?"

"Very much, I was good at sports, you see, and this made me popular with the others. I was a big boy for my age so I was never bullied."

"Were you a bully?"

"I think I was, don't we all enjoy power?"

"Were you punished often at school?"

"We would have to write out lines of Latin verse if we were caught," he answered evasively. "One time when I was ten or eleven

I was caught pinching sweets out of another boy's locker. Then I was punished."

He recalled standing in front of the headmaster feeling that he would soil himself as he was told his punishment. Thinking of making a dash for it, stopped by his numbed leaden legs and feet as he walked ahead of the master into the assembly hall. Looking out abashed by the sea of expectant faces gathered to witness his shame.

"How?"

"I was caned by the headmaster. It was terrible and I had a hard time not howling, all those other boys watching."

"You mean you were beaten in public."

"Yes; funny, but I enjoyed it when other boys got it. I realise now that I got sexually aroused when I saw them punished."

"So you treated Alex the same?"

Mr Jones did not answer. He thought back to the time when he was made a prefect at his senior school. He had become proficient and respected by the junior boys, remembering the cringing fear on their faces as he sent them to the dormitory. He liked those stalwart boys who took their punishment like men with their marble white faces rushing from the room just able to contain themselves in the pain he had inflicted and afterwards the quality of his coming as he relived the ever increasing intensity of the whipping he had applied.

"She had to be treated like a boy," he said limply.

"Did you make her howl?"

"Not Alex, she was tough. She never made a sound, not even that last time."

"Did you get aroused?"

"Yes, and when I took my wife that night I would be satisfied and relaxed." He was strangely composed.

"What did Alex do to deserve punishment?"

"Answering back, untidy room, failed to learn her scripture."

"Minor reasons for such severity."

The doctor couldn't stop the comment.

"Yes, you see I would manufacture the reason in the end to obtain sexual satisfaction. The last time..."

He paused for some minutes reliving the scene in her room, witnessing his awful cruelty and yet once more feeling the stirring of his desire and with it the justification for his action.

"The last time you said?" noticing his composure starting to dissolve.

"Just before she went on the sailing trip. The principal wrote a letter to say that she was not involved with painting red signs on the school walls. She did not know this and I told her she must be punished and let her decide either to cancel her trip or..."

"Go on."

"I must have hurt her because I saw her bound wrists tugging against the restraints but she was silent throughout."

Reliving the scene, entering her room, watching her wrists in their bonds strain with each lash of the cane as he tried to make her break. No sound came from her stubborn clenched jaw, not even as the blood stains soaked into her white cotton pyjamas.

Suddenly, thinking back to the paltry reasons for these punishments, he felt his eyes water and the tears of remorse flow down his cheeks.

Doctor Williams, seeing the shame of his actions reflected in his face, suggested a break.

"I think it's time for a break. Would you like coffee or tea?"

"Coffee please."

"After, I would like you to lie on the couch and tell me about your life after leaving school."

They got up and he stretched. While the doctor went to get them some refreshment he went to the window looking out onto the back street behind the institute in all its red brick grimness; similar to a Cardiff slum. 'Can I really go on with this?' he thought, 'can I tell him of my inner hell, can I bear the shame, especially knowing that tonight the thoughts will come flooding back and seem to be justified until lust is satisfied'.

As the doctor returned with the coffee they talked about his national service in the Welsh Guards as a private and later a Corporal. He had been posted to Malaya during the early days of the communist incursions and he described the disoriented fear of the jungle when on patrol. Not much of a time to indulge fantasy, he commented.

"Come and lie on the couch, Mr Jones, or would you prefer Arthur."

"Art, really."

"You may close your eyes if you prefer, Art. Do you remember when you first had thoughts of wanting to rape a young woman?"

"Whilst on leave in Malaya me and my mates went into Singapore to one of the brothels after dinner in the early afternoon. I had already thought about it before and we were all sitting in the room with the girls. One leaned over to me and asked, 'what does the corporal like?' I had been drinking and said 'I'd like to tie you up and rape you' and everyone laughed, not her though. We went up to one of those dinky rooms and she handed me two rope bonds, slipping off her clothes. She lay with her hands against the bed posts for me to tie her. She was some actress lying there writhing in fear so that I came almost as soon as I had my trousers off. 'Come again corporal,' she said as I paid her, 'I'll make it more fun next time'."

"Did you return?"

"No opportunity before the regiment returned from its tour and I was demobilised. I got a job with the Hudson's Bay Company soon after leaving the army and went to Vancouver. I was able to control my thoughts and desires by throwing myself into the work so that a year went by in Vancouver before..."

There was quiet in the room, the doctor said nothing and he had the sensation of talking to himself but out aloud.

"There was a pretty young girl at the notions counter I chatted up and she came to the movies with me. She asked me back to her rooms for coffee so I thought she wanted it too. I made her take off her dress, she was shaking and I kept insisting. She pleaded with me to leave her but I kept on watching her and feeling more potent and powerful as I pushed her back on to the bed. She said she would scream so I slapped her face and I remember her head going from side to side like a rag doll and she was silent as I had her. I told her I would kill her if she told anyone but I never saw her again, she wasn't there next morning."

"I was standing outside the Bay doors on Georgia Street when I first saw Vickie. I noticed men come up to her and sometimes she would go off with them so I knew she was a prostitute. She looked about fourteen years old and I learned later that she was seventeen but acted like this to attract a certain clientele. One evening coming off work I stayed watching her for nearly half an hour. She had no takers in that time so I went over to her asking if I could help her, 'only if you want a trick' she replied.

She told me she would charge $20.00 and I could choose. She was off-hand with me, also indicating her pimp across the street in case I thought of any funny stuff. As we walked to her room I told her what I needed and by the time we stepped into her room she looked and behaved like a young teenage kid. She would not remove her dress until I threatened her and seemed reluctant to do anything as I forced her onto the bed. She made the acting so real as she let me forcibly tie her arms to the bed post and as I pulled her knickers down started to cry out allowing me to muffle her. She looked prepubescent with her hair shaved and I took her as she struggled in the most realistic way. Over the next two years she serviced me each time the desires built up and provided the release I needed to remain in control. Then one day she wasn't there and I was desperate again."

"I remember it was a Friday night and I realised that I would have to contain myself all weekend. I toured downtown seeking someone who could replace Vickie. Eventually I got onto the bus to go home to my house in East Vancouver. There was a pretty young girl on the bus and I sat near watching her and imagining. She had long hair and a lovely face which compelled me to get off the bus with her. I intended to trap her and force her home with me so that I could have her. But a man came up to her, took her arm and I watched them walk away hand in hand. All weekend I went in search of a woman to satisfy my cravings without success. The fantasy daydreams getting stronger until eventually only excess drink would assuage them." Art's eyes counted the ceiling tiles, his mind recalling the terror of those desires. From a distance he heard a voice ask.

"Tell me about the content of your fantasies at the time?"

"They always start in a similar way, I am in a room, sitting room, with a young woman opposite me, usually somebody I had noticed during the day. She is fresh, pretty with long hair tied at the back of her head and has no make-up and an innocent look. We are finishing playing a game of cards which I win, allowing me to have her; the prize for winning. I bring her face towards me, loosen her hair so that it frames her face and kiss her. She responds at first and as I became more persistent she starts to struggle. The more she fights the more determined I become, forcibly removing her clothing and when she cries out I hit her across her face. She begs to leave but I force her all the more until undressed, her nubile body with small breasts, pink nipples and wisps of pubic hair, is exposed for my will. I tie her wrists and gag her mouth before I assault her. The pattern is the same each time with some variations; there is a gradual build up of the violence as the days pass until I act out those desires during sex."

He lay quiet, thinking of the variety in his fantasies and daydreams over the years, accepting that his description was just an example, one that was tame, knowing that he could not tell the doctor of his obsessive desire to whip a woman. He asked Vickie one day if she would allow it. She agreed to his request but would charge $20 a lash and insisted that her pimp be present to protect her from excessive punishment. That was more than he could afford.

"I left the Bay and started work at the main office of a real estate firm in Vancouver. I worked all hours which helped sublimate the desires and fantasies putting temptation out of the way. I was driving along 49th Avenue in one of those desperate phases and entered the Anglican church. As I sat and meditated James Hayward introduced himself asking if I needed help. He was a kind, contemporary man who I felt I could trust so I talked about my desires in a non-specific way. I started attending the church and over the next year became more active in its affairs. I found this strong commitment of faith helpful."

"Soon after I took over as manager of the new office I noticed a young secretary. When I asked about her the other men were all smiles indicating I would not have much luck with her, they had all tried but found her too goody goody. I was surprised when she told me she was twenty-two. She always dressed like a teen and did her hair in an unsophisticated single braid and I was attracted. At this time, my own fantasies were directed towards a more romantic content involving her, and the ugly fantasies seemed to fade into the background. She accepted my invitations and after going out for a few months I asked her to marry me. She seemed as grateful to accept as I was to ask. She had no family except for an aunt on the prairies who had brought her up. Her mother had died of tuberculosis before the war and her father was killed in action. James married us quietly at the church and we lived in an old east end house.

She enjoyed the sex with me and I indicated to her that I liked it when she played the little girl with me. I bought her teen nightdresses and she would plait her hair or put it up in a pony tail at night and act coy with me. She professed that she liked the feeling of being forcibly taken. I would let her hair down to frame her face and she even let me tie her hands to the bed posts and pretend to rape her. I could fantasise during making love to her, satisfying my desires and controlling them to keep me out of trouble although I was never able to tell her about myself. I would see her face become younger during sex until it was transformed into a young girl's, often some youngster I had seen in the preceding day. I could be violent in my imagination, undetected, and yet not harm my wife."

"Alex was born during the afternoon and my despair drove me to the bars and I got stinking drunk. Next day I went to talk with James to confess my disappointment but I don't think he understood. I was even more shattered when he told me a few weeks later that he was accepting a church in Toronto. With the help of the church and my wife, I was able to keep control of myself and devised the scheme to bring up Alex as a boy. I trained my wife to accept me as the total authority in our house. I made sure that Alex never wore a pretty outfit, only jeans or trouser suits. So she grew up a solitary child with only boys for chums and her appearance remained healthily scruffy. My doing."

"She grew very tall about the age of ten and I could no longer spank her across my knee. I remember sitting thinking one evening when the images of those school chastisements lead me to justify punishing Alex as a school boy. As the idea matured I would fantasise about her bending to a beating, wrists bound and cane in hand."

"I waited for a really justifiable reason to punish Alex and she provided it by breaking her Lenten vow. I could justify harsh punishment for religious reasons and when I sent her to her room did really think she deserved it. I had expected her to scream after the first stroke but she stayed passive and made no movement or sound as I increased the severity with each stroke."

'Oh Alex, if you had screamed I think I might have stopped and never hit you again,' he thought.

"Soon after I started to cane Alex I had a fantasy of a young girl being beaten until she removed her clothes and submitted to my sexual advances, serving me any way I wished. But Alex was safe from my sexual advances, with never a hint of her being the subject in my fantasies until I allowed her to be perverted on that sailing holiday."

"Why did you allow her to go sailing with her friend?"

"My wife suggested it that first time. As Alex got older my wife would not risk playing our sexual games in case Alex heard us. The long weekend was memorable as she played games with me. After that it was easy to encourage Alex to stay over with Andrew. They were like brothers anyway and her appearance remained scruffy. I wish I had never let her go on that bloody sailing trip."

Gareth could feel a belligerence trying to break through to justify his behaviour.

"What did happen after the sailing trip to so upset you?"

"I told you, I had to have her!" he shouted again, a crazy stare in his eyes.

"Art, just tell me quietly, what happened?"

There was a long pause as he stared at the ceiling. No movement, just his breathing, a glassy look to his eyes, then very quietly.

"She walked into the front room transformed, beautiful with grace of movement. Her hair was soft red, groomed and held in a pony tail. The tiny waist was accentuated with a belt, her breasts proud and firm, the nipples through her T-shirt pert and tempting. As she leant to buss my cheek I felt the breast touch my arm, setting me on fire. As she walked away, watching the movement of her body, torturing me with a lust I knew I could not and would not be able to resist. Then she punished me with her silence until I gave her my apology for unjustly caning her and I knew I had lost my authority over her and my control, two blows in one. I brooded in the solitude of my study thinking of ways to regain my control over her. I would imagine her tied to the pillar, her bare back waiting for my pleasure."

"All this was made worse by her new found show of affection, seeking me at night to hug and kiss me goodnight, allowing me to put my arms round her. I felt my hands stray to her buttocks, drawn like a magnet, or to her thighs when she sat close to me on the settee. I would go to her room at night to say goodnight and lean down to kiss her and my hand would seek to touch her breast. As the fantasies recurred in the evenings I would see Alexandra's face, hair, body and scented freshness with pinpoint clarity. She would turn towards me with a beckoning look after she had been over the chair and then submit to my sexual desires. One night, the fantasy of desire welled up inside me, Alex at the centre; nude, desirable and drawing me to her room. I sat on her bed looking at her peaceful face lost in sleep, slowly moving down the bedclothes as she stirred. She appeared frozen in time as I lifted her nightie and I knew she feigned sleep as my hand explored towards her india and as she murmured protests, I silenced her with one hand, forcing her legs apart with the other. I had to have her you see. I had to control her, force her, can't you understand?"

There was a long silence, his face contorted by the memories and the distaste for relating them.

"She should have kept quiet, she gave me my chance to release that horrible desire. When my wife accused me, I denied and made her agree that Alex must be punished for her iniquity. We took her to my study as planned and forcibly tied her to the pillar, blinded her in her shirt, her back exposed. I told my wife to get out; erect and unstoppable with my re-established power over her. The whip in my hand..."

He let out a great yell of despair. The doctor had never seen a man so stricken, tears rolling down both cheeks, an agony of grief on his face and his body racked in self pity. All arrogance dissolved, just a child-like quest for understanding as he lay there. In a strictured whisper he said,

"I nearly killed her."

Next morning Gareth sat at his desk summarising the content of the three hours of consultation, sifting the details and arranging them in chronological order. He sat back and dictated the report using the material from all three sessions. He handed the tapes to his secretary, asking her to make them a priority and to send copies to Doctors Mayhew and Jerald in time for the afternoon research meeting. The meetings they used to discuss new cases and their suitability for inclusion into their study. Doctor Jerald was from Mount Sinai hospital, an endocrinologist who provided the anti-androgen they were using to suppress the aberrant desires in their patients. After the meeting they met informally in Doctor Mayhew's office.

"That was a horror story," Doctor Jerald commented.

"I'd give it a ten for revulsion," Gareth replied, "I had a difficult time being non-judgmental during the consultations."

"I bet you did. What's your impression, Doctor Mayhew?"

"Sadism primarily; incest and pedophilia, although the infliction of pain on a helpless victim had to occur for satisfactory orgasm."

Gareth wondered if he would ever be able to detach himself in Doctor Mayhew's way. Even the scientific terminology could not reduce his autonomic revulsion.

"Would you imply that the youthful sight of infliction of pain was a cause?" Gareth asked.

"Oh no! Most public school boys, in England I mean, would be revolted by the sight. There has to be a deeper desire within the unconscious to be released by the stimulus."

They had had similar discussions before as they tried to understand each individual case. Sometimes they could almost feel compassion but not today.

"Is it potentially there in all of us?"

"Probably not. The research on fantasy content would suggest that sadomasochism is unusual and the mutual acting out of those fantasies rare. Mind you, the research is done mainly on university populations and may not be representative."

"What happens at puberty?" Doctor Mayhew turned to Doctor Jerald to consider his question. "Does testosterone unleash these aberrant desires and our giving anti-androgen cap them again?"

"By cap you mean inhibit or control I assume. Well, in this case, and I think most others, the patients tell us they were aware of them prior to puberty; once they enter puberty they understand what they were feeling. Testosterone potentiates the desire, making it difficult for the 'directory of the forbidden' to maintain control. I always think of the cerebral cortex as the inhibitor and the holder of that 'directory'. As the desires well up from the unconscious they are controlled in the self conscious brain."

"Is 'the directory' in the operating system or the software?" Doctor Mayhew smiled at his computer analogy, "Penfield never got sexual imagery from stimulating the cerebral cortex; he was surprised and commented on it. I would favour it in the unconscious knowing you can make a case for either at the present state of our knowledge."

"Do you think that his use of the prostitute to control his desires was rationalisation?"

"His story consistently reports it, Gareth. Certainly prostitutes provide services for men who perceive that their wives or sexual partners would find obnoxious. He has the recurring theme that he could prevent raping his daughter by making her male, inflicting pain on 'him' and controlling his desires by achieving orgasm with his wife. It could be either true or a justification of his behaviour."

"How old was the daughter?" Doctor Jerald asked Gareth.

"Thirteen when they left her in Vancouver. She must be over twenty by now."

"I wonder what she is like? We know so little about the victims in our research."

"Mentally sub-normal I'd bet," Gareth said.

"Not quite fair," Doctor Mayhew replied, "I agree with Doctor Jerald that we know too little about the victims and those we know about may be biased in favour of the mentally sub-normal. An intelligent child may be more capable of finding a stable family life within the foster parent program or even outside it."

"Doctor Mayhew, no normal child would take that sort of beating without complaining." Doctor Jerald sounded indignant.

"Tell that to the English public schoolboys of my generation."

"Maybe I should have said Canadian child. No, you're right, look what happened in the residential schools across Canada." He got up to put his coat on adding, "many of the puberty rites around the world are centred on endurance of pain as proof of manhood. He consistently said to her to 'take it like a man'."

CHAPTER 12

Sacrifice and Bliss

Standing in a line up, the notice ahead proclaimed, 'Canadian Economy', her heavy cases and back pack suggested that Alex was leaving for longer than six weeks. John arrived from parking the car and helped her with her cases onto the weigh scale. They went to the cafeteria for coffee having arrived far too early, a tendency of all first time flyers. Alex had been in float planes up and down the coast but not on an airline. She was going to Toronto to do her fourth year elective at Mount Sinai Hospital in Endocrinology, a subject that had interested her since first year medical school. They finished coffee and John saw her through security saying good-bye and good luck on her flight. Her apprehension, blamed on this flight, seemed inappropriate. She felt a foreboding hard to pin point almost a premonition which over coffee John had teased her for. Perhaps it was seeing Jim again? He was doing his internship at Toronto General and when she phoned, his new wife invited her to stay with them.

She settled into her elective at the hospital, her interest increasing with the variety. One morning she attended a lecture followed by a seminar given jointly by an endocrinologist and psychiatrist on the treatment of pedophilia. The two physicians were involved with the use of hormones which neutralised testosterone and were successful in counteracting their patients' unnatural desires. Subjectively she found difficulty remaining non-judgmental with those desires, whilst objectively she became interested in the results they were having in helping these patients. The seminar restarted after a break for coffee and took the form of a case presentation by the psychiatrist.

The young looking psychiatrist shepherded his patient into the room and introduced him by his initials A.J. to protect his identity. Alex looked up at the patient from the audience, noting from his profile that he was tall, in his mid fifties she guessed, his hair was grey and his beard a graying sandy colour. She thought 'probably sandy red when younger', and Doctor Gareth Williams asked him about his past history. As he started to speak she felt an adrenaline rush with palpitation and fear. She tried to analyse her overwhelming desire to leave the room. She forced herself to stay in her chair telling herself she was being stupid, behaving like 'a neurotic female'. As she felt her will overcome the urge to flight the reason for her reaction began to clarify. She listened to this patient tell 'her story' in an accuracy of detail that with each act of cruelty remembered left her nauseous with the fear of her youth. Those periods of tremulous waiting, the accurate description of his bonds, the passage of her gas added reality to the relived fear. Her anxiety slowly subsided as she listened, her objectiveness allowing an assessment of the courage it must take for this man to relate his inner most shame with such remorse. Not the remorse of a sickly sweet evangelist but that of a man of great sincerity, she heard his side of the agony of unnatural sexual desire and the voice of her mind.

"By the rivers of Babylon, there we sat down, yea, we wept, when we remembered." Alex obeyed.

If you had asked Alex what she felt she would have told you fear but not pain. Pain is not remembered, only the fear of pain to come. She would tell of the solitude of her spartan life and the careful assessment of all words spoken in his presence; the stress of avoidance of heresy. She would tell you that her God brought Andrew to her. She knew that she must stand up and be counted before he would dispense with his cruelty. She would tell you that 'life for life, eye for eye, tooth for tooth, hand for hand, burning for burning, wound for wound, stripe for stripe' was, in her bitter anger, what she had wished for this patient on the podium. But as he finished his story with the tale of his battered body and her mother's death all told with such directness and truth, the rehabilitation of her father had started in her mind.

She did not remember the discussion following his history. She did remember looking into the face of Doctor Williams and wondering if she could possibly tell him what had happened. Her independent nature gave way to a yearning for John, to talk to him and ask for advice. When she phoned John later that evening, she found she was unable to tell him what had happened, instead chatting lightly about her comfort with Jim and his wife.

Gareth Williams had looked out into his audience as he shepherded Art Jones into his place. He found his eyes fixed on the woman in the audience, wondering who she was and where she had come from. All through the presentation given by his patient with such continuity his eyes kept straying back to her face. He saw some initial discomfort; then a strange mask of blankness covered her face. He saw the tears drop down her cheeks and would remember making a snide judgement of the weakness of female medical students.

Over the ensuing days Doctor Williams found that he was not able to dismiss his attraction to the sandy haired woman and angled for an introduction from his Endocrinologist colleague. Alex was surprised by his directness in asking her to meet him for a drink that Friday evening in the tavern she already frequented. He was sitting waiting for her when they arrived and she introduced him to Jim and Audrey.

There was no strain to their conversation which ranged from her life in Vancouver to his upbringing in Ontario. She was not surprised when he asked her to see him over the weekend. He suggested she might like to drive out to the family farm and even stay overnight there. She accepted his invitation with a spontaneity that surprised him.

He arrived the next morning at the apartment, smiling when he saw her bed on the floor.

"At least you will have a bed tonight," he said, "which should be more comfortable."

Alex didn't argue, just hoped it would not be too soft!

She enjoyed the weekend on the farm, the friendly parents, his brother and sister at the family meal on Sunday after attending the local United Church.

"Can I ask you about the seminar I saw you at?" he asked as they drove back to Toronto.

"Yes," she replied, anxiety welling inside her.

"Why were you upset," he asked, "I couldn't help noticing the tears."

"Because," she was about to fabricate and then totally out of character looked at him, "he is my father."

She found herself telling him the story, reiterating the accuracy with which her father had recounted it at the seminar. Ever the good psychiatrist he had remained quiet, she thought, only to discover later that he had been rendered speechless.

"Entering the seminar room it never occurred to me that the initials A.J. would mean Arthur Jones. I thought my father was in Winnipeg."

"Why Winnipeg?"

"He wrote to me three weeks after Mother died, the only clue to his whereabouts the postmark," Alex told him and continued, "I only discovered that my mother killed herself at the seminar."

"Hence the tears. I thought you were just another over emotional female medical student," he confessed.

"You won't say anything to my father will you?" Alex asked, "I'm not ready to meet him yet. Better he doesn't know I now have his address."

"When I first met you, you said you had wanted to meet me. Was your father the reason; the only reason?"

"Yes," she said, appreciating the true meaning of his question adding, "and yes, I would like to!"

"Like to what?"

"See you again; that is what you are going to ask isn't it?"

"You're very direct," he answered, grinning at her.

"You forget, I was brought up to be one of the boys!"

An easy friendship developed between them over the next week. Alex did not recognise the intensity on his part, 'Andrew would have laughed at her' she thought.

Mid week and Alex was at dinner with him again.

"Will you stay the night, Alex?" One weekend and one evening out did not seem enough to merit such a suggestion.

Whilst she had sought his company to ask about her father she was enjoying Gareth for himself; and yet Alex, always easy in the company of men, had not considered this request in her mind. He was more than a decade older than her as tall, lean and... 'Ugh, don't think of it' flashed through her mind.

"I like your company, Gareth, I enjoy the company of men, but had not thought in terms of a sexual relationship. You've taken me by surprise!"

"Have I offended you?"

"Why do people keep asking me that?" she said, frustrated by this repeated question, "do I appear offended?"

"No, but..."

"But what?"

"Are you aware..." searching for words to match her directness, "just how attractive you are?"

"Yes, I like to attract, I'm a woman, I like to be looked at, noticed, desired and courted. I have resisted it in the past few years for good reason."

She felt trapped by her own easy manner with him, not expecting intimacy, used to unsullied male companionship.

"Taking advantage of your female students, Doctor Williams!"

"You're not studying psychiatry are you?"

"Certainly not," she replied, "Endocrinology, I hope. I will be back in July if I get the internship at Mount Sinai."

"You could come and live with me," he said hopefully.

"A coin has fallen into my lap before," she said, wondering if he would understand.

"At Lydia," he answered, "who was the lucky patron?"

"Jim; we met at fourteen and had an affair for a few years."

"Did he break it off?" Seeing her head shake. "You did. Is there someone else?"

"Yes."

"Still?"

"Yes."

Gareth thought about those other girlfriends who in the past gathered him in, coy, shy, manipulative kittens intent on entrapment in some cases, but never such candour before.

"Who is he?"

"The person?" she answered, "should a psychiatrist assume gender with such assurance?"

"Lesbian, Alex!"

He looked shocked, as she laughed at him wickedly.

"If I do tell you who he is then you will know that he has at last accepted me," she said, adding, "is your invitation still open?"

The evening before she returned to Vancouver she had dinner with Gareth. His companionship during the past three weeks which she had enjoyed and the intimacy, whose pleasure she had almost forgotten, made her accept his invitation to live with him should she get the internship. She wrote to him after she heard she would be going to Toronto.

655 #2 Road
Richmond, BC.

Dear Doctor Williams,

I will be coming to Toronto for my internship. Does your offer still stand?

I make no assumptions, writing to you rather than phoning so that you may write a refusal without pressure. I would enjoy and indeed look forward to your companionship and your gentle tender intimacy. But I make no bones about my duplicity knowing that I cannot offer you love in return.

Whether or not you accept I have another request of you. I would like to meet with my father. I think that if he knew that I was at the seminar and heard him perhaps he would find it easier to agree. I don't think he knows that I'm a medical student (Doctor hopefully). My minister Mr Roberts with whom my father has corresponded twice does not have his address, the social welfare people have failed to trace him and John (my guardian father) has never corresponded with him.

Gareth, if you agree to approach him be honest with him. I have not forgiven him his cruelty and doubt I will ever be able to. I do no longer hold that bitter anger of 'an eye for an eye' and believe I am now able to meet him with a neutral disposition.

I look forward to seeing you again,

Yours
Doctor Alexandra Jones!

Ten days later, by return mail in Canada, she got his reply.

The Clarke Institute.
Toronto, Ont.

Dear Doctor Alexandra Jones,

In addressing you thus, I refute the notion that you are one of the boys! Do, 'Come and live with me and be my love'. You may have your own room and I will enjoy your companionship more than your bed. I will always remain dumbfounded by your candour and do so respect you for it.

I met with your father the afternoon that I received your letter. You may not be aware that he has started a group with other pedophiles, incestuous fathers and teen rapists in association with the Rev James Hayward's church to which I was invited as a guest speaker. I stayed after the others had left in order to tell him of your request. I said that you were in the seminar and approached me after it had ended. Then I let him know about your interning here and read your message to him verbatim. His reaction, a ululation of emotion, sent James scurrying from the room! He asked so many questions that I was unable to answer and none such as 'how is she in bed' that I could have answered. The humour of the last statement should convey the eagerness with which his questions were asked.

your ever eager psychiatrist,
Doctor Gareth Williams!

"That's better, Gareth," she said sipping at the glass of beer, "I didn't mean to be antisocial at the airport. It always seems so uncertain until you get settled at home and feel the nice hard bed."

"That's all right," he answered, looking pleased with her compliment, "I'm the same at airports."

"At least I have a day or two to recover before starting work at the hospital."

"I thought we would eat out tonight so that we can relax and talk."

Gareth took her to a quaint French restaurant near the hospital and within walking distance of his house. The brick floors were cooling in the humid Toronto evening and the antiquated furniture gave the atmosphere of an old country farmhouse with excellent food into the bargain; the wine going to her head unloosing her tongue and flirtatious disposition.

"I've missed you," she confided, her lips pressed together, eyes narrowed and magnetic.

"And I you, Alexandra."

"Have you really, Doctor Barlow." She squealed with self embarrassed mirth at her Freudian slip. "I must explain, Gareth, that whenever John calls me Alexandra I always reply Doctor Barlow. It started on the first sailing trip with them."

"Your guardian father?" he asked to which she nodded. "How do you feel about meeting your real father?"

"Anxious," she shivered, "I know I must meet him, but every time I think of it I feel anxiety turn to nausea and fear. I wish it could just happen out of the blue, no warning, no build up."

He paid the bill, Alex taking the receipt and handing him her share. He tried to decline.

"Always dutch, Gareth."

They watched the news discussing the items. Alex felt at home with Gareth almost as if she had not been back to Vancouver. Their banter reminded her of Andrew with one difference; Gareth found her physically attractive. At the end of the Journal he got up, and put their glasses and cups into the dishwasher.

"Time for bed," he said, "anything you need, Alex?"

"You," she replied watching his face relax, "but after I'll sleep in the nice hard bed."

When she got up next morning she found a note from him asking her to shop for him. He was entertaining a couple of friends for dinner and he said he would be home at four.

He seemed relaxed and organised as they sat to watch the evening news.

"What time are your guests coming?" Alex asked.

"I suggested six thirty."

"Formal?"

"More or less. But not very."

"You're not much help!" she complained. "I'd better shower and dress then."

Alex liked the contrast of her red sandy hair and apricot skin against a dark dress chosen for its simplicity. This one chosen with Anne after lunch together a few days ago had a simple bodice and flared skirt. She hardly used make-up except around her eyes, preferring to adorn herself with the simplicity of her silver Indian motif ear rings and barrette. Tonight she could not resist adding Stephanie's pearls, wanting to make Gareth proud of her. She heard him answer the door still sitting at her dressing table, muffled voices of greeting as coats were accepted and hung, then silence as they went into the sitting room.

She admired herself in the mirror, grinning at the thought of her vanity but pleased with the result. She went downstairs to go into the sitting room to meet their guests. She was approaching the door, and when she knew he was behind it, a wave of anxiety hit her stomach, enormous the desire to turn and run. She took a deep breath and opened the door to look into his eyes as he sat facing her; Gareth crossing the room to lead her to him. She stood looking down at him wondering, 'whose eyes will break their contact first?', not noticing that Gareth and the other guest had left the room.

"Father."

"Alexandra," seeing her frown, "I thought that might allow a new start."

"How are you?" she asked at a loss for words, thinking of herself only, how stultified and awkward; then she saw him his eyes running with uncontrollable emotion. She got up to sit on the arm of his chair taking his head in her arms and held it gently. She remembered the time he sank back into his chair like a pricked balloon and now seeing the top of his head, a broken man. He was just the skeleton of his former self; gone his confidence in the seminar and gone her anxiety and fear. For some minutes he was silent, then drawing his head away looked up.

"That's better," a brief smile, "I had never expected you would want to see me."

"I wanted to see you in court and in my anger cruelly punished. I wanted revenge, I even convinced myself that God justified it. I was bitter for a long time."

"You're a doctor now, I hear."

"Yes, I passed my exams in May and start my first internship in a day or two."

"At Mount Sinai Hospital," he said, "I was a patient there."

"Yes I know," she answered, sensing unsafe ground, "shall we ask the others back?"

As she went to tell Gareth they would enjoy their company and to meet the Reverend James Hayward she was surprised how long it had taken them to say so little. The dinner was ready, the wine poured and the ice broken as she chatted with James. She watched out of the corner of her eye as her father talked comfortably with Gareth.

"Alexandra, how is Andrew?" her father asked from across the table.

"Andrew developed leukaemia in second year university," she said, "and he died eight months later."

"Who was Andrew?" Gareth asked.

Nobody had asked her that before. She wondered at first 'why didn't he know?', recovering to tell him.

"He was my brother."

"I thought you only had one offspring, Art."

"Not real," she said, "my adopted brother, John's son. Have I never told you about him?"

"No."

"Is your parish close by, James?" she asked, purposefully turning the conversation away from Andrew.

"St Mark's Anglican Church is just a few blocks away."

"May I become a temporary member of your congregation? I won't be able to give much time to the social side, I expect."

"You still go to church then?" Her father looked pleased. "Doctor Barlow was not a religious man if I remember."

"He and sometimes Flora would come with me and we discussed religion after church every Sunday morning," Alex said to him. "He has his own personal beliefs and I sometimes think he is more religious than me."

The evening passed in the safe territory of social conversation the past only touched on, never confronted. James told her about her father's continuing commitment to helping other men in similar circumstances.

Even though the evening had gone well once they had left she had a feeling of renewed freedom out of his company. It was still early, the meal and discussion had only lasted three hours. She was exhausted from the tension and still uptight.

"I could drink another glass of wine, Gareth."

"I hope," he said pouring her wine, "that you really meant out of the blue and no warning?"

"If you had told me I could not have come down to meet him. I knew he was in the room just before I opened the door and nearly bolted."

He brought her wine and sat next to her and took her hand, silent for a while.

"You never told me about Andrew. Did you love him?" he asked with professional curiosity.

"Andrew," she smiled at the thought of him, "oh, yes, I loved him like nobody else. He was my saviour."

"Was he a good lover?"

"He must have been; they fell for him left, right and centre!" She laughed seeing his puzzled look. "He was my beloved brother, no incest there. I loved the little runt with intense tolerance. I could tell him, discuss with him or argue with him about anything, I eventually told him about my life with graphic honesty, an abreaction which I knew sickened him almost as much as his first view of my back. I never had a girl friend, I had Andrew who I asked about my feelings, emotions, dreams wet and dry, day or night, argued religion, science and delved into literature with him. I pricked him with lances about his terrible treatment of women, a megalomaniac lecher, but I still loved him with sisterly tolerance."

Alex entered the church just before seven, the small congregation in the side chapel indicating that communion would be celebrated at its small altar. She saw her father alone in a pew and took her place next to him. The certainty of the familiar litany and prayers of the communion service gave her comfort. Sitting back during the communication talking to her God shyly asking if he approved. So deep in meditative thought.

"The peace of God which passeth all understanding..." She heard coming from the altar as James gave the blessing. Remembering that her father was beside her she stole a glance in his direction.

She followed her father out of the church and they went to the Rectory. Furnished with bachelor utility and comfort, the large kitchen table was already set for breakfast for three. James preparing the bacon and eggs, her father fixing the coffee and fussing with the toast, avoiding conversation. Sitting together, their plates in front of them, their eyes closed in an unspoken grace; they started to eat in silence.

"Butter and marmalade, Alex?"

"Thank you, James."

The terrible silence of her youth returned, regretted and now rejected.

"Art!" she had decided not to address him as father, "stop eating and tell me about your group," she said, thrown out like a challenge to surprise him.

"There are about twenty who attend the meetings."

"What do you discuss?"

"We run them like AA meetings. Sometimes a guest speaker, but usually one of us gets up and tells of his experience."

"All men, no women?"

"No women; others will respond to his experience giving ideas of their own, the meeting lasts about two hours."

"Do you all have similar problems?"

"Most are pedophiles, some have had incest with their daughters, in one case a son."

"Are you all on Cyproterone?"

"What's that?" James asked.

"A hormone that acts against testosterone and other androgens." She watched to see if James understood.

"We are all in the study group."

"Do they work well?"

"For most of us," he replied, "there are a few exceptions and they need to talk a lot."

As she questioned him he appeared to become more relaxed the answers given with ease. She was due at the hospital at ten, a good half-hour walk.

"It's after nine, Art, I should be walking back to the hospital. Would you like to walk with me?"

"I'd like that."

They walked in silence and after a few minutes she took his arm and saw a smile on his lips.

"Did my questions bother you?"

"At first, Alexandra."

"What about at second?"

"As you sounded more like a doctor I found myself relaxing."

"You seemed smaller at the seminar; today you have grown taller."

"Ah! I have a beautiful woman on my arm," he told her, looking pleased with himself.

Alex noted this first hint of humour with pleasure as they were approaching the entrance to the hospital.

"Will I see you at communion next Sunday, Art?"

"Will you come to breakfast after, Alexandra?"

Alex developed less and less anxiety with each Sunday breakfast spent in his company. Their conversations were held to a safe clinical objectivity with Alex learning that, as in her reading of Havelock

Ellis, there were no two cases alike. Those artificial attempts at classification into pre or post pubertal sexual or physical abuse would be defied by many individual cases. Judging by the twenty or so in his group the combinations of physical and sexual desires were myriad. He told her about the other men describing their confessions at his meetings, all reporting that their aberrant desires were insatiable, all trying to justify them until they were caught and had to face the consequences.

"They have all been in prison."

"Are you the only exception, Art?"

"Yes," he replied, "I think it delayed my getting help. I wonder if your mother would have taken her own life under different circumstances."

She looked at him and saw the pain in his expression, the beard covering his facial contortions, the sad eyes with their watery glaze and his turning away from her in his grief. She knew that this was no 'Swaggert' act and felt compassion for him.

"You have been in a prison of your own design, Art. Did you ever feel that the police were looking for you?"

"No," he said pensively, his chewing mouth giving him time to phrase his reply, "I didn't change my name, my private company is still with my name as director and uses my Toronto address."

"What private company?"

"I have a private company into which I placed all my property. Ever since going into real estate I have bought and sold on my own behalf. I lived off my salary until I left Richmond and since then on the proceeds of my investments."

"Is it registered in Ontario?"

"No. British Columbia."

"You mean the police could trace you through the company?"

"Yes."

"I had a feeling they were not trying when I so wanted revenge."

"I covered my tracks carefully in the first year but after that I stopped trying. I sold the house in Richmond through the company, your mother was a director and used her maiden name to sign the papers."

"Are you very broke? Do you need help financially?"

He was silent for some time looking embarrassed at the offer of assistance.

"You don't need to be ashamed of needing my help, Art."

"I'm not ashamed of needing your help, I'm ashamed of not needing it."

"I don't understand."

"The value of the assets is over five million now." He said it simply, no hint of pride or bragging.

With each successive Sunday breakfast their conversations became less objective and more searching. Alex told him about the sailing trip during which she resolved never to be physically abused again. They pieced their stories together weaving an intricate relationship of her need for an intimate family and his terror at his irresistible aberrant desire 'to have her'.

"What do you mean by have me?"

"My desires said 'you must have her'."

"To make love to me?"

"Oh no, force you, make you do what I want, control you. All wrapped into 'I must have her'. All masked with neat excuses for trying to get you. When not aroused my mind tells me clearly it would be wrong. Some men describe it as the beast inside us."

"I longed to have a father to whose arms I could fly for compassion and comfort."

"That just encouraged the beast to escape."

Alex had a final question that she was getting closer and closer to asking. She rehearsed his answers in her mind, 'I had been drinking', 'you made me so angry', 'my desire was too strong', or even 'you deserved it'. Her ultimate question was asked before Christmas.

"Why did you whip me, Art?"

Wondering which of her complex answers would be woven into his reply, the simplicity of his statement shocked her.

"Because I wanted to," he said quietly, "I had always wanted to whip a woman, to see her hand tied and defenceless like the times I beat you."

"Does the drug take that desire away?"

"Yes, the sadistic desire is part of my deviation," he looked at her, "but that was no excuse for my crime against you, Alexandra."

"Even trying to understand your behaviour as a physician I still cannot forgive you."

"Nor should you."

They were to return to this topic on other occasions with the same conclusion. Even after he discussed his wish to finance a foundation whose aim would be to identify men with pedophilia and give them preventive care she was unable to be as magnanimous as Jesus.

Soon after arriving in Toronto, Alex contacted Mary and went to dinner with them. Ann, now twenty, was studying business and commerce at the university and had moved out of home to an apartment not far from the hospital area. Alex told her about the tavern frequented by her crowd and Ann would join them from time to time. An easy friendship developed now that their age difference seemed so much less. David was in his last year of high school still uncertain of his career. Ted appeared more distinguished with age and she found him better company than she remembered from the visit for Christmas ten years before.

In coming to live with Gareth, Alex had a hidden agenda; she secretly hoped to overcome her obsession with John. She was not ready to talk to him about John. She knew that were it not for John she could easily learn to love Gareth and would consider settling down in marriage to him. Her pleasure in his company grew as she became wrapped up in her work at the hospital. Returning home to enjoy his company was a pleasurable relief from medical care. She was touched by his kindness cherishing his concern for her well-being. He never tried to deflect her from her Sunday morning breakfast meetings with her father, instead going off to the family farm for church and lunch. On Sunday evenings at supper he was ever ready to discuss her latest meeting with Art. As summer moved into fall she became very comfortable under his roof.

On Sunday evening she would phone John to tell him about her experiences at the hospital, never letting him know of her emerging comfort with Gareth. She found herself unable to talk to him about her meetings with her father. Then two events altered the comfortable course of this present life.

One Friday night in late November, desperately tired with the week's intensive work at the hospital, she arrived home expecting an early night looking forward to a relaxing hot tub followed by easy intimacy with Gareth. As she entered the house Gareth was putting the phone down.

"What's the matter?"

"Doctor Mayhew has been admitted to hospital with chest pain leaving a message requesting me to introduce the speaker at the Institute lecture tonight."

"Who is speaking?"

"An emeritus professor from Sarah Lawrence, quite notable in his way."

"Does he have a name?"

"Campbell, Joseph Campbell," he replied, a beseeching look, "would you come with me to help entertain him at dinner after the lecture?"

"I was so looking forward to my hot bath and..."

"You can still have it, there's time," he interrupted.

"And you afterwards!" she continued ogling him, laughing at him caught between a rock and a hard place. "Duty before pleasure. Okay, what time?"

"You bath and change. I'll get us a light snack and we need to be there at seven thirty. We can take him out to dinner afterwards on the institute."

She sat in the audience impressed by the full to capacity lecture hall, still asking herself 'what am I doing here when I could be at home relaxing; who needs yet another lecture?' She watched Gareth accompany a surprisingly robust man to the podium, introducing him with apparent ease, outlining his academic attainments as if he had known him for years.

"Professor Campbell has chosen 'Sacrifice and Bliss' as the topic for his lecture this evening."

There was a burst of applause, the lights dimmed and a slide of Salvador Dali's painting 'Crucifixion' was projected onto the screen, focusing audience attention on God's sacrifice of Jesus his son, then tracing various myths on the same theme from all over the North American continent. He then took his audience further afield pointing out the consistency of human inner thought from all parts of the world as expressed in their myths. She had never been swept up by a lecture before, totally engulfed, time meaningless and not wanting him to stop. The applause rang through the hall at the conclusion and as she clapped she thought 'and I'm to have dinner with this man, how intimidating'.

Gareth was now on his feet calling the audience to be quiet. "Professor Campbell has offered to answer questions from the audience," greeted by another burst of applause.

"In your book on *Joyce's Finnegan's Wake*, Sir, how did you come to the conclusion that 1132 represented a biblical text?"

Alex saw a slow smile of pleasure spread across Campbell's face at this question. He told of the time when he was preparing for a class on Joyce's book and he had been rereading St Paul's Epistle to the Romans. As he read he stumbled on the statement 'for God has assigned all men to disobedience, that he may show his mercy to all' only to discover that it was Romans chapter 11 verse 32. He went on to tell them that Luther had suggested that men should 'sin bravely' for however great the sin it would only challenge the greatness of God's mercy. She reflected on her father's sin against her, asking 'does he have that much mercy?' She wondered if it was a message for her, putting it aside for her discussion with God on Sunday.

All her tiredness was gone and replaced by anticipation of having dinner with this man. When they got to the restaurant there were just the three of them.

They settled with a bottle of wine circulating, all formality buried. She felt as if she were entertaining a favourite uncle and as the meal progressed he was telling them his favourite Iroquois myths; then Alex found herself replying with the story of Axelnadar which John had told at Minstrel Island.

"I've not heard that story before, Alex."

"It was made up by John when I was sailing with him in Kwakiutl country. I was a great friend of his son Andrew and when we were anchored in the deserted Indian village of Matilpi I had my first period. He made us make up our own stories each night. It was a magical cruise."

"Did you understand who Axelnadar was?"

"I asked John if it was me, but he did not reply."

"But of course it was you; its your anagram."

"Then who was Wrablord?"

"Ah, when you know that you will also know your bliss."

It was after midnight before they left the restaurant. As they were putting on their coats to get him into his taxi he turned to her.

"Thank you for an entertaining evening," he said, his eyes piercing her shield, "you know your bliss now, don't you, Alex?"

"Yes."

"Then follow it."

The taxi door closed and they watched him depart.

"An extraordinary evening, Alex." She nodded and walked home in silence under Gareth's steady gaze. They entered the house, sat for a while before she went upstairs to change for bed and joined him. In their lovemaking she was once again joined with her bliss and knew she was compelled to follow it.

On Sunday evening she phoned Vancouver telling John about her meeting and having dinner with Joseph Campbell, her excitement with his lecture, telling him she would like to have one of their Sunday morning discussions about its content. Then John told her that he had accepted Mary's invitation to come to Toronto for Christmas and he would be there in less than three weeks.

Mary asked her to stay with them over Christmas or New Year, depending which holiday time she would be permitted at the hospital. Gareth had asked her to go to the farm with him for Christmas. Now she felt she should accept Mary's invitation, not wanting to let Gareth know that John was the real reason. Lots were drawn among the staff and she had Christmas off and New Year on duty.

John visited her at the hospital the day after he arrived and she took him around after they had attended Grand Rounds together. The five days off for Christmas in his relaxed company exchanging news bringing her up to date on the home front, meeting at breakfast over coffee and discussing some of Joseph Campbell's ideas had been bliss. As his visit drew to a close she yearned to pack her bags and return to Vancouver with him, carefully avoiding difficult good-byes to keep it hidden.

Back with Gareth, working hard at her hospital duties to make the time pass quickly, he, always perceptive and thoughtful, realised that the break had disturbed her, guessing that John's visit had something to do with it.

"Did you tell John about meeting with your father?"

"No, I couldn't face it."

"Is that what has upset you?"

"Am I upset, Gareth?" she asked, playing for time.

"Unsettled at least," he replied and with a flash of insight that he thought might unravel her, "will you marry me, Alex?"

"I think, Gareth, that you know the answer to that and maybe the reason it must be no."

"John?"

"Why did you say that?"

"You did not want me to meet him and an educated guess."

"I thought 'if I get away and live with Gareth, John will become less of an obsession and that I might even fall in love with you'. After the dinner with Joseph Campbell, telling him the story of Axelnadar I knew who Wrablord was. I yearned to go back to Vancouver with him."

"At least you can now believe that he is not your father."

"I've taken advantage of you."

"It's a two-way street."

"Do you want me to move out?"

"I need the rent!"

"Can you accept me as 'one of the boys', eh!"

"Alex! What a suggestion."

At breakfast after communion near the end of her internship in Toronto she was with James Hayward; her father not yet returned from the church.

"Would you read a special epistle at communion next Sunday morning?"

"Depends what you request."

"From Romans eleven to include verse thirty two?"

"I'll consider it," he answered as her father came into the kitchen and they sat down for breakfast.

When James came to the epistle the next Sunday morning he announced that he had been asked to read from chapter 11 of St Paul's epistle to the Romans by Alexandra Jones.

"Alexandra," he announced, "will be returning to Vancouver next week and we will miss her."

At the end of the service the small but regular congregation stayed behind to wish Alex bon voyage, detaining her so that Art and James were waiting for her to start breakfast. They held hands for the silent grace.

"Thank you, James, for the epistle," she said as they started to eat.

"An interesting choice, Alex," James replied, "was it a message for your father?"

"Yes," she answered and turned to her father, "Art, I may be too human to be able to forgive, but I believe that God is merciful, however sinful we are."

She watched her father who seemed smaller again, bent over and defeated.

"Will you correspond with me now, Art?"

"I would like that, Alexandra."

CHAPTER 13

John *** Alex + + +

* * * * *

Pounding against the northwest wind early in the morning along the familiar channel from Forward Harbour to Forward Bay, the seas of the Johnstone Strait running even this early, tide against wind steep and crested, *Never Satisfied II* corkscrews her way past Gunner Point. "Should we take refuge in Blenkinsop?" I ask, to be told I'm getting soft in my middle years. Only seven in the morning, the fuel tank full and with the promise of a lessening sea off Port Neville we soldier on. Anyway I want to be in Matilpi tonight, or even Minstrel if the Chatham Channel permits, to meet Alex's plane in the morning.

News from Alex over the past year had been chattily inconsequential, her secretive nature uppermost in my mind when I heard from Anne and Doug that Jim approved of her friendship with Gareth Williams; 'although a little old for her,' he had commented, 'almost as old as John', he had said. I knew she was staying with him, certain now that there was more than friendship. A bitter sweet morrow on my mind for the news she would bring with her. The year without her an empty vessel, a time past year no present contentment and now an altered future. I shiver at the morbid thoughts, 'push them aside and savour the next four weeks' companionship together. Stop it, you self pitying old bugger' wondering what was reflected on my face, 'cheer up, cheer up, there no such thing as sweet sorrow, well not at my age.'

The soliloquy of thought continued unabated, a mixtured memory lane with daydreamt tomorrows, 'what if's, what if she were at the wheel, did she ever look back, remember the intensity in those eyes, she looked back just to make sure she was ahead, always racing.' The rhythm of movement certain now that Jesse Island is astern. The sun beginning to warm my back, my face cold from the head wind, nose atingle with ears unfelt. 'Will the rigged wheel hold now the sea is constant, try it, yes; ah sweet relief,' the steam rising from the bucket, the plastic warmed. Careful in this wind, the yellow stream from bucket to sea. Hot coffee in the thermos, feet working from side to side, calves contracting, circulate the heat from stomach to feet. 'Stimpson Reef in sight now, no chance of sleep this morning and no whale today to jump a greeting,' a reactive smile at the remembrance, 'I must be a cat, how many lives left,' I wonder.

Matilpi, at anchor now, swinging in the wind which comes first from port then from starboard, sitting in the late afternoon sun, memories extracted from my modular mind, her first menses, 'the white face tortured by the blood trickling down her thighs; something awful wrong, Dad!' Nobody told her to expect this, my unsmiling face wretched with having the responsibility of telling. Where are you Anne when I need you, remembered! Babbling Andrew questions, questions; shut up Andrew! Get through the channel first, she's beauty face asleep, the purchase of pads and belt, giggle to uncontrolled laughter. Intense faces watching for honesty, 'are you kidding me? I'd never do that'; St Peter? 'I saw Jim kiss you,' blush!

Tears were streaming down my cheeks, distress echoed in the loudly spoken cry, "she's not my daughter!" Then whispered time and time again to the andante agony of the music, "she's not my daughter."

A Rawson thirty came round the island into the bay providing relief from my memories, a boat of acquaintance, company for happy hour and the evening meal taking away the melancholy images as preparation of the meal assumes the mind's control. Memories tried to return briefly before sleep suppressed in part by food, wine and company.

Now it's morning, time to leave for Minstrel Island. 'She'll be here soon.'

The spray rising from the plane's floats on contact with the smooth sea.

'She's here, welcome, Alex, welcome. She'll be running, running towards my arms, swung around in joy, oh welcome.'

There she was, standing on the dock handing down her tote bag, as I walked over to her.

"Hi, Alex."

"Hi, John," she said, punching my shoulder, lightly.

"Good flight?" I asked, "you're early."

"Bumpy, like a leaf," she told me, "there's wind out there."

We walked to the boat, she stowed her bags and came up on deck. "Do you need anything here?" she asked brusquely.

"No, nothing, why?"

"Let's go then."

She stood looking towards the settlement, 'were her memories the same?'

"Where to?" I asked, and gave her a slip of paper, "no, write it. Will we be of like mind?" Two slips of paper and one common word; Mamalilaculla.

Across the bay from the rotting timbers of the Mamalilaculla pier a small inlet allows access into the forest. Entering this Emily Carr treescape, its tree trunk columns reaching to a canopy of evergreen fantail, the quiet atmosphere of religiosity enhanced by the muffled forest floor. No echoes here, just the movements of nature, and yet a holy place of unseen spirits where past and future gather. As we walked in the intense silence broken only by snapping twigs, the forest incense wafting our nostrils, I watched Alex, lithe body with grace of gazelle, move through the trees relaxed and carefree. Stopping at the huge cedar tree trunk, looking up reciting the Kwakiutl prayer:

'Look at me friend! I come to ask for your dress, for you have come to take pity on us: for there is nothing for which you cannot be used, because it is your way that there is nothing for which we cannot use you, for you are really willing to give us your dress.'

She stopped, "I can't remember how it finishes; can you, John?"

How silent she had been today up to this point.

"Are you too reliving the past in this Andrew-infested place?"

"It's like being in church."

I nodded and smiled at our telepathy.

"Can I make my confession with you here in this place? I'm in love," she said before I could answer. And so the moment I always feared. I felt the heckles rise in my neck; anxiety, almost terror, at the thought of losing her.

"I hope he is worthy of you."

"Oh, I will tell you with whom, this is a confession, remember."

"You don't have to if the abstract is easier." I was thinking Eliot again, 'What might have been is an abstraction remaining a perpetual possibility only in a world of speculation.'

She went ahead of me out of the trees onto the sea shore, silhouetted against *Never Satisfied II* swinging in the breeze, she sat down on the rocks.

"Let me tell you the problems first and then you will know who; he is older than I, could be my father," her voice cracking, "however much I tried, he keeps returning as the only person I need and I cannot deny it any longer."

"Did you meet at Med school," I asked, "one of your teachers?"

"No, a doctor and a teacher though."

The blessed afternoon wind from the northwest was starting to rustle the trees releasing me from this conversation; the conclusion I wished to evade.

"I think we are about to get our westerly and should row back," I said, conscious that I was becoming mawkish and trying not to show my wretchedness. In the boat as I rowed she looked at me through narrowed eyes and the set of her face warned me of the difficulty of expression for her. There was silence between us now, an unfinished confession, and the expected wind had died.

"I think I will see if I can get some rock cod for supper," she said, "do you want to come?"

"I think I'll read awhile."

"Pass down the outboard."

"Please, Alexandra," I said, trying to lighten my own tension.

"Thank you, Doctor Barlow."

I watched her go into Eliot Passage and settled back in the cockpit with my book. I read without concentration, knowing that I was absorbing nothing. Resting my head against the cabin sole my eyes closed I knew that Alex's confession had ruffled my feathers. 'Was I the father seeing his daughter taken away? Or a jealous Bartolo afraid of losing a dowry? Jealous, yes, and she was not my daughter and there was no dowry. Had I not encouraged independence? Now she was to take the last step, should I not be satisfied with my own success? Was I mourning for the past when I had been allowed to love her in nurturing; when did it change to melancholy daydreaming reminiscent of those perchancely planned meetings with Stephanie? Tickle or lust of an eleven year itch desiring to be assuaged? Now

must I accept the reality of an older man as a statutory son-in-law!
You're just a silly moralist, lacking in conviction or just frightened
by what the neighbours would think.'

I went forward restlessly to see her, she was off Clock Rock in
Knight Inlet fishing; I returned to the cabin to get the binoculars
intending to signal to her but as I watched it appeared that she was
alongside a black object in the water. Dismissing it as an illusion but
continuing to follow her she seemed to part from the object and then
a conical white shape came out of the water, which disappeared in a
ripple of wavelets.

+ + + + +

The little outboard smoothed her towards Pearl Island into Knight
Inlet where she hoped for action off Clock Rock. She had felt her
face reflect that bland look of pent-up emotion not appreciating that
John had deflected the confession. She saw the kelp of the rock
ahead dropping her Buzz Bomb over the side let it touch the bottom
some six fathoms below. 'A good place,' she thought, as the first
strike came almost immediately and a good size as well. It did not
take long for the gathering of supper and she allowed the dinghy to
drift back towards Eliot Passage. She longed for Andrew, to talk to
him, feeling that only he would understand. She did not see the fin
the first time it broke the surface half a mile away but heard the
exhaling of air and saw the waves on the water's surface. A few
minutes later the fin broke the surface a few feet from her as B-10
edged alongside the dinghy. Then the head, the blow hole issuing a
rush of halitosis, putting her hand down on the whale's back Andrew
came into her mind, that smile of welcome and recognition. At peace
and still, Andrew asked of John, and she assured him of his health.
He was puzzled by her need to see him until he comprehended her
love for his father.

"I just tried to tell John that I loved him. We were in the forest
cathedral as I started my confession."

"What did you say, Alex?"

"I told John I was in love with an older man," she said, "then that
he was a doctor. I saw his hurt face and could not continue in case
he rejected me."

"Alexandra, still so naive and now so selfish, don't you know he has always loved you? When you came to live with us you never accepted him as your father."

"He's not my father."

"Dad's a stern moralist, Alex. As your father, to express carnal desire for you would be for him incestuous. He has been holding it back and now you tell him you're in love with an older man, a doctor. You bet he looks hurt, he thinks he's missed his chance. It almost killed him to see you apparently in love with Jim and now this. Do you think he has not heard about your older companion in Toronto?"

"How did you know, Andrew?"

"Never you mind; more important, he knows. The afternoon when we discussed my will, I asked him if he would be upset if I left everything to you. He told me he had suggested a will for that reason. I tried to tell him that you loved him when he told me he had just changed his own to include you. I said 'you're struck on that girl' and he looked sheepish without replying. What sort of torturer are you anyway?"

"Andrew, stop it."

"Good, so you should be tearful."

"Oh, shut up."

"No I won't. You have been in love with him since you were fourteen. A crush at first, then the love of a daughter for her father. But it became much more didn't it? Sure, you enjoyed sex with Jim and Gareth, but you were never able to say 'I love you' to either of them. You don't have to tell me why. You're both as nutty as fruit cakes about each other. He can't tell you, Alex. It's your duty to tell him and put an end to this stupid fencing with each other's love. Is that clear?"

Alex found this passage of thoughts unworldly and, as previously, suspected that she was wish generating, but how did he know about the will and Gareth. Her hand rested on his head for some time until he breathed again showering her with blow.

"You haven't answered me yet!"

"I'll tell him after my shower. If you're wrong I'll come after you and shoot you with an explosive harpoon."

"Has he told you about Stimpson Reef?"

"Not that I recall."

"I bet he hasn't told anyone yet, too frightened people will think he's barmy! Last year he was powering north when I passed him at Port Neville. I jumped for him. Then I saw *Never Satisfied* seemed to be too close to shore. As I approached I realised that Dad was sleeping. I just managed to push the keel away from the reef before he would have hit. I jumped for him again, but I bet he hasn't twigged that it was me," then she sensed John's voice, "you can't prove it scientifically, Alex," making her laugh out aloud at the sensed mimicry.

She was laughing as his head drifted under water and she thought he had gone. His nose came slowly out of the water as he skyhopped his farewell. His great snout seeming to smile in happy ecstasy as his teeth showed and she knew she had talked to Andrew and not to herself.

* * * * *

I saw her go to shore with the filleting knife to clean the fish noticing her complete change in mood. As she returned to the boat I went forward to weigh anchor. As we powered the short distance to the anchorage between Maud and Pearl Islands I remembered the first story she told, about 'Big Figure', that had truly taken my attention, trying to remember its content.

"Are the sunshowers hot, Alex?" I called forward to where she was sitting.

"Just right."

"I'll shower now before anyone else gets here," I told her, looking forward to showering on deck so that I could soap myself better than being cramped in the cockpit corner. The sun was warm on the bathrobe as I went to the cabin. As Alexandra showered on the foredeck, washing her hair and luxuriating in the flow of hot water, I, spying on her from the cabin whilst getting the happy hors d'oeuvre, tried not to allow myself to think juxtaposition from guardian to lover, felt frustration tinged with jealousy at the thought of so lucky another man and stirred our Bloody Marys with a stick of celery.

I was passing up the drinks and snacks as she emerged in her bathrobe from the forward cabin.

"I'll pass the rest up to you if you go up there," I said, holding out her drink. She bypassed the drink, stayed in the cabin and stood looking at me, then put her arms on my shoulders gently pulling me towards her.

"You're the one in my confession, John."

At first unable to comprehend, or was it a refusal to comprehend.

"Oh Alexandra, what are you saying?"

"That I love you, we are made for each other and I want you. I have waited long enough for you to release me from your guardianship."

"But I am your guardian in law and have had to regard you as my daughter even against my will."

"Against your will!"

Her countenance was changing to reflect her dissipating tension.

Her hand passed down my back as she looked into my eyes. Her other hand held my chin, not allowing me to look away, insisting on an answer.

"Is it lust, Alex?"

My own guilt ridden desire reflected in the question.

"That too," she tendered, "I love you, have done since that first summer."

"Are you sure?"

Her hand pulling my chin towards her, her lips parting soft, her tongue exploring. Fighting the revelation of my desire she pressed against me, my response all too obvious, she released my chin.

"Yes, and so is your son," she replied, her hand dropped down to untie my bathrobe. Part bending, part kneeling, she opened the robe, looked at me and kissed me. "Thank you," she said, and closed the robe.

"What for?"

"For desiring me."

I was bewildered by the suddenness of her revelation that meshed with my own longings and yet not able to trust the reality pinching at myself against the fraudulence of a dream. Climbing up to the cockpit to join our drinks, pretending it was a happy hour like any other, but behaving now like shy children, brief glances at each other's face across the cockpit, wistful smiles, mine tinged by a lingering guilt. The tension in my arms shaking the Bloody Mary which, reaching my lips, jittered my teeth. The needed alcohol slowly soothing the tremor. I snatched glimpses of her demure face revealing her greater comfort.

"How am I to tell our friends that I..."

"Anne knows, so Doug will know; Jim, Jessica and Allison know and even Flora knows that I intended to tell you. Do you recollect that I went to consult Anne just before Andrew died?" I nodded. "She sensed that you were the reason I could never tell Jim I loved him. Anne took Andrew's place as my confidant at least until I met Allison. I enjoyed Jim's company in and out of his bed and after seeing Anne was very honest with him. He knew I would not stay with him. Gareth was my 'invitation to dinner!' a stop gap," she said, bending the truth of the past to justify the present, "I needed the intimacy after watching Jim and Audrey."

"I hated it when Jim stayed overnight," I heard myself say.

"My jealous Doctor Bartolo," she poked her tongue at me, "I told Gareth about you six months ago and never slept with him again. Like Jim he's become a good friend. Anyway my mind wasn't making love to them, it was always you I lusted after!" she said with narrowed eyes and a smug look full of saucy humour.

We finished our drinks, argued about who would get the supper, eventually allowing me to do so. I watched her gather her clothes from the forward cabin and move them onto my bed. We talked about destinations over supper, deciding on Waddington Harbour the next day.

+ + + + +

Love consummate she lay, head propped, looking down at his close eyed face and quoted almost imperceptibly, "for thy sweet love remembered such wealth brings." His eyes opened, a sour look crossed his face.

"Am I in disgrace with fortune in men's eyes?" he whispered, "look upon myself and curse my fate?"

"Unfortunate quote!" she said, "what's bothering you?"

"The neighbours."

"What they will say?" she grimaced, "who cares."

"Not what they say Alex, what they will think," he said pausing, silent, except to sigh, "what I think they will be thinking."

"John not comfortable with John?"

"H'm, no element of guilt, Alex?"

"Men! Always so much guilt about sex. None for me; I never let you be an intimate father. At first I did not trust fathers, you might have tried to force me as he did. Later when I had a terrible crush on you I was frightened to show any intimacy for fear of me. Lastly when I knew I loved you I feared your rejection."

"Mary asked why you never showed me affection when saying goodnight."

"That changed tonight!" Teasing him. "How come you don't turn over and go to sleep."

"You haven't said good night yet," he taunted and chucked her chin, "we used to have long, relaxed conversations."

"You and Stephanie?" she asked, and seeing him affirm, "how do I compare?"

A flash of anger crossed his brow.

"If you ever ask that again," he said tautly, "I'll put you over my knee."

Her face went blank, her eyes burned with fury.

"No man will ever do that again," she spat. "How do I compare!"

"Ooh! A justifiably raw nerve," he said, reaching for her face with his lips.

"Demon," she replied, her humour returned.

"I don't remember, Alex," he said seriously, "if it were not for her photograph I don't think I could even remember her face. I remember happiness, laughter, her nakedness, our conversations but not the act. Wilder Penfield in his brain stimulation experiments reported that nobody described memories of sex."

"I guess you're right," she replied, trying to conjure up Jim or Gareth, remembering only that they satisfied.

"Can I keep my dinner dates?" he asked, teasing her.

"Who was she?" Inquired with the accent on 'was'.

"She is married now. I was so delighted when she told me; she deserves to be happy and is by all accounts."

"But who was she?" An edge to the question.

"Unless she tells you, you will never know. No, Alex not Flora."

"Do I know her then?"

"You have met her," he replied with a finality that told her it was pointless to wheedle anymore. She left the bed for the head, struggling into her dressing gown.

"Can I get you anything?"

"Would you like hot chocolate?" he asked, getting up to join her.

"With or without?"

"With, just like old times although I still miss Andrew. He used to steal it," she pointed to the brandy, "but I've already told you."

"Before or after you told us your story."

"Long before. He used to put it in a little bottle during the day and kept in his bunk. It was a riot trying to put it in the chocolate at night without you seeing."

"What else did you get up to?"

"I'll tell you as I remember."

The kettle boiled and the chocolate liberally dosed with brandy, they settled back into the bunk.

"Will you always talk to me after?"

"Not if you keep reminding me with your misdeeds of youth when I was supposed to be your father."

"They weren't mine, they were Andrew's."

"Do you remember the day we were returning from Peter's office on the north shore?"

"Yes." She yawned, relaxed by the brandy, her eyes closed.

"You mimicked me, 'did she reason with you'. Do you recall what I said?" he asked, but he looked down to see she was asleep, leant down and touched her forehead, "you haven't changed."

* * * * *

Waddington Harbour, the northwest wind trying to blow us off our anchor, the wind coming in gusts making sleep impossible. One on watch and the other watching the watch, eventually we both sat in the cold cockpit and talked.

"This reminds me of the first night we spent in Clam Bay."

"You and Andrew?"

"Yes, so calm when we turned in then it started to blow after dark. I was quite concerned, we spent the night drinking hot chocolate. It seemed that one of us was always peeing over the side. Once I remember laughing at Andrew for not taking account of the wind. It took a while for him to see the funny side; we both felt mad at the wind."

"I could not equate his actually enjoying being with you. I thought you forced him to go with you. He was evasive when talking about you; then I came for the weekend and believed."

"Did you enjoy that first weekend or were you scared of sailing?"

"I wasn't scared of sailing!"

"Scared of what?"

"You and Douglas. Just as I gained confidence something would happen to dash it. I wasn't comfortable until after Pirates Cove, but once you knew what was happening to me that was understandable."

"What was I like?"

"Great. You kept on taking your clothes off!"

"No chance of that tonight."

The wind didn't moderate and I took the first two hour watch changing turn and turn about until morning when the wind dropped.

+ + + + +

In Joe Cove, a strange little anchorage entered through a rock strewn narrow channel, had a fresh water creek at its head. The ravens complaining in constant 'Gwas' interspersed with beak clacks. The reason clear in the trees; there were three juvenile and two adult eagles sitting looking down on the creek. The juveniles were restless children on and off of their perches, like kittens in a box swirling and weaving with each other in the air. As evening closed early in this bay surrounded by cliffs there was a long period of dusk after supper. Warm in sweaters we were entertained by the sounds and movements of nature.

"Put on some of your music, John."

'Then I will know your mood,' she told herself.

Faure's late piano quintet came from the speakers, the first movement listened to silently. The fast short second movement, Allegro vivo, was frenetic.

"One part of me feels free, energetic with romantic love; that youthful vibrancy of my whirlwind courtship with Stephanie. Andrew was conceived as a child of frenetic love. I feel twenty again, our whole life ahead confident and strong," he said, her contentment obvious.

Then the slow movement began his change in mood, his arm along the cockpit sole requesting her to move close. Her head rested against his shoulder, then slowly he slid her head onto his lap as he saw Andrew do at Hardy Island, stroking her hair. She tried to sit up but his firm hand restrained her.

"What's the matter?"

"I don't want to be seen."

"There must be tears on your cheeks, Doctor Barlow."

"Oh shut up, Alexandra," he snapped in imitation anger, "I used this music whenever you upset me."

"I heard it often."

"When I saw you could not trust me yet, if Jim stayed over, when you were working so hard at Med school and I did not see you often or this past year after Jim said, 'I approve of Gareth, although almost as old as John,' which stabbed like a mortal wound. In Matilpi the night before you arrived I listened saying over and over 'but she's not my daughter'. But it was still tinged by the guilt of wanting incestuous love." She moved her head as if about to speak. "Stay quiet and listen." The last movement full of hope rising to its crescendo, the future of the brave. "In my mind you have conquered that guilt; all that is left is for me to rid myself of my own."

* * * * *

In Cullen Harbour the wind had prevented us from getting to Well's Passage, the evening cloudy from the system that had passed giving the strong winds; the winds moderated as the evening approached and now the water was still. I lay on my back, my eyes relaxed with contentment when I heard her quiet voice.

"Do you think it will work?"

"We've lived together for years, nothing changed."

"I want more than that."

"Such as?"

"A husband."

"That all?"

"No secrets, no ulterior motives."

"You should talk."

I opened my eyes.

"What's hiding behind your mask, Alex?"

"I'm not taking the pill, haven't for six months. I thought, if I didn't tell you it would be a fait accompli! My period finished a few days ago; can you stand it?"

"You do pile it on, Alexandra; first guilt then nine months of terror," I said, trying to sound jocular.

"I have followed my bliss and it will be complete when I have borne your child." She stopped, eyes narrowed from a face of mischief, "Wrablord."

+ + + + +

They arrived at Napier Bay in Tracey Harbour after a beating sail against strong northwest winds. Glad to be at rest in a calm bay the wind still strong in the tree tops. The hard sail left them tired and it was late by the time they were anchored and bedtime after they had eaten.

"Time for bed?" he asked, seeing her go to the head.

He got undressed and lay on the bed waiting for her, eyes closed. A strange languor to her this evening dutifully going through the motions. Her hand ran across his chest, he opened his eyes to her mask.

"No secrets, no ulterior motives you said, what are you hiding?"

"For over a year," she said after a long pause and looking awkward, "I have been seeing my father."

Revulsion, bitterness mixed with hatred crossed his face with no effort to hide it from her. She waited for him to adjust before continuing.

Her revelation reminded him of Hardy Island and the time when she told Andrew and himself of her father's cruelty with simple accuracy. Then he remembered his conversation with Jessica about her edited version for his sake. 'Such premeditated cruelty, what did she expect me to think?' he asked himself. Now he was hearing her anger replaced by compassion for him and even pride when relating his latest achievement.

"Have you forgiven him?"

"No. I could never do so and I told him."

"What did he say?"

"That he did not seek or expect to be forgiven. He said that it was enough that I had arranged to see him. After the seminar I phoned you to ask for your advice but once you were on the line I shied away from telling you. Twice since then I started to tell you and couldn't."

"What stopped you?"

"I had the sensation that I would be kicking you in the teeth."

"Am I in that much need of protection?"

"Yes, if you could have seen your face of hatred when you were dressing my back, you might understand."

"I would have a hard time being civil to him, Alex."

"His return into my life allowed me to finally dismiss you as a father."

"How many more masks to strip away?"

"None," animation back in her expression, "want a drink?"

* * * * *

Listening to the weather forecast in the morning which predicted northwest winds of 10-20 knots we decided to make an early start. Powering out of Tracey Harbour the wind in our face we knew we had a hard day's sailing ahead of us. We put up the small jib and reefed the main at James Point helped by the ebbing tide reached out past the ominous Lewis Rocks before close hauling to try and clear the northwest end of the Numas Islands. Remembering Hiscock's advice we stayed in Labouchere Passage taking short tacks to our destination. As we worked our way to the Raynor Islands the wind strengthened above 25 knots and Alex put the second reef in the mainsail. I suggested we turn back to be confronted by her withering look. At Taylor Point the wind became more westerly allowing us easier progress on the port tack. As we approached the Raynor Group the wind moderated and shifted allowing us to make the entrance to Blunden Harbour.

I shook her hand as we entered the harbour before midday.

"We made it, John."

"Yeah!" I said delighted to be back in one of my favourite spots. "Pity we can't stay more than one night."

Our supplies were running low and I felt it would be wise to sail to Port McNeill the next day. We lunched and went on shore at the site of the Indian village.

She was notably subdued and preoccupied. Even the dinghy trip through the islets up to the rapids did not break through her silences and when asked if she wanted to go fishing she declined. I knew if I was patient she would tell me.

+ + + + +

Alex remembered flying up to Nimmo Bay and looking into Tracey Harbour, the place they had set out from in 1976 to sail up to Blunden Harbour. 'Where was it that Andrew found that piece about Well's Passage and the killer whales?' she asked herself. Then she remembered the Christmas present they had given John, a large book with a ring binder, maps covered with information on names, extracts from the ship's log of Captain Vancouver and the Kwakiutl customs translated for Franz Boas by George Hunt.

"Where is that book of maps with all the writing on them?"

"With the charts, Alex, I think."

She came back with it, sat down and put it on her knees. The determination in the set of her jaw told John that he was in for an argument. She relaxed back and laid out all the facts she had gathered since 1982 supporting her claim that B-10 was Andrew incarnate. Then she opened *'Exploring Puget Sound and British Columbia'* by Stephen Hillson and looked for the extracts she needed.

"Well's Passage is a Killer Whale area," she read, "the early Kwakiutl people recognised the sea as the home of Killer Whales and the place to which the souls of sea hunters go."

"Andrew was hardly a sea hunter!"

"Maybe the whales needed someone who could write their story! Both times I met B-10 he skyhopped his farewell, an event witnessed by Allison at Boat Bay and you at Mamalilaculla."

"Well, I saw a white conical shape through the binoculars," he admitted.

"At Boat Bay Andrew said 'I will jump for John if I see him', and you recorded it in the log in 1982 off Port Neville."

"Did I?"

"Yes, because I remember asking you if it happened and it's there!" He went down to the cabin returning with the log for 1982.

"Yes I did record it," he said, a look of triumph facing him. "Okay, okay," he said, putting up his arms in self defence.

"Andrew told me about his out of body experience, our ignoring him until I told you he was everywhere. The only influence he claimed with you was to lead you to the Blake poetry for the card in my Bible. You had never read Blake before, had you?"

"Well no, that's true."

"How long did it take for you to find the quotation; be honest?"

"I opened the book and it was there."

"In 1985 you were asleep, weren't you?"

"Yes, as stated in the log."

"Then he said I would have to deal with my father and in Toronto I understood him."

"He could have been referring to me; it is ambiguous, Alex."

"At Mamalilaculla Andrew said you knew about Gareth, I hadn't told you so how could that be wish generating?"

"You knew Jim and I had met; that would be a reasonable assumption."

"Have you ever discussed your will with me? Do you keep a copy that I might have snooped around the house and found?"

"Only the will is hard to explain," he answered and tried to deflect her attention. "You would have a strong ally in all this."

"Who?"

"Stephanie would have supported you."

"Were you 'struck on that girl', John?" Ignoring his attempted deflection.

"At that time."

"Yes, at that time." Taunting him with a grimace.

"I can't remember when my love for you as a woman replaced my love for you as a daughter. I never loved you as I did Andrew, there was always a difference. If I had had a daughter of my own I think I would have been more protective, not as prepared to give so much independence. I don't know how I would look at my own daughter, if I would be aroused by the sight of her."

"You were aroused by the sight of me?" she queried.

"Of course."

"Dirty old man!"

"Why should I remain impassive at the sight of a naked woman taking a shower on the foredeck just because she has the face of my daughter?" he looked at her quizzically, "of course you, you didn't make use of my naked body," and seeing her poker face added, "dirty old woman!"

"Touché," she replied laughing.

"This last year with you in Toronto I was so alone. Not like the solitude I enjoy single handing up here knowing that you would be at home, but a desperate loneliness. Then I realised I was missing you like Steph."

"So Andrew was right," she said looking triumphant.

"Such a furtive imagination!"

+ + + + +

A gentle wind took them to Port McNeill leaving them feeling robbed when they compared it to the first glorious crossing in 1976.

The slow crossing made it too late to shop for supplies after they had anchored. Instead they went ashore to walk and Alex phoned Doctor Ferguson to invite him and his wife for a drink. They had a leisurely supper together and went to the hotel at eight to meet their guests.

After their drinks arrived Alex turned to Mrs Ferguson.

"This is a special trip for us, Jenny."

"Why special?"

"We got engaged at Mamalilaculla," she said, watching John's embarrassment with amusement, thinking, 'well he's got to get used to it and they don't know about my childhood.'

"When did you meet her, John?" Doctor Ferguson asked.

"A long time ago now, Alistair."

"Cheers to both of you," Jenny said, and John looked saved.

The conversation spread out from their engagement, Alistair asking John about singlehanding and John asking Alistair about his flying experiences. As Alex went to the restroom she saw an old Indian sitting at a table by himself nursing a glass of beer. When she was returning she noticed a sparkle of recognition in his eye and stopped.

"Do you remember me; you took my cast off."

"At Nimmo Bay?"

"Yes."

"You used to tell Transformer stories for the children. Can I sit?" He indicated the chair. "Have you a new Transformer story for me?" His face crinkled with pleasure.

He told her the story of the woman who wanted the soul of a whale for her unborn son. When he had finished she looked at him and smiled.

"I must join the others. Come and join us if you like."

His old head shook as his eyes broke away from her.

Back at their table she asked Alistair if he remembered the trip to Nimmo Bay.

"Yes, it was a clear day, not much wind and I remember thinking you were good luck."

"There was an old Indian who took us up to the clinic room and I took his cast off for you."

"I can't say I remember. Why?"

"I was just talking to him at the table over there," she pointed to his table but he had already gone, "oh, he must have left. I wondered if I could get his name and address from the clinic records."

"Come up tomorrow morning and we'll dig them out."

By the time she got to the clinic in the morning Alistair already had the records out for her.

"There was no cast removed that day, Alex. Did we go up twice to Nimmo Bay?"

"No."

She shook her head, realising that she could not remember what the old man looked like, only the story remained in her memory. He was not there.

* * * * *

Alex was preparing to bring the anchor up at Port McNeill.

"Where are we going tonight?"

"Somewhere neutral without memories for you," I answered.

"Okay, but what is it called?"

"The anchorage south of Spoat Islet," I told her with smugness.

"Where, John?"

Accompanied by one of her fierce jabs to my shoulder.

"A small bay on the north side of Hanson Island," I said as I rubbed my shoulder.

"You shouldn't be obscure," she said, taking aim at my other shoulder.

"Ach, I'm not Andrew. I went there last year for the first time and was comfortable. There is a rock marked on the chart, I went in at high tide and was surprised to see it so close in the morning!"

We had a slow sail until we were past Haddington Passage where the wind picked up and blew us behind Cormorant Island almost into Blackfish Sound and our destination. Another cloudy day with a cold wind drove us into the cabin for happy hour and supper. A Sunday morning breakfast mood pervaded the cabin as we poured our coffee.

"You remember I stopped to speak to the old man last night?"

"You said so, yes."

"We could find no record of the old Indian at Nimmo Bay that day and no cast removed."

"Odd," I said, "you remember removing his cast, what did he look like?"

"I cannot remember what the Old Indian at Forward Bay looked like, nor at Nimmo Bay and now I just can't see him in the pub last night. All I remember is the Transformer story he told me. It went like this."

"During the Transformer's journey down the east coast of the island near Shushartie Bay there was a young woman calling out to the sea standing between two skulls, so he knew she was calling a whale. 'Why do you call to the whale to come?'

"'So his soul can enter my body to make my son a strong fisherman hunter knowing the ways of the whales. Then he will be a great chief of our tribe.'

"'Go home now.' The Transformer told her, 'the eagle will be his messenger.'

"The woman left the beach and walked the two miles to her house and as she was about to enter an eagle screeched to her from the totem. She opened the door and the bird flew down to enter the house. As he perched near the fire he changed into her young husband. They lay together and when her son was born he became the great whale hunting chief of his tribe."

"Isn't it similar to one I used to read to you on the first cruise up here?"

"My furtive imagination again?" she said with irony. "You old cynic, can't you believe, just once."

"Your use of the word believe gives me a point won in the argument."

"Surely our forefathers had spirits," she answered, "a spiritual thread throughout evolution; a guiding hand."

"I agree with Richard Dawkins that the watchmaker was blind," he replied, shaking his head. "The chance that we are here by luck may be improbable but still possible. Once over that hurdle of acceptance then the story is one of ever increasing genetic complexity driving the evolution of new organisms. I also agree with Alistair Hardy that this process is also molded by the environment."

"You! A Lamarkist."

"Surely as a physician scientist you agree with most of it," I said, ignoring her jibe.

"Yes, except for your initial giant leap of faithlessness!"

"And you accept chance in the genetic theory of natural selection?"

"Just as I accept I have free will and that my God is not almighty."

"How can you accept him as outside of you, Alex?"

"I talk to my God, he is not me, he's separate from me and so I always think of him as my soul who leaves my body after death, just as Andrew followed us up the coast and occupies another living organism. You too have a God within you, you just don't listen to him."

"If you accept God as a synonym for unconsciousness, yes. So much of our behaviour takes place on a level below our self consciousness; I think our consciousness resides in the cerebral cortex and is only capable of inhibiting our unconscious drives or drawing on them for action."

"You mean the control of our internal environment, breathing, heart rate and body chemistry. Anything else?"

Her inquiry sounded ominous.

"Other important things as well, such as our social behaviours, anger, response to pain or Cannon's fear, flight and fright reaction."

"Do you include sexual behaviour in others, John?"

"Yes, I cannot prevent some of my responses to sexual images. In one of his novels Marquez compared the penis to a first born son 'you spend your life working for him, sacrificing everything for him and at the moment of truth he just does as he pleases.'"

"I like that," she laughed, "but is it true?"

"Yes it's true in terms of response; most of us have inhibitions that make our overt behaviour socially acceptable. We are now imperfect examples!" I said, watching her expression, the lopsided smile develop in the left side of her upper lip spreading through her face.

"My father was without inhibition; that's all?"

"Which one, Alex?" But she wanted to be serious. "He also had unusual sexual desires. You could say that he was unable to hold them in his imagination alone."

"Suppose you, John Barlow, lusting after me on the foredeck, had ravaged me against my will. Should you be forgiven on the basis of a disorder; lacks inhibition."

"What are you driving at?"

"Should I exercise some compassion towards my patients with unusual desires? In Endocrinology I can treat them and alter those desires. Surely I must listen to their stories dispassionately in order to identify those areas in which I can try to help them."

"Certainly."

"Should I exercise some compassion towards Father. 'Father forgive him, he could not stop doing what he was imagining'?"

"I could never forgive him!"

Shot back at her like a knee jerk.

"Why so little compassion?"

I was beside myself as a deep well of anger and hatred rose inside me and prickled my eyes. A fury must have shone out of them at her.

"You never saw the little girl who did not stay in my house because of the fear of all fathers, or see the look of abject terror as a hand raced towards the side of her face, or the perforated ear drum, or the fear in her eyes at the thought of the twelve lashes to her friend's back, or the look of dismay at our nude bathing or the 'Noh mask' drawn over her face at being cowed into remaining quiet, or the sight of her back whipped into a coalescing hematoma. Not even compassion for myself for ignoring the obvious symptoms and signs of an abused child." 'H'mph' snorted from my nose in anger. "I could almost forgive him wanting to express sexual love for one so lovely if mutual." She remained still, masked, and I continued. "No I could never forgive your father those actions against you. Not even compassion... well... no, not even compassion."

Behind her mask I saw the enormous effort to resist public tears, her eyes fixed me.

"John," she whispered, secretively, "I would like him to give me away."

I was silent to let the pressure of my steam drop, bringing me back to reason. I pulled her towards me putting her head against my chest. "Oh, Alex, you surely know how to put me on trial."

* * * * *

We arrived at Boat Bay in the early afternoon, our final anchorage before leaving the Kwakiutl country with its spirits to whom Alex had assigned Andrew's. Thinking back to her arrival at Minstrel Island the weather had been unusually bad even for here; just two clear sun filled days at Blunden Harbour and here. Now I could look across the water to Robson Bight, the Tsitika river valley rising to the summit of heaven, the mountains evocative and full of memories. My sadness at leaving again recompensed by the certainty of the new memories added.

+ + + + +

Supper finished and cleared, both sitting in the evening sun in the cockpit, two purring cats of contentment. Events remembered and spoken, some funny some sad, a chemistry gathering force between them as the sun sank below the horizon. Hot chocolate served in the cabin, a romantic piano concerto of John's playing softly, her head nestled against his chest, touched by night's desire, anticipation rising and falling with his breathing, an uncanny sense of wonder induced by the music. The final crescendo to end the music, the shedding of clothes, taking him to her. Sweet scent of skin and hair, taste of saliva, feel of his tongue as her orgasmic vision opened the Tsitika Valley laid out in front of her, an eagle central wheeling in the sky, its beak a visible yellow point on its white head, now receding to a tiny dot of white rising into the summit of heaven; the dot bursting like a huge fireworks sparkling into a kaleidoscope of lights which changing shape became Andrew's head moving towards her the brightness an agony until it absorbed into her.

"John! Oh John!" the words coming out of her like a scream, her finger nails piercing his skin as they dug deep into him. Her body shuddered as a huge indrawn breath puffed out of her nose.

* * * * *

I eased away as I felt her nails release me, her body still except for her moth-wing eyelids in a breeze and a quiver of her upper lip as if to start a smile. The indrawn breath sighed out of her nose in a series of short exhausts. I thought for a moment that she was unconscious, then her slow steady breathing told of her deep sleep. 'Relaxed after the battle' I thought, gently singing the ending of Britten's War Requiem to her sleeping form.

"Let us sle-eep now."

+ + + + +

Alex awoke at six, gently easing over his sleeping body, pulling her robe around her to go up on deck. The sun was just rising down the straits, she recited aloud.

'Welcome Great Chief Father, as you come to show yourself this morning. We come and meet alive. O protect me that nothing evil may befall me this day, Chief, Great Father.'

She stared across the straits half expecting to see the B Pod leaving for the north. She was unusually alive with the ecstasy of her dream still recalled. She lit the stove to make them coffee, standing in the galley an emptiness of something missing. Smiling to herself when she realised that John was not hovering anxiously behind her. No time she could recall when he had not been up with her making sure there was no error in her lighting of the kerosene stove, or trying to displace her from getting the breakfast. There he was still asleep, no sign of prewaking stirring as she put his coffee down beside the bunk. She sat beside him and went to draw the comforter over his shoulder and saw the deep nails cuts through his skin. 'Not a dream' she mused. Her fingers running through his hair in unspoken apology as he stirred and awoke.

"Alexandra," he said, pulling her towards him and kissing her forehead, "a child conceived of love."

"You felt it too, Wrablord."

"For the third time." He stretched and handled his coffee mug to his mouth.

"When I awoke I thought I had been dreaming, but then I saw your back; my nails have cut your skin."

"If you had long nails they would have punctured my lung!" he said, punching her shoulder. "What dream?"

"Not a dream, a vision. It happened before I dug my nails into you."

"You let out a great scream of John."

"The dot of the eagle's head burst open like a fireworks display, formed into Andrew's head and passed into my body."

"So, you predict a boy?"

"Our son."

"After the vision you will want to name him Andrew?"
"No," she said, shaking her head.
"What then?"
"Jonah!"

EPILOGUE

In 1990 Doctor John Hall, a biologist in Alaska, was observing the killer whales and reported that B-10's fin had been clipped by a bullet, probably from a fisherman's rifle. The whales have found it rewarding to remove the Alaska black cod from the long line fishing tackle as an easy access to food. So like Andrew to have found a ready made meal knowing his dislike for fishing from the sea for himself!